"So, Dad, how did dinner go with Mrs. Sommars?"

James asked as he poured his corn flakes.

Alex cupped his mug of coffee, considering his son's question. "Dinner went fine." It was afterward that clung to his mind. Someone had hurt Carol, and hurt her badly. He barely touched her and she'd trembled. Her eyes had clouded, and she couldn't seem to get out of his car fast enough. The crazy part was, Alex was convinced she was attracted to him.

"Mrs. Sommars is a neat lady," James continued. "She's a little weird, though."

Alex pulled his gaze from his coffee. "How's that?"

"She listens to opera," James explained between bites. Alex laughed, finished his coffee and set the mug in the sink. He was on his way to the front door when James stopped him.

"Don't forget to pick me up at practice, okay?"

"I'll be there."

"Hey, Dad?"

"What now?"

James shrugged. "In case you're interested, Mrs. Sommars will be t

Alex was intereste

Dear Reader,

The name Silhouette **Special Edition** represents a commitment—a commitment to bring you six sensitive, substantial novels every month, each offering a stimulating blend of deep emotions and high romance.

This month, be sure to savor Curtiss Ann Matlock's long-awaited *Love Finds Yancey Cordell* (#601). And don't miss Patricia Coughlin's unforgettable *The Spirit Is Willing* (#602), a deliciously different novel destined to become a classic. Four more stellar authors—Tracy Sinclair, Debbie Macomber, Ada Steward and Jessica St. James—complete the month's offerings with all the excitement, depth, vividness and warmth you've come to expect from Silhouette **Special Edition**.

Deeply emotional, richly romantic, infinitely rewarding—that's the Silhouette **Special Edition** experience. Come share it with us—six times a month!

From all the authors and editors of Silhouette **Special Edition**,

Best wishes,

Leslie Kazanjian
Senior Editor

DEBBIE MACOMBER
The Courtship of Carol Sommars

 Silhouette Special Edition

Published by Silhouette Books New York

America's Publisher of Contemporary Romance

In loving memory of
David Adler, Doug Adler and Bill Stirwalt
Beloved Cousins
Beloved Friends

Special thanks to:
Pat Kennedy and her endearing Italian mother,
and Ted Macomber and Bill Hall
for the contribution of their rap music
and all the lessons about living with teenage boys

SILHOUETTE BOOKS
300 East 42nd St., New York, N.Y. 10017

ISBN: 0-373-09606-2

First Silhouette Books printing June 1990

Books by Debbie Macomber

Silhouette Romance

Mail-Order Bride #539
*Cindy and the Prince #555
*Some Kind of Wonderful #567
*Almost Paradise #579
Any Sunday #603
Almost an Angel #629
The Way to a Man's Heart #671

*Legendary Lovers trilogy

Silhouette Special Edition

Starlight #128
Borrowed Dreams #241
Reflections of Yesterday #284
White Lace and Promises #322
All Things Considered #392
The Playboy and the Widow #482
Navy Wife #494
Navy Blues #518
For All My Tomorrows #530
Denim and Diamonds #570
Fallen Angel #577
The Courtship of Carol Sommars #606

Silhouette Christmas Stories 1986

"Let It Snow"

DEBBIE MACOMBER

hails from the state of Washington. As a busy wife and mother of four, she strives to keep her family healthy and happy. As the prolific author of dozens of best-selling romance novels, she strives to keep her readers happy with each new book she writes.

Vancouver

WASHINGTON

Hayden Island

Columbia River

Portland International Airport

Government Island

Interstate 5

PORTLAND, OREGON

Willamette River

West Hills

City
Center

Ross Island

Ford Memorial

Interstate 205

Underlined places are fictitious.

Chapter One

Carol Sommars swore the entire house shook with her fifteen-year-old son's cassette player blasting out the words to his favorite rap.

I'm the Wizard MC and I'm on the mike
I'm gonna tell you a story that I know you'll like
Cause my rhymes are kickin', and my beats do flash
When I go to the studio, they pay me cash

"Peter," Carol screamed from the kitchen, covering her ears against the racket. A squad of dive-bombers would have made less commotion.

Knowing Peter would never be able to hear her above the din, she marched down the narrow hallway and pounded on his door.

Peter and his best friend, Jim Preston, were sitting on top of Peter's water bed, their heads beating out the tempo to the music. They both looked shocked to see her.

Peter turned down the volume. "Did you want something, Mom?"

"Boys, please, that music is too loud."

Her son and his friend exchanged knowing glances, silently commenting on her advancing age, no doubt.

"Mom, it wasn't that bad, was it?"

Carol boldly met her son's cynical look. "The walls and floor were vibrating."

"Sorry, Mrs. Sommars."

"No problem, Jim. I just thought I'd save the stemware while I had the chance." Not to mention warding off any internal injuries to herself.

"Mom, can Jim stay for dinner tonight? His dad's got a hot date."

"Not tonight, I'm afraid," Carol said, casting her son's friend an apologetic glance. "I'm teaching my birthing class, but Jim can stay some other time."

Peter nodded, accepting her reasoning, then in an apparent effort not to be outdone by his friend, he added, "My mom goes out on hot dates most every weekend herself."

Carol did an admirable job of disguising her laugh behind a cough. Oh, sure! The last time she'd gone out had been...she had to think about it...two months earlier! And that had been as a favor to a friend. She wasn't looking to remarry. Bruce had died nearly thirteen years earlier, and if she hadn't found another man in that time, she wasn't going to now. There was a good deal to be said for the benefits of living independently.

She closed Peter's bedroom door and braced her shoulder against the wall while she sighed. A flash of deafening music jolted her upright once more. It was immediately lowered to a respectable level, and she continued on her way back to the kitchen.

At fifteen, Peter was advancing into the most awkward teenage years. Jim, too. Both boys had recently obtained their learner's permit from the Department of Motor Vehicles and were both in the same fifth-period driver training class at the local high school.

Checking the time, Carol hurried back into the kitchen and turned on the oven, before popping two frozen chunky meat pies inside.

"Hey, Mom, can we drive Jim home now?"

The operative word was *we*, which of course, meant Peter would be doing the driving. He was constantly reminding her how much practice he needed if he was to pass the driving portion of the test when he turned sixteen. The fact was, Peter used any excuse he could to get behind the wheel of a car.

"Sure," she said, forcing a smile. These "practice" runs with Peter demanded nerves of steel. No one had ever stopped to ask Superman how he'd gotten so strong. Carol knew. He was the father of a fifteen-year-old with a driver's permit.

Actually Peter's driving skill had improved drastically in the last few weeks, but not before the armrest on the passenger side of the car had permanent indentations. Their first times on the road together had been more hair-raising than a teenage fright show.

Thanks to Peter, Carol had been spiritually renewed when he'd run the stop sign at Jackson and Bethel. As if to make up for his mistake, he slammed on the brakes as soon as they were through the intersection, catapulting them both forward. They'd been saved from injury by their seat belts.

"Can Jim sit in the front seat with us?" Peter asked as they approached her ten-year-old Ford.

"As long as you've got enough space to drive comfortably."

"Hey, Mom, no problem."

Carol was squashed between the two boys, but being the congenial mother she was, she didn't complain.

"My dad's going to buy me a truck as soon as I get my license," Jim said. "A red four-by-four with flames painted along the sidewalls."

Peter tossed Carol an accusing glare. With their budget, they were going to have to share her cantankerous coupe for a while. The increase in the car insurance premiums with an additional driver was enough to set them back to frozen meat pies every third night as it was. As far as Carol was concerned, nurses were overworked, underpaid and rarely appreciated.

"Mom—hide."

The panic in her son's voice vaulted her heart to her throat. "What is it?"

"Melody Wohlford."

"Who?"

"Mom, please, just scoot down a little, would you?"

Still not understanding what was happening, she scooted down until her eyes were level with the dashboard and her knees were scrunched up under the radio.

"More," Peter instructed between clenched teeth, and braced his hand against the top of her shoulder, pushing her down even farther. "I can't let Melody see me driving with my mother!"

Carol muttered beneath her breath and did her best to keep her cool. She exhaled slowly and reminded herself that this too shall pass.

Peter's speed decreased to a mere crawl. He inadvertently poked her in the ribs as he hurriedly rolled down the window and draped his elbow outside. Carol bit her lower lip to keep from yelping, which no doubt would have ruined everything for her son.

"Hello, Melody," he said casually, raising his hand as if doing so demanded supreme effort.

The soft feminine greeting drifted back to them. "Hello, Peter."

"Melody," Jim said, in a suave voice Carol barely recognized.

"Hi, Jimmy," Melody called. "Where you guys headed?"

"I'm driving Jim home."

"Yeah," Jim added, half leaning over Carol and blocking off her already limited supply of oxygen. "My dad's ordered me a truck, but it hasn't come in yet."

"Boys," Carol said in a strangled voice. "I can't breathe."

"Just a minute, Mom," Peter muttered under his breath, pressing down on the accelerator and hurrying ahead.

Carol struggled into an upright position, dragging in several deep gulps of oxygen. She was about to deliver a much-needed lecture when Peter pulled into his friend's driveway. No more than a moment later, the front door banged open.

"James, where the hell have you been? I told you to come home directly after school."

Carol blinked. Since this was the boys' first year of high school and they'd both come from different middle schools, Carol had never met Jim's father. Now, however, didn't seem the appropriate moment to leap out and introduce herself.

Alex Preston was so angry with Jim that he barely glanced in their direction. When he did, he dismissed both her and Peter without so much as a word. His dark brows lifted derisively over gray eyes as he glared at his son.

Carol was certain if Jim hadn't gotten out of the car on his own, Alex would have taken delight in pulling his body through the window.

Carol couldn't help but note that Alex Preston was an imposing man; he had to be easily six-two. His forehead was high and his jaw well-defined. But his eyes were what immediately captured her attention. They held his son's with uncompromising authority.

There was an arrogant set to his mouth that Carol found herself disliking, which wasn't like her. Normally she didn't make snap judgments, but one look told her she wasn't going to get along with Jim's father, which was unfortunate since the boys had become such immediate and fast friends.

Not that it mattered all that much. Other than an occasional generic phone conversation, there would never be any reason for them to have contact with each other.

"I told you I was going out tonight," Alex blared. "The least you could do is have the consideration to let me know where you are. You're damn lucky I don't ground you until the year 2000."

Jim dipped his head with a guilty look. "Sorry, Dad."

"I'm sorry, Mr. Preston," Peter called out.

"It's not your fault."

To his credit, Alex Preston glanced apologetically toward Peter and Carol as if to say he regretted this scene.

"It might be a good idea if you hurried home yourself," Alex called out to her son.

Carol stiffened in the front seat, doing her best not to leap out of the car and inform him that they had no intention of staying anyway. "Perhaps we should leave now," she said to Peter, with as much dignity as she could muster.

"Later," Peter called to his friend.

"Later," Jim called back, looking chagrined.

Peter had eased the car out of the driveway and was headed toward the house before either of them spoke.

"Did you know Jim was supposed to go home directly after school?" Carol drilled.

"How could I know something like that?" Peter flared. "I asked him over to listen to my new tape. I didn't know his dad was going to come unglued over it."

"He's just being a parent."

"Maybe, but at least you don't scream at me in front of my friends."

"I try not to."

"I've never seen Mr. Preston blow his cool before. He sure was mad."

"I don't think we should be so hard on him," she said, feeling generous since she was a parent herself. Adults needed to stick together. "He was obviously worried."

"But, Mom, Jim is fifteen! You shouldn't have to know where a kid is every minute of every day."

"Wanna bet!"

Peter was diplomatic enough not to respond to that.

By the time they had returned to the house and Carol had changed clothes for her class, the oven timer had dinged, indicating their dinner was ready.

"Mom," Peter said thoughtfully as she delivered the fresh green salad to the table. "You should think about going out more yourself."

"I'm going out tonight."

"I mean on dates and stuff."

"Stuff?" Carol questioned, swallowing a smile.

"You know what I mean. You haven't lost it yet, you know."

Carol wasn't entirely sure she did know. But whatever "it" was had come as the result of a good deal of thought on her son's part. She was fairly certain he meant to compliment her, so she responded appropriately. "Thanks."

"You don't even need to use Oil of Olay."

She nodded, although she wasn't entirely sure she appreciated him studying her skin tone.

"I was looking at your hair and I don't see any gray, and you don't have fat folds or anything."

Carol couldn't help it—she laughed. "No fat folds? Then for heaven's sake, who's going to hold back Don Johnson?"

"No, Mom, I'm serious. You could probably pass for thirty."

"Thanks . . . I think."

"I'm not kidding. Jim's dad is going out with someone twenty-one tonight, and Jim told me that she's tall and blond and pretty with great big . . . you know." He cupped his hands over his chest.

Carol sat at the table and, bracing her elbows on the top, dangled her fork above her plate. "Are you suggesting I find myself a twenty-one-year-old with bulging muscles and compete with Jim's dad?"

"Of course not," Peter said, looking at her as if she were being ridiculous. "Well, not entirely. I'm just saying that you're not exactly over the hill. You could be dating a whole lot more than you do. And you should before . . . well, before it's too late, if you know what I mean."

Carol pierced a fork full of lettuce and offered a convenient excuse. "I don't have the time to get involved with anyone."

Peter took a bite of his own salad. "If the right guy came along, you'd make time."

"Perhaps."

"Mr. Preston does. Jim says his dad is always busy with work, but he finds time to date lots of women."

"Right, but most of the women he sees are too young for pantyhose." Instantly feeling guilty for the catty remark, Carol shook her head. "That wasn't nice, I apologize."

"I understand," Peter said, sounding mature beyond his years. "The way I see it though, you need a man."

That was news to her. "Why? I've got you."

"True, but I won't be around too much longer, and I hate the thought of you getting old and gray all alone."

"I won't be alone. Grandma will move in with me and the two of us will sit side by side in our rocking chairs and crochet afghans. For entertainment we'll play bingo every Saturday afternoon." Even as she spoke, Carol realized that sounded ridiculous.

"Grandma would drive you crazy in three days," Peter said with a know-it-all smile and waved his fork in her direction. "Besides, you'll get fat eating all her homemade pasta."

"Maybe so," Carol agreed, unwilling to argue the point. "But I have plenty of time before I need to worry about it. Anything can happen in the next few years."

"I'm worried now," Peter countered. "You're letting your life slip through your fingers like the sand in an hourglass."

Carol's eyes connected with her son's. "Have you been watching soap operas again?"

"Mom," Peter cried, "you're not taking me seriously."

"I'm sorry," she said, doing her best to hide the smile that lifted up the corners of her mouth. "It's just that my life is full. I'm simply too busy to spend time developing a relationship." One look from her son told her he wasn't going to accept her explanation. "Sweetheart," she countered, setting her fork aside, "you don't need to worry about me. I'm a big girl. When and if I ever decide to seriously date again, I promise it'll be with someone muscular so you can brag to your friends. Would a wrestler be all right?"

"The least you could have done was get married again," he said, his patience clearly strained. "Dad would have wanted you to find happiness again, don't you think?"

Any mention of Peter's father brought with it a feeling of terror and guilt. They'd both been far too young and foolish to have married. They were high school seniors when Carol learned she was pregnant. In those days, marriage was the only option. Either that or disgrace, and so, believing her love and their baby would change Bruce, Carol had agreed to marry him. From that point to the moment Bruce had died in a terrible car accident three years later, Carol's life had been a living hell. She would be crazy to even consider seriously dating again.

"Peter," she said, pointedly glancing at her watch and pushing her plate aside. "I'm sorry to end this conversation so abruptly, but I've got to get to class."

"I think you're just being stubborn, but that's your decision."

Carol didn't have the time to argue. She dumped the remainder of her meal in the garbage, rinsed off her plate and stuck it in the dishwasher. She left Peter after giving him instructions to take care of his own dishes, then she headed for the bathroom.

She freshened her makeup and ran a brush though her shoulder-length dark hair. On impulse, she turned sideways to examine her reflection in the full-length mirror that hung on the back of the bathroom door.

She sucked in her stomach, straightened her shoulders and flattened her hand over her firm abdomen. There were curves in all the appropriate places, some more shapely than others.

She examined several poses, trying to find her best, but quickly gave that up. No matter how she stood, she wasn't going to look twenty-one again. As she turned away, she caught sight of her profile and couldn't resist further examination. Her breasts weren't bad. As though to prove her point, she cupped them to lift them slightly higher. Her legs were rather attractive, too. She twisted her right foot around and examined her calves and trim ankles. An inch or two added to her five-five frame certainly wouldn't hurt, though.

"Not bad," she muttered, eyeing herself critically. Thirty-four wasn't exactly retirement age.

Releasing her breath, Carol let her shoulders sag forward. "Who are you kidding?" she muttered with a depressed sigh. She faced the mirror and glared at her image once more. Peter may not think she needed Oil of Olay, but the dew was definitely off the rose. Most definitely.

Tugging at the skin at her cheekbones until it was stretched taut, she squinted at her reflection, trying to remember what she'd looked like at eighteen. Young. Pretty. Stupid.

She wasn't any one of those three now. And even if the opportunity was afforded her, she wouldn't go back. She'd made plenty of mistakes along the road, but there wasn't a single, solitary thing she would change about her life. Not now, anyway. After Peter got his driver's license, she could easily modify that thought.

No, the only option left open to her was the future, and she would face that, sagging bosom and all.

"Hey, Mom," Peter's voice cut into her musings. "Can I invite a friend over tonight?"

Carol opened the bathroom door and frowned at her son. "I can't believe you'd even ask that. You know the rules. No one is allowed over here when I'm not home."

"But, Mom," he whined.

"No exceptions."

"You don't trust me, do you?"

"We're not discussing this now. I have a class to teach, and I'm already five minutes behind schedule." To her way of thinking, that was Peter's fault, too. If he hadn't tried to convince her how attractive she was, and how if she didn't act within the next twenty minutes, she would lose it all, then she wouldn't be late in the first place.

Class went well. They were into the third week of the eight-week course sponsored by Ford Hospital in a suburb of Portland, Oregon. The couples were generally first-time parents, and their eagerness and excitement for the adventure that lay before them filled each session with infectious enthusiasm.

If Carol had known when she was carrying Peter that he was to be her one and only pregnancy, she would have taken time to appreciate it more.

Since she was the last one to leave the building, Carol turned off the lights and hauled her material out to her car. The parking lot was well lit, and she hurried through the rain, scooting inside the car. She drew in a deep breath and turned the ignition key. The Ford coughed and objected a couple of times before roaring to life. Her car had been acting a little funny lately, but it was nothing she could pinpoint. Satisfied that there wasn't anything too terribly wrong, she eased into the traffic on the busy street.

It wasn't until she stopped for the red light at the first intersection that her compact released a series of short pathetic coughs, only this time it sounded sick...real sick.

"What's wrong?" she cried as the light turned green. Pushing down on the accelerator, she leaped ahead, but it was apparent that whatever it was, the trouble was serious.

"All right, all right," she said, "I get the message. You need a mechanic and fast." A hurried glance down the business-lined thoroughfare revealed there wasn't a single service station in sight.

"Great," she muttered. "How about if I promise not to let Peter behind the wheel for a while, will that help?"

The ailing car belched loudly and a plume of black smoke engulfed the rear end.

"Okay, so you're not interested in a deal." Turning into the first driveway she happened upon, Carol found herself in a restaurant parking lot. The minute she eased into an empty space, the car uttered one last moan and promptly died.

For a full minute Carol just sat here. "You can't do this to me!" she muttered. Her pathetic coupe disagreed. Climbing out, she walked around her car a couple of times as if she would magically discover a cure lying on the sidewalk. The rain was coming down in sheets, and within a minute, she was drenched.

In an act of angry frustration, she kicked a tire, then yelped when the heel of her pump broke off. It was enough to make her want to break down and weep.

With no options left open to her, she limped into the restaurant, intent on heading for the ladies' room. Once she composed herself, she would deal with the car and call Peter to tell him she was going to be late.

Alex swore if his date giggled one more time, he was going to walk away from the table. The woman was driving him absolutely insane. He should know by now never to accept a blind date.

The first thing Bambi did when they were seated at the restaurant was to pick up the salt shaker and start listing the amazing qualities of crystal.

It took Alex five minutes to make the connection. The salt shaker was made of crystal.

"I'm crazy about hot tubs," Bambi said, leaning forward to offer him a generous view of her ample breasts.

"They're . . . hot all right," Alex murmured, examining the menu without much enthusiasm. His friend—at least someone he *used* to consider a friend—claimed Bambi was every man's dream come true. Her name should have told him all he needed to know. Once they'd met, he'd learned her given name was Michelle, but she'd started calling herself Bambi several months back because she loved forest animals so much. Animals like pigeons, and doggies and hamsters.

Alex didn't have the heart to tell her that in all the years he'd been camping, he'd yet to stumble upon a single family of hamsters grazing in a meadow.

The waitress came to take their order, and it took Bambi five minutes to explain how she wanted her alfalfa sprouts served. Okay, Alex admitted, he was exaggerating, four minutes. He ordered a steak and asked for it rare.

"I'm on a diet," Bambi explained, once the waitress had left their table.

He smiled benignly.

"Do you think I'm fat, Alex?" she asked softly.

Her big brown eyes appealed to him to lie if he must. Once more she bunched her full breasts together and leaned toward him. It was more than apparent that she wasn't wearing a bra. He suspected that he was supposed to swoon at the sight she was offering him.

"You do think I'm fat, don't you?" Bambi asked, pouting prettily.

"No," Alex told her.

"You're just saying that to be kind," she purred, and demurely lowered her lashes against the high arch of her cheek.

Alex smoothed out the linen napkin on his lap, thinking he was getting old. Far too old for someone like Bambi/Michelle. His teenage son might appreciate her finer qualities, but then he suspected that even James had better sense than that.

"Do you have a hot tub?"

Alex was so caught up in his thoughts, mentally figuring how long it would take to get through dinner so he could take her home, that it took him several moments to realize she'd directed the question to him.

"I love hot tubs," she reminded him. "I even carry along a swimsuit with me just in case my date has a tub. See?" She reached inside her purse and held up the skimpiest piece of material Alex had seen in his entire life. It was all he could do not to leap up, grab it out of her hand and demand that she put it back inside her purse.

"I don't have a hot tub," he said, doing his best to remain civil.

"Oh, that poor, pathetic thing," Bambi said, looking past him to the front of the restaurant. Her eyes were round as saucers.

"I beg your pardon?"

Bambi used this golden opportunity to lean as far forward as humanly possible, drape her breasts over his arm and whisper, "A bag lady just came into the restaurant. She's drenched to the bone, and I think she might be hurt because she's limping pretty bad."

Although he really wasn't interested, Alex glanced over his shoulder. The instant his gaze connected with the woman Bambi was referring to, he twisted his chair around for a better view. "That's no bag lady," he said.

"I realize she isn't carrying a shopping bag." Bambi raised her voice slightly, defending herself.

"I know that girl."

"You do?"

"Yes, she was with my son and his best friend this afternoon. I think she might be in some kind of trouble." He wasn't in the business of rescuing maidens in distress, but someone had to do something. "Will you excuse me a moment?"

"Alex," Bambi cried, reaching out for his arm, stopping him. Half the restaurant turned to stare at them—including the girl at the front. Even from half the distance of the room, Alex could feel her stare.

"You can't involve yourself in other people's problems," Bambi insisted.

"She's just a kid." He pulled his arm free.

"Honey, one look at her and I can tell you she's been around the block more times than the mailman."

Disregarding Bambi's unsought advice, Alex dumped his napkin on the table, stood and walked away.

"Hello, again," he said when he reached her. Bambi was right about one thing. She looked terrible—nothing like what she had looked earlier in the afternoon. Her hair fell in wet tendrils that dripped on her jacket. Her mascara was trailing in black streaks down her face, and she held the heel to her shoe in one hand. "I'm James's dad— we met briefly this afternoon." He held out his hand to her. "Do you remember me?"

"Of course I do," she said stiffly, clearly resenting this intrusion. She glanced longingly toward the ladies' room.

"Is something wrong?"

"Wrong?" she echoed. "What could possibly be wrong?"

She thrust out her chin proudly, but he resisted the urge to shake some sense into her. Sarcasm always set his teeth on edge. "I'd like to help if I could."

"I appreciate the offer, but no thanks. Listen, I think you'd better get back to your date." She glanced toward Bambi, and a smile quivered at the corners of her mouth. She had trouble meeting his eyes.

Briefly Alex wondered what she found so amusing. Then again, he knew.

"I thought she was supposed to be tall and blond," she said next, and it sounded like she was having a difficult time not laughing outright. Alex didn't appreciate her sense of humor, either, but he wasn't going to respond in kind. She was the one standing there looking like a drowned rat. Not him.

Her brows lifted as she studied Bambi. "Actually two out of three isn't bad."

Alex didn't have a clue what she was talking about. His look must have said as much because she added, "Jim was telling us how your date for this evening was tall and blond and had great big—"

She stopped abruptly, and Alex could swear she was blushing. A bright pink color started creeping up her neck and invaded her cheeks. "I'm sorry, that was uncalled for."

Bambi apparently wasn't about to be the center of their conversation while sitting down. She pushed back her chair, joined them near the hostess's desk and looped her arm through Alex's. "Perhaps you'd care to introduce us, Alex darling."

Alex resisted the urge not to roll his eyes at the way she referred to him as "darling." They barely knew each other. He doubted that Bambi would know his last name. Hell, he certainly didn't remember hers.

Since he wasn't sure of everyone's name, Alex gestured toward her and said, "This is a friend of my son's . . ."

"Carol Sommars," she supplied.

Alex was surprised. "I didn't know Peter had a sister."

Carol shot a look at him with surprised bright brown eyes. "I'm not his sister. I'm his mother."

Chapter Two

His mother," Alex echoed, clearly distressed. "But I thought . . . I assumed when you were with the boys that . . ."

"She's got to be way over thirty!" the ditsy blonde with her arm wrapped about Alex's exclaimed, eyeing Carol as possible competition.

Unwilling to be subjected to any debate over her age, Carol politely excused herself and blindly headed toward the ladies' room. With the way her luck had been going this evening, it shouldn't be a surprise that she would run into Alex Preston and his infamous hot date.

As soon as Carol viewed herself in the mirror, she groaned and reached for her purse, hoping to repair the worst of the damage. It wasn't any wonder Alex had mistaken her for a teenager. She looked like Little Orphan Annie on a bad day.

To add to her consternation, Jim's father was waiting for her when she left the rest room.

"Listen," he said, looking apologetic. "We got off to a bad start here. I'd like to help if I could."

Carol thanked him with a smile. "I appreciate that, but I don't want to ruin your evening. My car broke down, and I'm just going to call the auto club and have them deal with it." She already had the phone number and a quarter in her hand. The pay phone was just outside the rest rooms.

"All right." Carol was grateful when he left. She couldn't believe the way she'd spoken to him earlier and would like to apologize for that. Later, however, would definitely be more appropriate. Alex had caught her at a bad moment, but he'd quickly made up for it by believing she was Peter's sister. That was almost laughable, but exceptionally flattering.

She finished making her call and tried three frustrating times to get through to Peter, but the line was busy. Sitting in the restaurant foyer, she decided to give her son a few more minutes before calling again.

Alex strolled toward her. "Is the auto club coming?"

"They're on their way," she answered brightly, flashing a smile Little Miss Sunshine would envy.

"Did you get a hold of Peter?"

Her facade quickly melted. "I tried three times and can't get through. He's probably talking to Melody Wohlford, the one true love of his life."

"I have call waiting, so I'll contact James and have him get in touch with Peter for you. That way, you won't have to worry about trying to get through yourself."

"Thank you." She was more gracious this time. "Knowing Peter, he could be on the phone for hours."

Alex returned a minute later. "Jim was talking to Peter. Apparently they're doing their algebra homework together, which is probably good because Jim can use all the help he can get."

"In this case it's the blind leading the blind."

Alex grinned, and the mouth she'd found so arrogant and haughty earlier slowly lifted at the edges. His smile was sensual and earthy, and Carol found herself liking it a whole lot. It had been a good many years since she'd found herself staring at a man's mouth and thinking how nice it looked. Self-conscious now, she dragged her gaze away and glanced past him into the restaurant.

Alex gazed uncomfortably toward his table, where the other woman was waiting impatiently. "Would you like to join us and have something to eat?" he asked eagerly.

"Oh, no," Carol said, shaking her head for emphasis, "I couldn't do that."

Alex's gray eyes reached out to hers in blatant appeal. "*Please*, join us."

Carol wasn't exactly sure what was going on between Alex and his date, and she was even more uncertain if she should put herself in the middle of it, but then she always was a sucker for a sexy smile.

"All right," she agreed.

Alex immediately looked grateful. He glanced back to the woman who was glaring at him, clearly displeased that he was paying so much attention to Carol.

However, if her disapproval bothered Alex, he didn't show it. He led Carol back to the table and motioned for the waitress to bring a menu.

"I'll just have coffee."

As soon as the waitress left, Alex introduced the two women. "Bambi, Carol. Carol, Bambi."

"I'm pleased to make your acquaintance," Bambi said formally, holding out her hand. Carol swore she'd never seen longer nails. They were painted a fire engine red and were a good two inches in length.

"Alex and I have sons the same age," Carol explained. Her coffee arrived, and she quickly took a sip to disguise her uneasiness.

"Eat your dinner, Alex," Bambi instructed. "There's no need to let our evening be ruined by Carol's misfortune."

"Yes, please," Carol said hurriedly. "By all means, don't let me keep you from your meal."

Alex reached for the steak knife. "Is Peter trying out for track this year?"

"He wouldn't miss it. I swear that's the only reason he managed to keep his grades up the last tri. He knows the minute he gets a D, he's off the team. Lord knows what will happen next year when he takes chemistry."

"Jim has decided to take chemistry his junior year, too."

"I took chemistry," Bambi told them brightly. "They made us look inside a worm."

"That's biology," Carol explained kindly.

"Oh, maybe it was."

"I need to apologize for the way I blew up this afternoon," Alex continued. "I felt bad about it afterward. Yelling at Jim in front of his friends was not the thing to do. It's just that there are times when my son frustrates me to no end."

"Don't worry about it. I feel the same way toward Peter when he does something I've specifically asked him not to do." Feeling guilty for excluding Bambi from the conversation, Carol turned toward her and asked, "Do you have children?"

"Heavens no, I'm not even married."

"Children can be extremely wonderful and extremely frustrating," Carol advised Bambi, who seemed far more interested in gazing lovingly at Alex.

"Jim only has one chore around the house during the week," Alex went on to explain. "He's supposed to take out the garbage. I swear, every week it's the same thing. Garbage starts stacking up against the side of the refrigerator until it's as high as the cabinets, and Jim doesn't even notice. I end up having to plead with him to take it out."

"And two days later he does it, right? Peter's the same way."

Alex leaned forward and braced his forearms against the table, pushing his untouched steak aside. "Last week, I didn't say a word, wanting to see how long it would take for him to notice. Only when something started stinking up the kitchen did he so much as—"

"Pass the salt," Bambi said, stretching her arm between Carol and Alex and reaching for it herself. She shook it with a vengeance over her salad and then slammed it back down on the table.

Apparently Alex felt contrite for having ignored his date. He motioned toward her salad. "Bambi's on a diet."

"I am not fat," Bambi cried. "You said so yourself."

"I . . . no, I didn't mean to imply that you needed to be on a diet, I was just . . . making small talk."

"Well, if you don't mind, I'd prefer it if you didn't discuss my eating habits."

"Where's the protein?" Carol asked, examining Bambi's plate of greens. "You should be having protein—eggs, lean meats, that sort of thing."

"Who are you?" Bambi flared. "Richard Simmons?"

"You're right, I'm sorry. It's just that I'm a nurse, and I work with pregnant women, and nutrition is such an important part of pregnancy that my feelings just spilled out."

"Are you suggesting I'm pregnant?"

"Oh, no, not in the least." Every time Carol opened her mouth, it seemed she made an even worse mess of the situation. "Look, I think the auto club might need some help finding me. If you'll both excuse me, I'll wait outside."

"You should," Bambi said pointedly. "If you're over thirty, then you're old enough to take care of yourself."

Carol couldn't get away fast enough. The rain was coming down so hard that it was jitterbugging across the asphalt parking lot. Standing just inside the restaurant doorway, Carol buried her hands in her pockets and shivered. She hadn't been there more than a few minutes when Alex joined her.

Before she could say anything, he buried his hands in his own pockets, sighed and said, "I gave her money to take a taxi home."

Carol wasn't sure how to respond. "I hope it wasn't on account of me."

"No." He gifted her with another of his warm sensual smiles. "It was a blind date. I should have known better than to allow myself to get talked into it."

"I got stuck going out on one a while ago, and it was a disaster, too." It got worse the longer she was single. Her friends seemed to believe that since she'd been alone so many years she would be willing to lower her standards. "How long have you been single?" she asked Alex.

"Two years. What about you?"

"Thirteen."

His gaze jerked toward her. "That's a long time."

"So Peter keeps telling me. According to him, I'm about to lose it and need to act fast. I haven't exactly figured out what *it* is, but I have a good idea."

"Jim keeps telling me the same thing. Between him and Barney, that's the guy that arranged this date, they're driving me crazy."

"I know what you mean. My brother's wife calls me at least once a week and reads me ads from the personal columns. Last week's really got me. It was something like—Male, thirty-five, dull and insecure, seeks exciting, wealthy female any age who's willing to love too much. Likes string cheese and pop tarts. If you can solve the crossword puzzles in *TV Guide*, I'm the man for you."

"Maybe we should introduce him to Bambi."

They laughed together, and it felt natural.

"Give me your car keys," Alex said. "I'll check it out and if it's something minor, I might be able to fix it."

"I don't think it is. When the engine died, it sounded serious." Nevertheless, she handed him her key ring and stood under the shelter while Alex ran across the parking lot to test her car. She stood on her tiptoes and watched him raise the hood, disappear for a few moments and then promptly close it and come running back to her.

"I think you're right," he said, rubbing the black grease from his hands with a white handkerchief.

"Excuse us, please," a soft feminine voice purred from behind Carol. Bambi shot past them, her arm looped through that of a much older gentleman. She cast Carol a dirty look and then smiled softly in Alex's direction before turning her attention to her most recent admirer. "Now, what were you saying about your hot tub?"

The two were barely out of earshot when Alex started to chuckle. "It didn't take her long, did it?"

"I really am sorry," Carol felt obliged to say. "I feel terrible . . . as though I personally ruined your whole evening."

"No," he countered. "Quite the contrary, you saved me. By the time you arrived, I was trying to figure out how long my patience was going to hold. I had the distinct impression before the evening was out I was going to become involved in a wrestling match."

Carol laughed. It didn't take much imagination to place Bambi in the role of an Amazon. Come to think of it, Carol had been left to deal with a handful of Bambi's male counterparts over the years.

It was drizzling when the auto club van arrived. Alex walked the driver to Carol's car, and together the two men tried to determine what was wrong with her faithful Ford. They decided that whatever the problem was, it couldn't be fixed there and that the best thing to do was call a tow truck.

Carol agreed and signed on the dotted line.

"I'll give you a lift home," Alex volunteered.

"Thanks." She was already in his debt, one more thing wouldn't matter.

Within a couple of minutes, they were sitting inside Alex's car with the heater running full blast. Carol ran her hands up and down her arms to ward off a chill.

"You're cold."

"I'll be fine in a minute. If I wasn't such a slave to fashion, I would have worn something heavier than this cotton jacket, but it's the same pale green as my slacks and they go so well together."

"You sound just like Jim. It was forty degrees yesterday morning, and he insisted on wearing a shirt from last summer. Did you know sleeves are definitely out? Apparently, no one wears them anymore."

They smiled at each other, and Carol was conscious of how close they were in the snug confines of Alex's sports car. Her dark Italian eyes met his warm gray ones. Without warning, the laughter faded from Alex's lips, and he studied her face. After viewing the damage earlier, Carol knew her dark hair hung in springy ringlets that resembled a pad used to scrub kitchen kettles. She'd done the best she could with it, brushing it away from her face and securing it at the base of her neck with a wide barrette she found in the bottom of her purse. Now she was certain the tail that erupted from her nape must resemble a show horse's.

A small lump lodged in her throat, as though she'd tried to swallow a pill without water. "You never did get your dinner, did you?" she asked hastily.

"Don't worry about it."

"Listen, I owe you, please ... stop somewhere and let me treat you. It's after nine—you must be starved." She glanced at her watch and felt a blush tint her cheeks. It had been longer than she could recall since a man had unsettled her quite this much.

"Don't worry about it, I'm a big boy. I'll make myself a sandwich or something once I get home."

"But—"

"If you insist, you can have me over to eat sometime. All right? When it comes to dinner, Jim and I share the duties. A good home-cooked meal would be welcome."

Carol didn't have any choice but to agree, and she did so by nodding her head briskly several times until she realized she was watering the inside of his car the way a sprinkler does a lawn. "Oh, sure, I'd like that." She thought to comment that she came from a large Italian family and was an excellent cook, but that would sound too much like the personal ads her sister-in-law, Paula, insisted on reading to her.

"You *do* cook?"

"Oh, yes." Once more she held her tongue. Whereas a few moments earlier, she'd been cold, now she felt exceptionally warm. Her hands were clammy and her stomach was filled with what seemed like a swarm of yellow jackets.

They chatted amicably on the remainder of the drive to her house, and Carol was surprised when Alex pulled into her driveway. She turned and smiled at him, her hand on her door handle. "I'm really grateful for all your help."

"No problem."

"And...I'm sorry about what happened with Bambi."

"I'm not," he countered, and then chuckled. "I'll give you a call later, all right?...to check on your car."

The question seemed to hang between them, heavy with implication. It was the "all right" that clued her in to the fact he was referring to something beyond the sure-I'll-send-Jim-home-now conversations they'd had up to that point.

"Okay," she said almost flippantly, feeling more than a little light-headed.

"So, tell me about this man who stirs color back into my little girl's cheeks," Angelina Pasquale said to Carol as she delivered a huge steaming plate of spaghetti to the table.

Carol's mother didn't know how to cook for three or four, it was twelve or fifteen servings for each and every Sunday meal. Her two older sisters lived in California now, and there was only Tony and Carol and their families who religiously came for Sunday dinner. Her mother, however, continued to cook as if two or three families might walk in unannounced and state they'd arrived for the evening meal.

"Mama, Alex Preston and I just met last week."

"That's not what Peter said." The older woman wiped her hands on the large apron that was tied around her thick waist. Her dark hair was neatly tucked behind her head and streaked with gray and white. She wore a small gold crucifix around her neck that had been given to her by Carol's father forty-two years earlier.

Carol brought the long loaves of hot bread from the oven. "Alex is Jim's father. You remember Peter's friend, don't you?"

"He's not Italian."

"I don't know what he is. Preston might be English."

"English," Angelina said the word as if she was spitting out dirty dishwater. "You gonna marry a non-Italian again?"

"Mama," Carol said, silently laughing, "Alex helped me when my car broke down. I owe him dinner, and I insisted on taking him out to repay him. We're not stopping off at the church to get married on the way."

"I bet he's not even Catholic."

"Mama," Carol cried. "I haven't the faintest clue where he attends church."

"You taking a man to dinner instead of cooking for him is sin enough, but to not even know if he's Catholic is asking for trouble." She raised her eyes as if to plead for patience in dealing with her youngest daughter. When she lowered her gaze, they fell to Carol's feet. Once more she folded her hands in prayerlike fashion. "You wear pointed-toed shoes for this man?"

"I didn't wear these for Alex. I happen to like these—they're in style."

"They're gonna deform your feet. One day, you'll trip and end up facedown in the gutter like your cousin Celeste."

"Mama, I'm not going to end up in a gutter."

"Your cousin Celeste told her mother the same thing, and we both know what happened to her. She had to marry a foot doctor in order to live."

"Mama, please don't worry about my shoes."

"Okay, but don't let anyone say that your Mama didn't warn you."

Carol had to leave the room to keep from laughing. Her mother was the delight of her life. She drove Carol crazy with the loony things she said, but Carol knew her advice was deeply rooted in love.

"Carol," Angelina said, surveying the table, "tell everyone dinner's ready."

Peter was in the living room with his younger cousins, who were watching the Dodgers play Kansas City in a hotly contested baseball game.

"Dinner's on the table, guys."

"Just a minute, Mom. It's the bottom of the eighth, with two outs." Peter's intense gaze didn't waver from the screen. "Besides, Uncle Tony and Aunt Paula aren't back from shopping yet."

"They'll eat later." Carol's brother Tony and his wife had escaped for the afternoon to Clackamas Town Center, a large shopping mall south of Portland, and Carol wasn't expecting them until much later.

"Just a few minutes more," Peter pleaded.

"Mama made zabaglione," Carol prompted.

The television went off in a shot, and four bodies rushed into the kitchen, taking their places at the table like a rampaging herd of buffalo. Peter was the oldest by six years, which gave him an air of superiority over his cousins.

Sunday dinner at her mother's was tradition. They were a close-knit family and helped one another without question. Her brother had loaned her his second car while hers was being repaired. Carol didn't know what she would do without him.

Mama treasured these times with her children and grandchildren, generously offering her love, her support and her pasta. Being close to her family was what had gotten Carol through the difficult years following Bruce's death. Her parents had been wonderful, helping her while she worked her way through college and the nursing program, caring for Peter when she couldn't and introducing her to a long list of nice Italian men. After three years of dealing with Bruce's mental and physical abuse, she wasn't interested. The scars from her marriage ran deep.

"I'll say the grace now," Angelina said. Each one in turn bowed their heads and closed their eyes.

No one needed any encouragement to dig into the spaghetti drenched in a sauce that was like no other. Carol's mother was a fabulous cook, from the old school. Angelina Pasquale insisted on making everything from scratch, and she'd personally trained each one of her three daughters.

"So, Peter," his grandmother said, tearing off a thick piece from the end of the loaf of hot bread. "What do you think of your mother marrying this Englishman?"

"Ah, Grandma, it's not like that. Mr. Preston called and Mom insisted on treating him to dinner because he gave her a ride home. I don't think it's any big deal."

"That was what she said when she met your father. 'Ah, Ma,' she told me, 'it's just dinner.' The next thing I know, she's standing at the altar with this non-Italian and six months later the priest was baptizing you.''

"Ma! Please," Carol cried, embarrassed at the way her mother spoke so freely. By now, however, she should be used to it.

"Preston." Once more her mother muttered the name, chewing it with her bread. "Now I could accept the man if he had a nice name like Prestoni. Carol Prestoni has a good Italian ring to it . . . but Preston. Bah."

Peter and Carol shared smiles.

"He's real nice, Grandma."

Angelina expertly wove the long strands of spaghetti around the tines of her fork. "Your mama deserves to meet a nice man. If you say he's okay, then I'll have to take your word for it."

"Mama, it's only one dinner." Carol wished she'd never said anything to her mother. Alex had called the night before, and although he sounded a little disappointed that she wouldn't be making the meal herself, he'd agreed to let her repay the favor with dinner at a local restaurant Monday night. Her big mistake was mentioning the evening to her mother. Carol usually didn't say anything to her family when she was going out on a date. But for some reason, unknown to even herself, she'd mentioned Alex almost immediately when she walked in the door after church Sunday morning.

"What color eyes does this man have?"

"Gray," Carol answered, and poured herself a glass of ice water.

Peter's gaze scooted to his mother. "How'd you remember that?"

"I . . . I just recall they were . . . that color." Already Carol's cheeks were tinged with color. She devoted her attention to her meal, but when she looked up, she noted her mother was watching her closely. "His eyes are sort of striking," she said, mildly irritated by the attention her mother and her son were lavishing on her.

"I never noticed," Peter insisted.

"A boy wouldn't," Angelina muttered, discounting his words, "but your mother, well, she pays attention to such things."

That wasn't entirely true, but Carol wasn't about to claim otherwise.

As soon as they were finished with the meal, Carol's mother brought out the zabaglione, a rich sherry-flavored Italian custard thick with eggs. Angelina promptly dished up six bowls.

"Mama, zabaglione's filled with cholesterol." Since her father's death from a heart attack five years earlier, Carol worried about her mother's health, although she wasn't certain her concern was appreciated.

"So zabaglione's got cholesterol."

"But, Mama, cholesterol clogs the veins. It could kill you."

"If I can't eat zabaglione then I might as well be dead."

Smiling wasn't the thing Carol should have done, but the fact was, she agreed.

When the dishes were washed, and the kitchen counters cleaned, Carol and her mother sat in the living room. Angelina rocked in the chair her mother's mother had brought directly from Italy seventy years earlier. Never one to have idle hands, she reached for her crocheting.

It was a rare treat to have these moments alone with her mother, and Carol sat on the sofa, her feet tucked under her, her head back and eyes closed.

"When am I gonna meet this Englishman who stole your heart?"

"Mama," Carol said with a sigh, opening her eyes, "you're making me sorry I ever mentioned Alex."

"You didn't need to tell me about him. I would have asked, because the minute you walked in the house I could see something in your eyes. It's time, my bambina. Peter is growing and soon you'll be alone."

"I . . . I'm looking forward to that."

Her mother discredited that comment with a hard shake of her head. "You need a husband, one who will give you more children and bring sparkle to your eyes."

Carol's heart started thundering inside her chest. "I . . . I don't think I'll ever remarry, Mama."

"Bah!" the older woman said and laughed loudly. A few moments later, she murmured something in Italian that Carol could only partially understand, but it was enough to make her blush hotly. Her mother was telling her there were things about a man that she shouldn't be so quick to forget.

The soft Italian words brought a vivid image to Carol's mind of Alex holding her in his arms, gazing down at her and making love to her. The image shocked her so much that she quickly made her excuses, collected Peter and drove home.

Her pulse rate hadn't decreased by the time she arrived back at her own small house. Her mother was putting much too much emphasis on her dinner date with Alex . . . far more than necessary.

As soon as Peter went over to a neighbor's to play video games, Carol reached for the phone. When the answering machine picked up her call on the fourth ring, she quickly hung up.

On second thought, this way was better, she decided, and dialed again. "You're a coward," she muttered as she pushed down the buttons. "Admit it!" She waited for someone to do so, but when no voice boomed from the ceiling, she said it herself. "All right, I'll admit it, I'm a coward."

Once more the answering machine acknowledged her call. She waited for the message, followed by a long beep.

"Hello...Alex, this is Carol...Carol Sommars. About our dinner date Monday night...I'm sorry, but I'm going to have to cancel. Something...has come up. I apologize that thisissuchshortnotice. Bye." The last words were all meshed together in her haste to finish.

Her face was flushed, and a thin sheen of moisture had beaded on her upper lip by the time she hung up the phone. With her hand biting into the telephone receiver, she slowly expelled her breath and closed her eyes.

Her mother was right. Alex Preston was the one who could bring the light back into her eyes, and she'd never been more frightened in all her life.

Chapter Three

Carol's hand remained tightly closed around the telephone receiver as she heaved in a giant breath. She'd just completed the most cowardly act of her life.

Almost immediately regretting her actions, she punched out Alex's phone number again, listened to the recorded message a third time while tapping her foot. At the beep, she paused, then blurted out, "I hope you understand . . . I mean . . . oh . . . never mind." With that, she replaced the receiver, pressed her hand over her brow, more confident than ever that she'd just made a world-class idiot of herself.

A half an hour later, Carol was sorting through the dirty clothes in the laundry room when Peter came barreling into the house.

He paused in the doorway, watching her neatly organize several loads. "Hey, Mom, where's the *TV Guide*?"

"By the television?" she offered, more concerned that his jeans' pockets were empty before putting them in the washer than anything as mundane as the location of the weekly magazine.

"Cute, Mom, real cute. Why would anyone put it there?"

Carol paused, holding a pair of dirty jeans to her chest. "Because that's where it belongs?" she suggested hopefully.

"Yeah, but when was the last time anyone found it there?"

Not bothering to answer her fifteen-year-old's question, she dumped his jeans into the washing machine. "Did you look on the coffee table?"

"It's not there. It isn't by the chair, either."

"What is it you're so keen to watch, anyway? Shouldn't you be doing your homework?"

"I don't have any... well I do, but it's a snap."

Carol added another pair of jeans to the churning water. "If it's so easy, do it now."

"I can't until Jim gets home."

At the mention of Alex's son, Carol hesitated. "I... see."

"Besides, it's time for wrestling, but I don't know what channel it's on."

"Wrestling?" Carol cried. "When did you become interested in that?"

"Jim introduced me to it. I know it looks phony and stuff, but I get a kick out of those guys pounding on one another and the crazy things they say to each other on the air."

Carol turned and leaned against the washer, crossing her arms over her chest. "Personally I'd rather you did your homework, and if there's any time left over you can watch television.''

''Of course you'd prefer that,'' Peter echoed. ''You're a mom—it's your God-given duty to think that way. But I'm a kid, and I'd much rather watch Spiderman take on Jack Beanstalk.''

Carol considered her son's argument for less than a moment. ''Do your homework.''

Peter sighed, his youthful shoulders sagging. ''I was afraid you'd say that.'' Reluctantly he headed toward his bedroom.

With the wash taken care of, Carol ventured into the back yard, surveying her neatly edged flower beds. Every year she grew Italian parsley, basil and thyme and a few other herbs in the ceramic pots that bordered her patio. One of these days she was going to dig up a section of her lawn and plant an honest-to-goodness garden.

''Mom...'' Peter was shouting her name from inside the house.

She turned, prepared to answer her son's call, when she saw Alex walk out the back door toward her. Her heart did an immediate somersault, then vaulted into her throat and stayed there for an uncomfortable moment.

''Hello, Alex,'' she managed to say, confident her face held the look of a cornered mouse. She would have gladly given six months' mortgage payments to have discovered a way to remove her messages from his answering machine. It required a good deal of poise just to stand there calmly and not run for the fence.

''Hello, Carol.'' He walked toward her, his gaze holding hers.

He sounded so...casual, so collected, but his eyes were a different story. Carol swore the man had the eyes of an eagle. They'd zeroed in on her as though he was about to swoop down for the kill.

For her part, Carol was a wreck. Her hands were clenched so tightly at her sides that her fingers ached. "What can I do for you?" she asked, shocked by how her voice pitched and heaved with the simple question.

A brief smile flirted with the edges of Alex's mouth. "You mean you don't know?"

"No... well, I can guess, but I think it would be best if you just came out and said it." She took a couple of steps toward him, feeling extraordinarily brave for having done so.

"Will you offer me a cup of coffee?" Alex asked instead.

The man was full of surprises. Just when she was convinced he was about to nail her for behaving like an utter fool, he casually suggested she make coffee. Perhaps he often confronted emotionally insecure women who left nonsensical messages on his answering machine.

"Coffee? Of course... come inside." Pleased to have something to occupy her hands with, Carol hurried into the kitchen and her coffee maker. Once she'd added the grounds to the filter and filled the machine with water, she turned and braced her back against the counter, hoping to look poised and positive. She did an admirable job for the first few moments. After all, she'd spent the last thirteen years on her own. She wasn't a dimwit, although she'd gone out of her way to give him that impression, and she hadn't even been trying. That disconcerted her more than anything. It was a wonder he wanted anything to do with her.

"No, I don't understand," Alex said. He opened her cupboard and brought down two ceramic mugs.

"Understand what?" Carol decided playing dumb might help. It had worked with Bambi, and who was to say it wouldn't with her? However, she had the distinct notion that if she suggested they try out a hot tub, Alex would be more than willing.

"I want to know why you won't have dinner with me."

Carol was completely out of her element. She dealt with pregnancy and birth, soon-to-be mothers and terrorized fathers, and she did so without a pause. But faced with one devilishly handsome single father, she was a worthless mass of frazzled nerves. Fearing her knees might give out on her, she walked over to the table, pulled out a chair and slumped into it. "I didn't exactly say I wouldn't go out with you."

"Then what was it you did say?"

She lowered her gaze, unable to meet his. "That... something came up."

"I see." He twisted the chair around and straddled it. The coffee maker was making gurgling sounds from behind her. Normally she didn't even notice it, but now it seemed to fill her compact kitchen like the roar of a jet plane.

"Then we'll reschedule. Tuesday evening at six?"

"I... I have a class... I teach a birthing class to expectant parents on Tuesday evenings." Now that was brilliant! Who else attended those classes? But it was an honest excuse. "That's where I'd been when my car broke down in the parking lot of the restaurant where I met you... last Tuesday... remember?"

"The night I helped you," Alex reminded her. "As I recall, you claimed you wanted to repay me. Fact is, you insisted upon it. You said I'd missed my dinner because of you and that you'd like to make that up to me. At first it was a home-cooked meal, but that was quickly reduced to us meeting at a restaurant in separate cars, and now you're canceling altogether.''

''I . . . did appreciate your help.''

''Is there something about me that troubles you? Do I have bad breath?''

''Of course not.''

''Dandruff?''

''No.''

''Then what is it?''

''Nothing,'' she cried. She couldn't very well explain that their one meeting had jolted to life a part of her that had lain dormant for more years than she could remember. To say Alex Preston unsettled her would be a gross understatement. She hadn't stopped thinking about him from the moment he'd dropped her off at the house. Every thought that entered her mind was linked to those few short minutes they'd spent alone in his car. She was an adult, a professional, but when she was around him she forgot everything. In thinking about it, Carol supposed it was because she'd married so young and been widowed shortly afterward. It was as though she didn't know how to behave with a man, but that wasn't entirely true, either. For the past several years, she'd dated numerous times. Nothing serious of course, but friendly outings with ''safe'' men. One second with Alex, and she'd known instantly that a date with him could easily send her tranquil, secure world into a whirlwind.

''Wednesday then?''

Carol looked warily across the kitchen, wanting to weep with frustration. She might as well be a good sport about it and give in. Alex wasn't going to let her off the hook without putting up one hell of a fuss.

''All right,'' she said, and for emphasis, nodded. ''I'll see you Wednesday evening.''

"Good." Alex stood and twisted the chair back around. "I'll pick you up at seven." He gifted her with one of his sensual, earthy smiles and was gone even before the coffee had finished brewing.

Once she was alone, Carol placed her hands over her face, feeling the sudden urge to cry, which was ridiculous. Closing her eyes, however, was a mistake, because the minute she did, her mother's whispered words, reminding her of how good lovemaking could be, saturated her thoughts. That subject was the last thing Carol wanted to think about, especially when the one she wanted to be making love to her was the one who had so recently vacated her kitchen.

Abruptly she stood and poured herself a cup of coffee. It didn't help to realize that her fingers were shaking. What was so terrific about men and sex, anyway? Nothing that she could remember. She'd been initiated in the back seat of a car at eighteen with a boy she was crazy in love with. Or the boy she *thought* she was crazy about. More likely it had been hormones on the rampage for them both.

After she learned she was pregnant, Carol was never certain Bruce had truly wanted to marry her. Faced with having to deal with her hotheaded father and older brother, Bruce clearly had regarded marriage as the more favorable option.

If Carol and Bruce had made love before they were married, they had sex afterward. Two weeks after they were married, Carol had learned how vulgar sex could be.

In the last year of her three-year marriage, Bruce had been drunk more than he was sober—abusive more than he was considerate. Lovemaking had become a nightmare for her. He knew better than to approach her while she was awake. Instead, he would wait until she was asleep and mount her before she was ready, and be finished before there was any possibility of her enjoying the act. Feeling violated and vaguely sick to her stomach, she would curl into a tight ball and lie awake the rest of the night. Then Bruce had died, and mingled with the grief and horror had been an almost giddy sense of relief.

"I don't want a man in my life," she cried forcefully.

Peter was strolling down the hallway to his room and stuck his head around the doorway. "Did you say something?"

"Ah..." Carol said, wanting to swallow her tongue. "Nothing important."

"You look nice," Peter told Carol on Wednesday when she finished with her makeup.

"Thanks," she said, smiling confidently. Her attitude toward this evening out with Alex had improved now that she'd had time to properly sort through her confused emotions. Jim's father was a nice guy, and to be honest, Carol didn't know what had been wrong with her Sunday to have caused her to react the way she did. She was a mature adult, and there was nothing to fear. It wasn't as though she was going to fall into bed with the man simply because she found herself attracted to him. They would have the dinner she owed him and that would be the end of it.

As much as she would have liked to deny it, Alex was special. For the first time in more years than she could remember, she was physically attracted to a man. And what was wrong with that? It only went to prove that she was a red-blooded woman. In fact, she should be grateful to Alex for helping her realize how healthy she was.

"Where is Mr. Preston taking you?" Peter asked, plopping himself down on the edge of the bathtub, watching her fluff out the ends of her eyelashes with a thin coating of mascara.

"Actually I'm taking him, and I thought we'd go to Jake's." Jake's was a well-known and well-loved Portland restaurant renowned for their Cajun dishes.

"You're taking Mr. Preston to Jake's?" Peter cried, his voice thick with envy. "Are you planning on bringing me back something?"

"No." As it was, she was stretching her budget for the meal.

"But, Mom, Jake's? You know that's my favorite restaurant in the whole world." He made it sound as though he were a global traveler and a connoisseur of fine dining.

"I'll take you there on your birthday." The way she had every year since he was ten.

"But that's another five months," Peter grumbled, not easily appeased.

She hesitated and gave him what she referred to as her "Mother Look", which generally worked to silence him.

"All right, all right," he muttered. "I'll be more than happy to eat frozen pot pie for the third time in the past week. There's no need to worry about me."

"I won't."

Peter sighed with feeling. "You go ahead and enjoy your *étouffée.*"

"I'm sure I will." She generally ordered the shrimp dish, which was a popular item on the menu.

Peter continued to study her, his expression revealing mild surprise. "Gee, Mom, don't you have a heart anymore? I used to be able to get you with guilt, but you hardly bat an eyelash anymore."

"Of course I've got a heart. Unfortunately I don't have a pocketbook to support it."

It looked for a moment as though Peter was about to say something else, but the doorbell chimed and he rushed out of the tiny bathroom to answer it as though something dire would happen if Alex were forced to wait more than a few seconds.

Expelling a sigh, Carol surveyed her appearance in the mirror one last time, confident that she looked her best. With a prepared smile on her face, she headed for the living room where Alex was waiting.

The instant she appeared, Alex's gaze rushed to hers . . . and held. The impact of seeing him again was immediate and strong. He was tall and long-limbed. It was difficult to take her eyes off him. Instead, she found herself thinking that his build suggested finely honed muscles. His shoulders were wide and his chest heavy, and Carol found him incredibly good-looking in his pinstriped suit. His face was weathered from working out of doors, his features sculptured and bronzed by the sun.

So much for the best-laid plans, Carol mused, shaking from the inside out. She'd planned this evening down to the smallest detail. They would have dinner, during which Carol would subtly inform him she wasn't interested in anything more than a casual friendship, then he'd take her home, and that would be the end of it. Five seconds after she walked into the living room, she was thinking about silk sheets and long, slow, heart-melting kisses.

Her mother was responsible for this. Her outrageous, wonderful mother and the softly murmured Italian words that reminded Carol she was still young and it was time to live and love again. She was alive all right. From the top of her head to the bottom of her feet, she was all the way alive.

"Hello, Carol."

"Alex."

"Mom's taking you to Jake's," Peter said, not bothering to hide his envy. "She can't afford to bring me anything home, but that's okay."

"Peter," she chastised, doubting that Alex had heard him.

"Are you ready?"

She nodded, taking a couple of additional moments to gather her composure while she reached for her jacket and purse. Glancing in her son's direction, she felt obligated to remind him, "You know the rules. I'll call you later."

"You don't need to phone," he said, making a show of rolling his eyes as if to suggest she was going way overboard on this parental thing.

"We'll be back early."

Alex cupped her elbow in his hand as he directed her toward the front door. "Not too early," he amended.

By the time they were outside, Carol had managed to bridle her fears and present an imperturbable facade. Her years of medical training played heavily in her ability to present a calm, composed front. And really, there wasn't a reason in the world why she should panic this way.

They talked amicably on the drive into the downtown portion of Portland, commenting on such natural subjects as the weather, when her car would be fixed and the approach of summer, which they both dreaded because the boys would be constantly under foot.

Alex managed to find parking on the street, which was something of a feat in its own right. He opened her car door for her and gave her his hand, which he didn't release.

Since Carol had made a reservation, they were seated immediately in a high-backed polished wood booth and greeted by their waiter, who recited the specials of the day.

"Jim tells me you're buying him a truck," Carol stated conversationally once they'd placed their order.

"So he'd like to believe."

Carol hesitated. "You mean you haven't?"

"Not to the best of my knowledge," Alex admitted, grinning.

Once more, Carol found herself fascinated by his smile, which was little more than a lopsided slashing of his lips. She found herself wondering how his mouth would feel and taste over hers. As quickly as the thought entered her mind, she discarded it.

"According to Jim it's to be the latest model, red with flames decorating the sidewalls."

"The boy likes to dream," Alex said, leaning back and relaxing. "If he drives any vehicle for the next two years, it'll be because he's impressed me with his grades, and his maturity."

"Oh, Alex," Carol said with an abbreviated sigh, "you don't know how pleased I am to hear that. For weeks, Peter's been making me feel as though I'm an abusive mother because I'm not buying him a car...better yet, a truck. Time and time again he's reminded me that *you're* buying one for Jim and how sharing the Ford with me could possibly damage his self-esteem, which might result in long-term counseling."

Alex laughed outright, the robust sound filling the crowded room and garnering them attention.

"By the way, Jim isn't Jim anymore, he's James."

"James?"

"Right. He noticed for the first time his learner's permit stated his name as James Preston, and he's insisting that everyone call him that. Actually I think he came up with the idea after I spoke to him about driving and his level of maturity. James is apparently more mature-sounding than Jim."

"Apparently," Carol returned, smiling. "Well, at least if Peter does end up having to go to a counselor, he'll have company."

Their meal arrived. The steaming *étouffée* was placed before her, and she didn't experience the least bit of guilt when she sampled the first bite. It was as delicious as she remembered.

"Have you been a nurse long?" Alex asked, when their conversation lagged.

"Eight years. I returned to school after my husband was killed, and nursing was a natural for me. I was forever putting Band-Aids on my dolls and treating everyone from my dog to my tolerant mother whenever anyone was sick."

"The next time I have the flu, I'll know who to call," Alex teased.

"Oh, good. When I'm ready to put the addition on the house, I'll contact you," Carol returned.

They both laughed.

The evening wasn't nearly as difficult as Carol had dreaded. Alex was easy to talk to, and with the boys as common, fertile ground there was never a lack for subject matter. Before Carol was aware of it, it was nearly ten.

"Oh, dear," she said, sliding from the booth. "I told Peter I'd check in with him. Excuse me a minute."

"Sure," Alex said, standing himself.

Carol was at the pay phone waiting for Peter to answer when she looked over and noted that Alex was using the second pay phone.

"Hello."

"Peter, it's Mom."

"Mom, you said you were going to phone," he accused, sounding offended. "Do you know what time it is? When you say you're going to phone you usually do. James is worried, too. Where have you guys been?"

"Jake's—you knew that."

"All this time?"

"Yes. I'm sorry, sweetheart, time got away with us."

"So I see," Peter said and paused. "So you like Mr. Preston?"

Carol hedged the question by responding, "He's very nice."

"Do you think you'll go out with him again? What did you guys talk about all this time? Just how much time does it take to eat dinner, anyway?"

"Peter, this isn't the time or the place to be having this discussion."

"I don't suppose there were any leftovers."

"None."

Her son sighed as if he'd actually been counting on her bringing home her untouched dinner as reward for the supreme sacrifice of having to eat chicken pot pie, which just happened to be one of his favorites.

"When will you be home? I mean, you don't have to rush on my account or anything, but you'd never let me stay out this late on a weeknight."

"I'll be back before eleven," she promised, ignoring the comment about the lateness of the hour. Sometimes Peter forgot who was the adult and who was the child.

"You *do* like Mr. Preston, don't you?" The question was too smug for comfort.

"Peter," she moaned. "I'll talk to you later." She was about to replace the receiver when she heard him call her name. "What is it now?" she said sharply, impatiently.

He hesitated, apparently taken back by her brusqueness. "Nothing, I just wanted to tell you to wake me up when you get home, all right?"

"All right," she said, feeling immediately guilty.

She met Alex back at their table. "Is everything all right at home?" he asked.

"Couldn't be better." There was no need to inform Alex of the inquisition Peter had wanted to give her. "What about Jim—James?"

"He's surviving."

"I suppose we'd better think about getting home," Carol suggested, eager now to leave. The evening had flown. At some point during dinner, her guard had slipped and she'd found herself enjoying his company with none of the terrible tension that had plagued her earlier.

"I suppose you're right," Alex said with enough reluctance to alarm her. He'd apparently enjoyed their time as much as she had.

They had a small disagreement over the check, which Alex refused to let her take. He silenced her protests by reminding her that she owed him a home-cooked meal, and he wasn't accepting any substitutes. After a couple of glasses of wine and a good dinner, Carol was too mellow to put up much of an argument.

"Just don't let Peter know," she said as they walked toward the car. Alex held her hand, and it seemed far too natural. It would have been unnatural for her to object.

"Why?"

"If Peter discovers you insisted on paying, he'll want to know why I didn't bring him something home."

Alex grinned as he unlocked his car door and held it open for her. He closed his hands over the curve of her shoulder, and his warm gaze closed over her. "You will cook me that dinner sometime, won't you?"

Before she realized what she was doing, Carol found herself shaking her head. The realization hit her like a lead balloon. She hadn't had time to compose herself by the time he'd walked around the front of the car and joined her.

Neither of them spoke on the drive back to her house. Carol's mind was filled with the things she'd planned to tell him. The things she'd carefully thought out beforehand—about what a nice time she'd had, and how she hoped they would stay in touch and what a good boy Jim—James—was and how Alex was doing an admirable job raising him. But the trite, prepared words refused to come.

Alex pulled into her driveway and turned off the engine. The living room was dark and the drapes pulled. The only illumination was the dim light on the front porch. When Alex turned to face her, Carol's heart exploded with dread and wonder. His look was warm, tender and eager enough to cause her blood to run hot . . . and then immediately cold.

"I had a good time tonight." He spoke first.

"I did, too." How weak she sounded, as though she were only recently recovered from a life-threatening illness.

"I'd like to see you again."

The words she'd feared, and longed for in the same thought, collided in her mind. The deep restlessness she'd experienced since the night her car had broken down reverberated within her, echoing like a sonic boom through the empty years she'd spent alone.

"Carol?"

ı don't know." She tried to remind herself of what her life had been like with Bruce. The tireless lies, the crazy brushes with danger as though he were courting death. The anger and impatience, the pain that gnawed at her soul. She thought of the wall she'd so carefully constructed around her heart. A wall years thick and so high no man had ever dared to challenge it. "I . . . don't think so."

"Why not? I don't understand."

Words could never explain the fear.

"Let me revise the statement," Alex said. "I need to see you again."

"Why?" she cried. "This was only supposed to be one night . . . to thank you for your help. I can't give you any more . . . I just can't and . . ." Her breath scattered, and her lungs burned within her chest. She couldn't explain, nor could she deny the things he made her feel.

"Carol," he said gently, softly. "There's no reason to be afraid."

But there was, only he wouldn't understand.

He reached up and placed his calloused palm against her cheek.

Carol flinched and slammed her eyes closed. "No . . . please, I have to go inside . . . Peter is waiting for me." She closed her hand around the door handle, and it was all she could do not to leap from the car and rush toward the house.

"Wait," he said huskily, removing his hand from her face. "I didn't mean to frighten you."

She nodded, and her startled gaze collided with his. She watched as his eyes slowly appraised her, taking in her flushed face, and then lowered as he watched the uneven rise and fall of her breasts. A frown settled over his face.

"You're trembling."

"I'm fine...really. Thank you for tonight, I had a marvelous time."

His hand settled over hers. "You'll see me again."

It wasn't until she was safely inside her living room and her heart was back to normal that Carol realized his parting comment had been a statement of fact.

Chapter Four

So, Dad, how did dinner go with Mrs. Sommars?'' James asked as he poured himself a huge bowl of cornflakes. He added enough sugar to make eating it worth his while, and then for extra measure added a couple of teaspoons more.

Alex cupped his steaming mug of coffee as he considered his son's question. "Dinner went fine." It was afterward that clung to his mind. Someone had hurt Carol, and hurt her badly. He'd barely touched her and she'd trembled. Her dark chocolate eyes had clouded, and she couldn't seem to get out of his car fast enough. The crazy part was, Alex was convinced she was attracted to him. He knew something else—she didn't want to be.

They'd spent hours talking over dinner, and it had seemed as though only a few moments had passed. There was no need for pretense between them. She didn't pretend to be something she wasn't, and he was free to be himself as well. They were simply two single parents who shared a good deal in common. After two years of dealing with the single's scene, Alex found Carol a refreshing change. He found her alluringly beautiful and at the same time scandalously innocent. During the course of their evening, she'd argued with him over politics, surprised him with her wit and challenged his intelligence. In those few hours, Alex learned this intriguing widow was a study of absorbing and charming contrasts, and he couldn't wait to see her again.

"Mrs. Sommars is a neat lady," James added, claiming the kitchen chair across from his father. "She's a little weird, though."

Alex pulled his gaze away from his coffee. "How's that?"

"She listens to opera," James explained between bites. "Sings it, too—" He paused, planted his elbows on the tabletop, leaned forward and whispered "—in Italian."

"Whoa." Alex was impressed.

"At the top of her voice. Peter told me she won't let him play his rap tapes nearly as loud as she does her silly opera stuff."

"The injustice of it all."

James ignored his sarcasm. "Peter was telling me his grandmother's a real kick, too. She says things like—'Eat your vegetables or I'm calling my Uncle Vito in Jersey City.'"

Alex laughed, glanced at his watch and reluctantly stood. He finished off the last of his coffee and set the mug in the sink. "Have you got your lunch money?"

"Dad, I'm not a kid anymore. You don't have to ask me dumb stuff like that."

"Do you?" Alex pressed.

James stood and reached inside his hip pocket. His eyes became round and flew to his father's. "I . . . guess I left it in my room."

"Don't forget your driver's permit, either."

"Dad!"

Alex held up both hands. "Sorry."

He was all the way to the front door when James's sudden shout stopped him.

"Don't forget to pick me up from track practice, all right?"

Alex pointed his finger like a pistol at his son and calmly said, "I'll be there."

"Hey, Dad."

"What now?" Alex complained.

James shrugged and leaned his shoulder against the doorjamb leading into the kitchen. "In case you're interested, Mrs. Sommars will be there, too."

Alex was interested. Very interested.

He left the house and climbed inside his work van, sitting in the driver's seat with his hands on the steering wheel while he mulled over once more the events from the night before. He'd dated several women recently. Beautiful women, intelligent women, wealthy women. He didn't like to think he was conceited, but he could have bedded any one of them without a pause. A couple of them had come on hot and heavy to him. But not one of them had appealed to him as strongly as this widow with the dark, frightened eyes and the soft, delectable mouth.

A deep part of him yearned to stroke away the pain she held on to so tightly, whatever its source. He longed to watch the anxiety fade from her eyes when she settled into his arms. He craved to have her look at him and feel secure enough to relax and smile. The urge to hold and kiss her was strong, but for whatever reason, he sincerely doubted that Carol would let him.

"Okay, Peggy, bear down...push...hard as you can," Carol urged the young mother-to-be, holding on to Peggy's hand. She did as Carol asked, gritting her teeth, arching forward and lifting her head off the hospital pillow. She gave it everything she had, whimpering softly with the intensity of the labor pain. When the contraction had passed, Peggy's head fell back and she took in several deep breaths.

"You're doing a good job," Carol said, patting her shoulder.

"How much longer will it be before my baby's born?"

"Soon," Carol assured her. "The doctor's on his way now."

The woman's eyes drifted closed. "Where's Danny? I need Danny."

"He'll be back in a minute." Carol had given her patient's husband a set of surgical greens and suggested he change clothes now instead of when they transferred his wife into the delivery room.

"I'm so glad you're here."

Carol smiled. "I'm glad I'm here, too."

"Danny wants a son so much."

"I'm sure he'll be just as happy with a little girl."

Peggy smiled, but that quickly faded as another contraction started coming on. She reached for Carol's hand, her face marked by the long hours she'd struggled to give birth. Carol had spent the past hour with her. She preferred it when they weren't so busy and she could dedicate herself to one patient. But more days than she cared to remember, the hospital's five labor rooms had been full, and she spent her time racing from one to the other.

Peggy groaned, shooting her gaze to a focal point on the wall. The technique was one Carol had taught in her classes. Concentrating on a set object helped the mother remember and practice the breathing techniques.

"You're doing just fine," Carol said softly. "Take in a deep breath now and let it out slowly."

"I can't do it anymore...I can't," Peggy cried. "Where's Danny? Why is it taking him so long?"

"He'll be back any second." Carol's gaze skipped to the monitor, which indicated the fetal heartbeat and the length and intensity of the contractions. Now that her patient was in the final stages, the labor pains were stronger and closer together.

Danny walked into the room, looking pale and anxious...and so very young. He walked around the side of the bed and reached for his wife's hand, holding it to his cheek. He seemed as relieved as his wife when the contraction eased.

Dr. Adams, old and wise, and a hospital institution, sauntered into the room, hands in his pockets, smiling. "So, Peggy, it looks like we're going to finally have that baby."

Peggy grinned sheepishly. "I told Dr. Adams yesterday I was sure I was going to be pregnant until Christmas. I didn't think this baby ever wanted to be born!"

Phil Adams gave his instructions to Carol, and within a few minutes the medical team had assembled in the delivery room with the about-to-be first-time parents. From that point on, everything moved like precision clockwork, and before the hour, a squalling Danny, Jr., was placed in his father's waiting arms.

"Peggy...oh Peggy, a son." Tears of joy rained down the young man's face as he sobbed unabashedly, holding his son close to his breast.

Although Carol witnessed scenes such as this day in and day out, the thrill of helping bring a tiny being into the world never left her.

When her shift was completed, she showered and changed clothes, keeping her eye on the clock. She had to pick Peter up from track practice on her way home, and she didn't want to keep him waiting, although she was the one likely to be left twiddling her thumbs.

The first thing Carol noticed when she pulled into the school parking lot was a van with Preston Construction printed in large black letters on the side. Alex. She drew in a shaky breath, determined to be friendly, but reserved. After the way she'd escaped from his car the night before, it was doubtful he would want to have anything to do with her, anyway.

The fact was, she couldn't blame him. She wasn't exactly sure what had come over her. Well, then again, she did know... and she didn't want to dwell on it.

She parked a safe distance away, praying that either Peter would soon be finished and they could leave or that Alex wouldn't notice her arrival. She turned off the ignition and reached for a magazine, burying her face in its pages. For five minutes nothing happened.

When the driver's side of the van opened, Carol realized that her luck wasn't going to hold. She did her best to concentrate on a recipe for stuffed pork chops and pretend she hadn't seen Alex approach her. When she glanced up, he was standing alongside her car. Instinctively their eyes met. Brown eyes to gray, and gray eyes to brown, for what seemed the longest moment of her life.

"Hello again." He leaned forward and rested his hands along the inside of her window.

"Hello, Alex."

"Warm day, isn't it?"

"Lovely." It wasn't only his smile that intrigued her, she realized grudgingly, but his eyes as well. Their color was like a cool mist rising off a pond. Would this attraction never stop? She continued to discover a new facet of this man that intrigued and excited her each time they met. Three brief encounters, and she was already tied up in knots so tight she couldn't think clearly.

"How was your day?" His eyes were relentless, searching for answers she couldn't give him to questions she didn't want to remember.

She glanced away. "Good. How about yours?"

"Fine." He rubbed a hand along the back of his neck. "I was going to call you later."

"Oh?"

"To ask if you'd like to attend the Home Show with me Friday night. I thought we could have dinner and do the tour."

Carol opened her mouth to refuse, but he stopped her, laying his finger across her lips, silencing her. The instant his hand came in contact with her skin, the warm, dizzy feeling began. As implausible, as preposterous as it seemed, a deep physical sensation flooded her body. Her breasts felt exquisitely heavy, and the part of her that was uniquely feminine started to pulse. And all he'd done was lightly press his finger to her lips!

"Don't say no," Alex said, his voice husky and deep.

She couldn't, at least not then, if her life had depended upon it. "I . . . I'll have to check my schedule."

"You can tell me tomorrow."

She nodded, although it demanded a supreme effort.

"Good . . . I'll talk to you then."

It wasn't until he'd removed his finger, sliding it across her moist lips, that Carol breathed again.

"What do you mean you can't pick me up from track practice?" Peter complained the following morning. "How else am I supposed to get home? Walk?"

"From track practice. The horror of it all." She added an extra Twinkie to his lunch because despite everything, she felt guilty about asking him to find another way home. She was such a coward.

"Mom, coach works us hard—you know that. I was so stiff last night I could barely move. Remember?"

Regretfully, Carol did. A third Twinkie made its way into the brown-paper sack.

"What could possibly be more important that picking me up?"

Escaping a man. If only Alex hadn't been so gentle. Carol had lain awake half the night, not knowing what was wrong with her or how to deal with it. This thing with Alex, whatever it was, stunned, perplexed and bewildered her. Italians were demonstrative people. For most of her life, Carol had given and received countless hugs and kisses—from relatives, from strangers. Touching and being touched were a natural part of her personality. But all Alex had done was press his finger to her lips, and her response... her response still left her stunned.

As she lay in bed, recalling each detail of their brief exchange, her body had reacted again. He didn't even need to be in the same room with her! Alone, in the wee hours of the morning, she was consumed by the need to be loved by him.

She woke with the alarm, in a cold sweat, trembling and frightened, convinced more than ever that she would be a fool to give a man that kind of power over her life a second time.

"Mom," Peter said impatiently. "I asked you a question."

"Sorry," she said, dragging her gaze back to her son's. "What was it you wanted to know?"

"I asked why you aren't going to be at the track this afternoon. It's a simple question."

Intuitively Carol knew she wasn't going to be able to escape Alex, and she would be a bigger fool than she was already even to try.

"I'll be there," she said softly, and handed him his lunch.

Peter stood frozen, studying her. "Are you sure you're not coming down with a fever?"

If only he knew.

When Carol pulled into the school parking lot later that same day, she saw Alex's van parked in the same space as it had been the day before. Only this time he was standing outside, one foot braced against the side, fingertips tucked in his hip pockets. His jeans hugged his hips and fit tight across his thighs. He wore a checked work shirt with the sleeves rolled up past his elbows.

When she appeared, he lowered his foot and straightened, his movement leisurely and confident.

It was all Carol could manage to slow down and park her car next to his. In an effort not to be placed at a disadvantage, she opened her door and climbed out.

"Good afternoon," she said, smiling so brightly her mouth felt as though it would crack.

"Hello, again."

A lock of his dark hair fell over his forehead, and he threaded his fingers through its thickness, pushing it away from his face. It was in her mind to tell him to leave it there. It was charmingly boyish.

Once more his gaze tugged at hers until their eyes met briefly, intently.

"It's warmer today than it was yesterday," she said conversationally.

"Yes, it is."

Carol lowered her gaze to his chest, thinking she would be safe if she practiced what she preached. Find a focal point and concentrate. Only it didn't work as well in matters such as this. Instead of saying what had been on her mind most of the day, she became aware of the pattern of his breathing, and how the rhythm of her own had deviated from the norm.

"Have you decided?"

Her eyes rushed to his, not understanding.

"About Friday night." If only it could be the way it had been in the restaurant when they'd talked and eaten. There was something about being with a crowd that relaxed her. She hadn't felt the least bit intimidated.

"I...don't think our dating is such a good idea. It'd be best if we...stayed friends. I can foresee all kinds of problems if we were to start seeing each other, can't you?"

"The Home Show's going to cause problems?"

"No...our seeing each other will."

"Why?"

"The boys—"

"Couldn't care less. If anything, they approve of our dating each other. I don't understand why there would be any problems. I like you and you like me—we've got a lot in common. We have fun together, and what could be so unhealthy in that?"

Carol couldn't very well explain that when he touched her, even lightly, tiny atoms started exploding inside her; her reaction to him was nuclear. Whenever they were within ten feet of each other, the air crackled with sensuality that grew more intense with each encounter. Surely he could feel it, too. Surely he was aware of it.

Carol pressed a hand to her brow, not knowing how to answer him. If she were to point out the obvious, she would sound like a fool, but she couldn't deny it, either.

"I . . . just don't think our seeing each other is a good idea."

"I do," he countered. "In fact, it appeals to me more every minute."

"Oh, Alex, please don't do this."

Other cars were filling the parking lot, and the two of them had quickly become the center of attraction. Carol glanced around self-consciously, praying he would accept her refusal and leave it at that. She should have known better.

"Come in here," Alex said, opening the side panel to his van. He stepped inside and offered her his hand. She joined him before she had time to determine the wisdom of doing so.

Alex closed the door. "Now where were we . . . ah yes, you'd decided you didn't want to go out with me again."

That wasn't quite accurate, but she wasn't going to argue the point. She'd rarely wanted anything more than to continue seeing him, but she wasn't ready. Dear God . . . Bruce had been dead for thirteen years. If she wasn't ready by now, she never would be. The knowledge hit her hard, like an unexpected blow, and her eyes flew to his.

"Carol?" He stepped toward her, the confines of the van already tight. The walls seemed to close in around her. He was so close, she could smell the scent of his aftershave and the not unpleasant effects of the day's labor. So close she could feel the heat coming off his body.

Emotion thickened the air, and the need that washed through her was both pagan and primitive.

She backed as far as she could against the orderly rows of tools and supplies stacked on the shelves. Alex towered above her, his eyes studying her with such tenderness and concern that she had to repress the urge to weep.

"Are you claustrophobic?"

She shook her head.

His eyes settled on her mouth, and once more Carol felt the clinging tightness come over her breasts, weighing them down. Her nipples beaded and stabbed at the thin material of her silky blouse. She'd unconsciously held her breath so long that when she released it, it burned her chest. If she hadn't been so terrorized, Carol would have marveled at what was happening between them, enjoyed the flood of sensations.

Gently Alex whisked back a strand of hair from her face. At his touch, Carol's breath scattered. He seemed to gain confidence when she didn't flinch away from him, and he cupped her cheek in his calloused palm.

Carol's eyes momentarily drifted shut, and she pressed her own hand over his.

"I'm going to kiss you."

She knew it and was unwilling to dredge up the determination to stop him.

His hands slipped to her shoulders as he slowly drew her forward. It was in her mind to end this now, to pull away. With the least amount of resistance he would have released her, she didn't doubt that for a second. It was as if this moment had been preordained, and she would be tempting the Fates to have denied him . . . denied herself this moment.

At first all he did was press his lips to hers. That was enough, more than enough. Her fingers curled into the broad expanse of his chest as he rubbed his mouth over hers in sweeping forays, using the tip of his tongue in ways she'd never learned.

She whimpered when he paused.

He sighed.

Her breathing was shallow.

His was harsh and choppy.

He hesitated and lifted his head, his eyes wide and shocked, his brow pleated with a dark frown. Whatever he had decided, he didn't share, letting her draw her own conclusions.

Her hands were braced against his chest when he sought her mouth again. This time, the force of his kiss tilted back her head, as he fused their lips together. The heat, hot enough to scorch them both, intensified. Alex continued grinding his lips over hers, giving her no choice but to respond. When her mouth opened, he groaned and thrust his tongue inside the inviting warmth, mating his tongue with hers until Carol was convinced they were both going to burst into flames.

He kissed and held her, and her lungs forgot it was necessary to breathe. Her heart no longer found it important to beat. Her soul refused to remember all the barren years of loneliness.

From somewhere far, far away, Carol heard voices. Her ears closed out the sound, not wanting anything or anyone to destroy this precious moment.

Alex groaned, but it wasn't to communicate pleasure, but frustration. Carol didn't understand. Nor did she realize what was happening when he released her gradually, pushing himself away from her. Then he turned away and called.

"The door's locked."

"The door?" she echoed. It wasn't until then that she realized Alex was talking to the boys. Peter and Jim were standing outside the van, wanting in. Dear God, she'd been so involved with Alex that she hadn't even heard her own son call her name.

"Open that door immediately," she demanded, amazed as hell at how composed she sounded. The trembling hadn't started yet, but it would soon, and the faster she made her escape, the better.

"I will in just a minute." He turned back to her and braced his hands on her shoulders. "You're going with me Friday night. Understand?"

"No..."

He cradled her face with his hands and kissed her once more, forcefully.

She gasped with shock and pleasure.

"I'm not going to stand here and argue with you, Carol. We've got something good going between us, and I'm not about to let you run away from it."

Standing stock-still, it was all she could do to agree.

He kissed the tip of her nose, then turned and slid open the van door.

"What are you doing with Mrs. Sommars?" Jim demanded. "I've been standing out here for the past five minutes trying to get inside."

"Hi, Mom," Peter said, studying her through narrowed eyes. "Everyone else has already gone home. Did you know you left the keys in the ignition?"

"I...Mr. Preston was showing me his...van." She was sure her face was as red as a fire truck, and she dared not meet her son's eyes for fear he would know she'd just been thoroughly kissed. Good heavens, he probably already did.

"Are you feeling all right?" Peter asked her.

"Sure. Why?" She felt as graceful as a hippo as she stepped down onto the pavement. James climbed in as she climbed out and walked over to her car.

"I think you might be coming down with something," Peter said as he automatically sat himself in the driver's seat, assuming he'd be doing the duties. He snapped the seat belt into place. "There were three Twinkies in my lunch, and no sandwich."

"There were?" Carol distinctly remembered spreading peanut butter over the bologna slices—Peter's favorite sandwich. She must have left it on the kitchen counter-top.

"Not to worry, I traded off two of the Twinkies." He readjusted the rearview mirror and turned the key. He was about to pull out of the parking space when a huge smile erupted over his youthful face, and it looked as if he was having trouble not laughing outright. "I'm glad you and Mr. Preston are getting along so well."

Alex sat at his cluttered desk with his hands cupped behind the back of his head, staring aimlessly into space. He'd finally kissed her. Dear God, he felt like a kid again. A slow, easy smile spread across his face, a smile so full, his cheeks ached with it. And what a kiss it had been. Satisfying enough to hold him until he could see her again. He was going to kiss her then, too, long enough for her to blossom in his arms. By God, he could hardly wait.

The intercom buzzed. "Mr. Miller's here."

Alex's smile brightened. "Send him in." He stood and held out his hand to Barney, his best friend. They'd been in college together, roommates their senior year, and had been close ever since. Barney was a rare kind of friend, one who'd seen him through the bad times and the good times and had been there for both in equal measure.

"Alex, it's good to see you." He helped himself to a butterscotch candy from the bowl on the edge of the desk and took a seat. "How you doing?"

"Good." It was on the tip of his tongue to tell Barney about Carol, but everything was so new, he didn't know if he could find the words to explain what he was feeling.

"I've decided to forgive you."

Alex arched his eyebrows. "For what?"

"Bambi. She said you dumped her at the restaurant."

"Oh, that. It wouldn't have worked, anyway."

"Why not?" Barney said, unwrapping the hard candy and popping it inside his mouth.

"I don't have a hot tub."

"She claimed you left with another woman. A bag lady?"

Alex chuckled. "Not exactly."

"Well, you needn't worry, because ol' Barn has met Ms. Right and is willing to share the spoils."

"Barn, listen . . ."

He raised his hand, stopping him. "She's perfect. I swear to you she's bright, beautiful and buxom. The three *b*'s—who could ask for anything more?"

"As I recall, that's what you told me about Bambi," Alex countered, humored by his friend's attempts to find him a wife. It wouldn't be quite so amusing if Barney could stay married himself. In the past fifteen years, his friend had gone through three wives. Each one of them beautiful, bright and buxom.

They might have been the best of friends, but when it came to women, their tastes were as dissimilar as could be. Barney went for breasts, whereas Alex was far more interested in brains. Nice breasts, like Carol's, were a bonus.

"You're going to let me introduce her to you, aren't you? I mean, the least you can do is meet Babette."

"No thanks, Barn."

"You won't even have a drink with her?"

"Sorry, I'm not interested."

Barney leaned back and crossed his legs, and sucked on the butterscotch candy a few seconds before he spoke. "She was first runner-up for Miss Oregon several years back. Does that tell you anything?"

"Sure," Alex said, reaching for a candy himself. "She looks terrific in a swimsuit and plays the piano."

Barney slowly shook his head. "I don't understand it. I thought you were ready to get back into the dating scene."

"I am."

"Listen, buddy, take a tip from a good friend. Play the field, sample the riches available and then settle down. I'm happier when I'm married, and you will be, too. Frankly, with your looks and money, I don't think you'll have much of a problem. There are plenty of willing chicks out there. Only I notice you aren't doing anything to meet one."

"I don't have to, you're worse than a matchmaker."

Barney ignored that. "It's time, Alex. You said so yourself. Just how long are you going to wait? Gloria's been gone two years now. She wouldn't have wanted this."

"I know." At the mention of his late wife, Alex felt a small twinge of pain. Time had healed the worst of it, but he would always remember the agony of being forced to watch the beautiful woman he loved die.

"You want me to give you Babette's phone number?" his friend asked gently.

Alex shook his head. "Don't bother to introduce me to any more of your woman friends."

Barney's mouth sagged open. "But you just admitted that I was right, that it's time to get out there and—"

"Remember the bag lady Bambi was telling you about?" Alex asked, interrupting his friend before he delivered the entire five-minute lecture.

"Yeah, what about her?"

"I'm going to marry her."

Chapter Five

"You know, Mom, I like Mr. Preston," Peter announced over dinner as though this were a deep, dark secret he'd been waiting to share.

"He seems very nice," Carol agreed, reaching for a slice of tomato. She didn't want to say anything more to encourage this topic, so she changed it. "How was school?"

"Fine. James was telling me about all the neat things him and his dad do together, like camping and fishing and stuff like that."

"Your Uncle Tony takes you with him."

"Not camping or fishing and besides, it's not the same," Peter fussed. "Uncle Tony's my *uncle*."

Carol paused, her fork poised over the plump red tomato. "Now that was profound."

"You don't know what I mean, do you?"

"I guess not," Carol admitted.

"Going camping with Mr. Preston would be like having a dad."

"How's that?" She took a bite of roast, and braced her elbows against the tabletop.

"You know."

"I don't," she countered.

Peter lapsed into silence as he mulled over his thoughts. "I guess what I'm trying to tell you is that James and I talked it over and we decided that we'd like it if the two of you want to get married."

Carol was so shocked by her son's statement that she stopped eating. Peter was staring at her, studying her for any sign or reaction.

"Well?" he pressed. "Is it going to happen? You two obviously like each other."

Chewing furiously, Carol dramatically waved her fork at her son, letting it speak for her. The meat, which had been so tender a few moments before, took on the quality of leather. The faster she chewed, the more there seemed to be.

"You may think I'm still a kid and I don't know much," Peter continued, "but it didn't take James and me long to figure out what was going on inside his dad's van."

The piece of meat slid down Carol's throat like a lead weight. She blinked a couple of times, uncertain if she could speak normally.

Peter was grinning ear to ear. "I wish you could have seen your face when Mr. Preston opened the door of the van." Peter didn't even bother to disguise his amusement. "If I hadn't been arguing with James, I would have started laughing right then."

"Arguing with James?" Three words were all she could engineer from her lips. From the moment the two boys had met the first day of high school, they'd been the best of friends. In all the months since September, Carol couldn't remember them arguing once.

"We had words when we couldn't get his dad to open the van," Peter admitted. His mouth wobbled with barely restrained amusement. "Your face was so red, and you wore this stunned look, like an alien had hauled you inside his spaceship." Peter's deepening voice vibrated with humor; he dabbed at the moisture that had collected at the corner of his eyes, still having trouble containing his enjoyment derived from the scene outside the high school track.

"Peter," she demanded, spearing another piece of meat with fury. "What did you argue about?"

"We argued over exactly what his father was doing with you in that van. What kind of son would I be if I didn't defend your...honor?"

"What did James say?"

Peter shrugged. "That his dad wouldn't be doing anything you didn't want him to."

"Those were fighting words?"

Peter shrugged. "It was the way he said them."

"I see."

Peter reached for a second helping of the scalloped potatoes. "Getting back to the marriage part. What do you think?"

"That you need to finish your peas and carrots."

Peter's eyes rushed to hers, but only for a moment. Then he grinned. "Oh, I get it—you want me to mind my own business. Right?"

"Exactly."

"But think about it, Mom. Promise me you'll at least do that much. Meeting Mr. Preston could be the greatest thing that's ever happened to us."

"And when you're finished with your dinner, I want you to stack the dirty dishes in the dishwasher," Carol said, without a pause, and finished the last bite of the roast, although it tasted a good deal like rubber.

"Every time I mention Mr. Preston you're going to give me another job to do?" Peter demanded.

Her son was a quick study, Carol would grant him that much.

"But you *are* going to see him again, aren't you?" he asked hopefully.

"The garbage should be taken out, and I've been noticing how the front flower beds need to be weeded. I know you worked out there last Saturday, but—"

"All right, all right," Peter cried, throwing his hands into the air. "Enough—I get the message."

"I certainly hope so," she said and stood to deliver her plate to the sink, her appetite gone.

Carol waited until Peter was busy with his homework and the dishes were done before she snuck into the kitchen and dialed Alex's phone number. She wasn't exactly sure what she was going to do if James answered.

"Hello."

"Alex?" She cupped her hand over the receiver and kept her eye on the doorway in case Peter strolled past.

"I can't talk long. Listen, did James happen to have a heart-to-heart discussion with you about . . . us?"

"Not exactly. He said something about the two boys having a talk about you and me. Why?"

"That's exactly what I'm talking about," she whispered furiously, ignoring his question. "Over dinner Peter rolled a grenade at my feet."

"He did what?"

"It's a figure of speech—don't interrupt me. He explained the two of them had argued when you didn't open the van door and afterward decided it would be just great if the two of us...that's you and me...got *married*." She could barely get the words past the growing knot in her throat.

"Now that you mention it, James did say something along those lines."

Carol pressed her back to the kitchen wall, suddenly needing its support. "How can you be so casual about this?" she burst out.

"Casual?"

"My son announced that he knew what was going on inside the van and that I should have seen my face and that fishing and camping with you would be like having a father." She paused long enough to draw in a breath.

"Carol?"

"And then when I try to calmly warn you what these two are plotting, you make it sound like...I don't know...like we're discussing basketball or something."

"Carol, slow down, I can barely understand you."

"Of course you can't understand me...I'm Italian and I'm upset."

"Listen, this is clearly something that's disturbing you. We need to talk about it. Can you meet me for lunch tomorrow?"

"I can't go out for lunch, for Pete's sake—I'm a nurse."

"An Italian one at that," Alex reminded her. "I'll meet you in the hospital cafeteria at noon. All right?"

Just then Peter casually strolled into the kitchen. He paused in the doorway, turned on the light and stared curiously at his mother.

"Sure, Mama, whatever you say," Carol said brightly...too brightly.

"Mama?" Alex echoed chuckling. "Okay, I get the picture. I'll see you tomorrow at noon."

Agreeing to meet Alex at the hospital was a mistake. Carol should have realized it immediately, but she'd been so concerned with the bombshell Peter had delivered over dinner that she didn't pause to consider what could happen once Alex slid his orange tray next to her own in the gossip-rich floors of Ford Memorial.

"I'm sorry I'm late," Carol murmured as she joined Alex at a table for two in the crowded cafeteria. A couple of nurses from surgery strolled past, glanced at Alex and then at Carol, and then back at Alex. Carol offered her peers a weak smile. Once she returned to obstetrics, she was in for an inquisition that would teach the Spaniards a lesson.

"I haven't been here long," Alex grinned and reached for his ham sandwich. "How much time do you have?"

Carol checked her watch. "Forty-five minutes."

Alex opened a pint-sized carton of milk. "All right, do you want to tell me what upset you so much about last night?"

"I already did."

"Refresh my memory."

Carol released a slow sigh. Several more of her friends had noticed her and Alex, including Joyce Mandle, her partner in the birthing classes. By this time, the probing stares being sent their way were rattling Carol's already shaky composure. "Apparently James and Peter have come to some sort of agreement...about you and me."

"I see." Humor flashed through his eyes like a distant light.

"Alex," she cried. "This is serious. We've only gone out to dinner once and our sons are talking about where the four of us are going to spend our honeymoon."

"And that bothers you?"

"Of course it does, and it should you, too. They already have expectations about how our relationship's going to develop. I don't think it's a healthy situation, and furthermore, they know about Friday night." She took a bite of her turkey sandwich and reached for her coffee.

"You mean that we're going to the Home Show?"

Carol shook her head. "I think we should forget the whole thing. We're looking at some potential trouble here, and I for one have enough problems in my life without dealing with the guilt of not giving my son a father who takes him fishing." She breathed deeply, then added as means of an explanation, "My brother doesn't camp or fish. Actually no one in our family does."

Alex's sandwich was poised in front of his mouth. He paused, his eyes studying hers, before he lowered his hands to the plate. "I beg your pardon?"

Carol shook her head, losing patience. "Never mind."

"No," he said after a thoughtful pause, "I'm sure I'll come up with the connection in a minute. But for now I can't understand what taking Peter fishing has to do with us seeing each other Friday night and your brother Tony—isn't it?—who doesn't camp and hunt."

"Fish," Carol corrected, "although he doesn't hunt, either."

"That part makes sense."

Curious stares seemed to come at Carol from every corner of the room. Alex had finished his sandwich, and Carol wasn't interested in eating any more of hers.

"Do you want to go outside?" she suggested.

"Sure."

Once they'd taken care of their dirty dishes and the trays, Carol led the way onto the hospital grounds. The weather had been beautiful for April. It wouldn't last much longer. The rains would return soon, and the "Rose City" would blossom into the floral bouquet of the Pacific Northwest.

With her hands buried in the front pocket of her hospital uniform, Carol strolled in the sunshine, directing them away from the concrete building and toward the parking lot. She spied his van in the second row and turned abruptly in the opposite direction. That construction van would be nothing but a source of embarrassment to her now.

"There's a pond this way." With its extensive rolling green lawns, it offered relative privacy.

An arched bridge stretched between the two banks of the oblong-shaped reservoir, and a school of feisty goldfish swam in the cold water. Sunlight rippled across the pond, illuminating half in golden brilliance, while the other half remained in enigmatic shadow. In many ways, Carol felt her budding relationship with Alex was like sun and shadow. When she was with him, she felt as though she were stepping into the light, that he drew her away from the shade. Only the light was brilliant and discomfiting, and it illuminated the darkest corners of her loneliness, revealing all the imperfections she hadn't noticed while standing so comfortably in the shadows.

Although gentle, Alex had taught her painful lessons. Until she met him, she hadn't realized how hungry she was to discover love in a man's arms. The emptiness inside her seemed to echo like a shout in a dark, deep well when she was with him. The years hadn't lessened the pain her marriage had brought into her life, but seemed to have enhanced the haunting self-doubts. She was more hesitant and uncertain now than she had been the year following Bruce's death.

With his hand guiding her elbow, Alex directed her to a park bench. Once they were seated, he reached for her hand, lacing their fingers together.

"I don't want you to worry about the boys," he said.

She nodded and lowered her gaze. She couldn't help being concerned, but Alex didn't understand her fears and revealed no distress of his own. That being the case, she couldn't continue to harp on the issue.

Gently he raised her fingers to his mouth. "I suppose what I'm about to say is going to frighten the hell out of you all the more."

"Alex...no."

"Sh-h, it needs to be said." He used his finger across her lips to silence her, and who could blame him, she mused, it had worked so well the first time. "The boys are going to come to their own conclusions," he continued, "and that's fine, they would anyway. For Peter to talk so openly with you about his expectations for our relationship is a compliment. Apparently he felt comfortable enough to do so, and that speaks well of the kind of mother you are."

Carol hadn't thought of it in those terms, but he was right. She and Peter were close.

"Now, about you and me," Alex continued, "we're both adults."

But Carol felt less mature than an adolescent when it came to dealing with him. She trembled every time she thought of him, and that was far more often than she would have liked. When he touched and kissed her, her hormones went berserk, and her heart experienced a nuclear meltdown. It wasn't any wonder she was frightened by the things Alex caused her to experience.

"I like you, and I'm fairly confident you like me."

She agreed with a sharp nod, knowing it wouldn't do any good to deny it.

"The fact is, I like everything about you, and that feeling intensifies every time we're together. Now, if it so happens this attraction between us continues, then so be it. Wonderful. Great. It would be a big mistake for us to allow two teenage boys to dictate our relationship. Agreed?"

Once more, Carol nodded.

"Good." He stood, bringing her with him. "Now we both have to get back to work." Tucking her hand in the crook of his arm, he strolled back toward the parking lot, pausing when he came to his van. He opened the door and then turned to face her.

"It seems to me we should seal our agreement."

"Seal it? I don't understand." Then again she did. His wonderful, mist-gray eyes were spelling out exactly what he intended.

He caressed her cheek, carefully and unhurriedly, then traced the outline of her lips. Whatever it was about his touch that sent her heart into such chaos, Carol couldn't understand. She reacted by instinct, drawing his finger between her lips, touching the tip of her tongue to it and sucking gently. The impact of her action showed in his eyes with devastating clarity.

He leaned forward and slipped his finger aside, replacing it with his mouth. His kiss was slow and gentle and wildly erotic. His tongue swept her mouth in long, broad strokes. He worshiped her, sliding his lips against hers in a wet, circular pattern.

When he broke away they were both shaking. Carol stared up at him, her breath ragged, her lips parted and eager. They felt as if they were starting to swell, and she moistened them.

"I've got to get back to work...."

"I know," Alex said and exhaled slowly, "me, too." But he didn't make any effort to break away from her, and Carol hadn't the strength to try.

He angled his head and dropped tiny kisses to her neck, then to her ear, taking the lobe in his mouth and sucking gently, before trailing his lips in heart-stopping increments back to hers. She was ready for him this time, more than ready. When his open mouth met hers, her tongue responded to him in a primitive mating dance, curling and coiling, tasting and exploring.

The sound of a car door slamming somewhere in the distance forcefully and abruptly brought them back into the real world. Carol leaped back, her eyes round and startled, her breathing harsh and uneven. She smoothed her hands down the front of her white uniform, as though she were brushing off germs. She was certain her cap was askew. Dear heavens, she'd been kissing him like a lover and in broad daylight. To her chagrin, Alex didn't look the least bit dismayed by what was happening between them, only pleased.

"I wish you hadn't done that," she said, knowing he wasn't the only one to blame—but at the moment, the one most convenient.

"Oh, baby, I'm not."

She folded her arms over her chest as a barrier to his appeal. "I've got to get back inside." But by the same token she was forced to wait until the flush of desire had left her face and her body had stopped trembling.

"It seems to me," Alex said with a smile of supreme confidence, "that if kissing you is this good, then when we finally make love it'll be downright dangerous." With that he climbed into the driver's seat, closed the door and started the engine.

"You didn't call me," Carol's mother complained Friday afternoon. "All week I waited for you to phone your mama and tell her about your date with the non-Italian."

"I'm sorry, Mama," Carol said, glancing at the kitchen clock. Alex was due to pick her up for the Home Show in ten minutes. Peter was staying overnight with a friend, and she was running behind schedule as it was. The last thing she wanted to do was argue with her mother.

"You should be sorry. I could have died this week and you wouldn't have known. Your uncle in Jersey City would have had to call you and tell you your mother was dead."

"Mama, Peter started track this week, and we've gotten home late every night."

"So don't keep me in suspense, tell me."

Carol paused. "About what?"

"Your date with that Englishman. Did he take you to bed yet?"

"Mama!" Sometimes the things her mother said shocked Carol. "Of course not."

"It's a shame. Are you seeing him again? For the sake of St. Teresa, don't wear those shoes with the pointed toes, he'll think you're a loose woman, and to be on the safe side, don't mention your cousin Celeste."

"Mama, I can't talk now. Alex will be here any minute—we're going to the Home Show. His company has a booth there, and it'd be impolite to keep him waiting."

"Do you think he'll convert?"

"Mama, I'm not marrying Alex."

"Maybe not," her mother said with a breathless sigh, "and then again, who knows?"

The doorbell chimed, and Carol, who had been dreading this evening from the moment she'd agreed to it, was flooded with a sense of relief.

"Bye, Mama."

Angelina said her farewell in Italian, and added something about bringing Alex over to sample her pasta. Carol was lowering the receiver into its cradle by the time her mother had finished issuing her advice.

The doorbell chimed a second time as Carol hurried into the living room. She rushed to open the door. "I'm sorry it took me so long to answer, my mother was on the phone."

"Did she give you any advice?" Alex teased.

"Just a little. She said it might not be a good idea if I mentioned my cousin Celeste."

"Who?"

"Never mind." Carol laughed a little nervously. Alex looked too good to be true, and the warm, open appreciation that shone in his eyes did wonders for her self-esteem.

"You were worth the wait."

Carol could feel the blush flower in her cheeks. She wasn't used to having men compliment her, although her family was free with praise, and always had been. This was different, however. Alex wasn't family.

His eyes compelled her forward, and she stepped toward him without question, then abruptly halted, realizing that she had very nearly walked into his arms.

"I'll . . . get my purse." She turned away, but his hand at her shoulder turned her back.

"Not yet."

"Alex . . . I don't think we should . . ."

But that was all the protest she was allowed. He ran his hand through the hair at the back of her head as he directed her mouth to his with tender restraint. He kissed her lightly at first, until she was pliant and willing in his arms, then he slipped his tongue inside her mouth.

Carol felt her body go limp. Her hands were trapped between their bodies, and her nails curled into his hard flesh, not with any need to hurt him, but in an instinctive, catlike reflex.

He repeatedly dipped his tongue in a series of delicious forays between her lips. Carol heard her own murmur of desire and humbling need. The heat of his arousal burned against her abdomen, and the impulse was strong to move against him and relieve the mounting pressure of her own appetite.

He slid his mouth back and forth over hers as he withdrew slowly. His tongue left her mouth, but hesitated to flirt with her upper lip. When he pulled away from her, she slowly, languorously, opened her eyes to meet his. Her dark eyes swam in his until she was convinced if he didn't kiss her again, she would drown.

"Don't look at me like that," he groaned. "Come on, let's get out of here before we end up doing something we're both not ready to deal with yet."

"What?" Carol asked, blinking, still too dazed to think coherently.

"I think you know the answer to that." He trailed his finger over the tip of her breasts, which had beaded into tight pearls, pouting embarrassingly hard through her light sweater. His touch, although gentle, heightened the already-sensitized nipples, and she gasped and bit into her lower lip. She leaped back and whirled around, interested only in locating her purse. It was all she could do not to cover her face with her hands.

They were in Alex's car before either of them spoke again after what seemed like aeons. "If you don't mind,

I've got to stop off at the shop and pick up some more brochures," Alex said, "we're running low already."

"I don't mind," Carol told him. It was a good thing she was sitting down because her legs had liquefied. She was sure her face was flushed, and she'd rarely felt this shaky.

Her mind became her enemy as Alex headed toward the freeway. Try as she might, she couldn't stop thinking about how he'd felt against her. So strong and warm. A thin sheen of perspiration moistened her upper lip, and she gnawed at it, eager to dispel the image that refused to leave her mind. She wished to God he'd never touched her breasts. Hot sensations continued to rush over her even now. Her breasts felt swollen and heavy and needy. It was far too easy to imagine what it would feel like to have Alex take a nipple in his mouth and suck on it the way he had her earlobe. Hot, sweet excitement cascaded over her.

Carol snapped her eyes open, furious with herself. This was neither the time nor the place to indulge her fantasies.

"How far is your office?" Carol asked after several strained minutes passed. Alex seemed unusually quiet himself.

"Ten more minutes."

Not knowing how else to pick up the conversation, she dropped it at that.

"Peter's staying with Dale tonight?"

"Yes. James, too?"

"Yes."

Immediately Carol wished she hadn't asked. This kind of information wasn't good for them. It presented temptations best ignored.

Carol curled her fingers around the armrest when Alex exited the freeway and stopped at the first red light. The district was an industrial area and well lit.

When Alex pulled into a side street, she saw his company sign. She'd never asked about his business and was impressed when she saw a small fleet of trucks neatly parked in rows outside. He was apparently far more successful than she'd assumed.

Unlocking the door, Alex let her precede him inside. He reached for a switch, and light immediately flooded the office. One entire wall was made up of filing cabinets. Three desks divided the room. Carol didn't have time to give the area more than a fleeting glance as Alex directed her past the first desk and into another room that was apparently his office.

The room was spacious and cluttered. The top of his desk looked like a cyclone had hit it.

"The brochures are around here someplace," he said, lifting up a file on the corner of the credenza. "Help yourself to a butterscotch candy."

"Thanks." Carol reached for one when her gaze fell on the two framed photographs hidden behind a stack of papers. The top of a woman's head showed on one, but that was all. The second one was of James.

"I've got to get organized one of these days," Alex muttered.

Curious, Carol moved toward the credenza and the two photographs. "Who's this?" Carol asked, lifting the one of the woman. She was hauntingly beautiful. Blond. Blue-eyed. Wholesome. Judging by the styles, the picture appeared to have been taken several years earlier.

Alex paused. "That's Gloria."

"She was your wife?"

Alex nodded, pulled out the high-backed cushioned chair and sank into it. "She died two years ago from cancer."

It was all Carol could do to hold on to the frame. The pain etched in his voice stabbed through her like a hundred pins, scratching at her soul.

"I . . . I thought you were divorced."

"No," Alex answered softly.

Carol continued to study the beautiful woman in the photo. "You loved her, didn't you?"

"So much that when the time came I wanted to die with her. Yes, I loved her."

With shaking hands, Carol replaced the photograph. Her back was to Alex, when she briefly closed her eyes. By the sheer force of her will, she was smiling when she turned around to face him.

He frowned. "What's wrong?"

"Nothing," she said breezily.

"You look pale all of a sudden. I thought you knew . . . I assumed that James or Peter had told you."

"No . . . neither mentioned it."

"I'm sorry if this comes as a shock."

"No . . . there's no reason to apologize."

Alex nodded, sighed and reached for her numb fingers, pulling her down into his lap. "I figured you'd understand better than most what it is to lose someone you desperately love."

Chapter Six

Gloria had problems when James was born," Alex continued. His hold on Carol's waist tightened almost painfully, but she was sure he wasn't aware of it. "The doctors said there wouldn't be any more children."

"Alex, please, there's no need to tell me this."

"There is," he countered strongly. "I want you to know—it's important to me that you do."

Carol closed her eyes and pressed her forehead against the side of his head. The emotion in his voice twined its way around her like thick ropes. Intuitively she realized that he didn't often speak of his late wife, and to do so now was difficult in the extreme.

Alex wove his fingers into her hair. "In the years following Jim's birth, Gloria's health was never good, but the doctors couldn't put their finger on what was wrong. She was weak and tired most of the time. It wasn't until Jim was in junior high that we learned she had leukemia—myelocytic leukemia, one of the most difficult forms to treat." He paused and drew in an unsteady breath, gathering his resolve.

"Alex," she pleaded, her hands framing his face. "Don't, please . . . this is obviously painful for you." But the moment her eyes met his, she knew nothing she said or did would stop him. It was as though he were wearing his pain around his neck, and the weight of it was dragging him down. Only sharing it now, with her, would lessen the trauma of the ordeal.

"We did all the usual things—the chemotherapy, the drugs—but nothing helped, and she grew steadily worse. Later, when it was apparent that nothing else could be done, we opted for a bone-marrow transplant. Her sister and mother flew in from New York, and her sister was the better match. But . . . that didn't work, either."

Carol stroked his cheek, yearning to do everything she could to lessen the pain that mauled at him like bear claws.

He hesitated and drew in a quivering breath. "She suffered, dear God, how she suffered. That was the worst for me to deal with. I was her husband, and I'd sworn to love and protect her, and there wasn't a damn thing I could do . . . not one single, solitary thing."

Tears moistened the edges of Carol's eyes, and she struggled to keep them at bay.

Alex's voice remained firm and controlled, but Carol knew the pain he was experiencing. "I didn't know what courage was until I watched Gloria die," he whispered. He paused and closed his eyes. "The human heart is a funny thing. The last three weeks of her life, it was apparent that she wasn't going to make it. Finally she slipped into a coma and was placed on a respirator. The doctors knew she would never come out of it and so did the nurses. I could see them emotionally removing themselves from her, and I couldn't bear it. I became a crazy man, refusing to leave her side, letting no one care for her but me. I held on to her hand and silently willed her to live with every breath I drew. I honestly believe I kept her alive by the sheer force of my will. I was afraid to leave her, afraid that when I did, she would silently slip into death. Eventually that was exactly what happened. I left her because Jim needed me and because I knew that inevitably I would be forced to go. I sat in the hospital waiting room with my son, telling him about his mother, and suddenly an intense laserlike pain shot through me—'' he hesitated and drew in a ragged sigh ''—and in that instant, I knew she was gone. It was like a knife had pierced my soul—I've never felt anything to compare with it. Within a few minutes a nurse came for me. I can remember so vividly that scene—my mind has played it back so many times.

''I stood and Jim stood with me, and I drew my son as close to my side as I could, looked the nurse in the eye and said, 'She's gone, isn't she?' The nurse nodded and Jim started to weep and I just stood there, dazed and numb. I don't remember walking back to Gloria's room, but somehow I found myself there. I lifted her into my arms and held her and told her how sorry I was that I'd been so stubborn and so selfish to hold on to her those three weeks, to refuse to allow her to die. I told her how I would have much rather been with her, how I'd wanted to hold her hand as she stepped from one life into the next.''

By now Carol was weeping softly, unabashedly.

Alex's fingers stroked her head. ''I didn't mean for you to cry,'' he whispered, and his regret was genuine. ''You would have liked her.''

Carol had felt the same way from the first moment she'd noticed Gloria's photograph. Nodding, she hid her face in the strong curve of his neck.

"Carol," he whispered, caressing her spine, "look at me."

She sniffled and shook her head, unwilling for him to witness the strength of her emotion. It was one thing to sit on his lap in his office, and entirely another to look him in the eye after he'd shared such a deep and personal part of himself.

His lips grazed the line of her jaw.

"No," she cried softly, her protest faint and nearly inaudible, "don't touch me...not now." He'd come through hell, suffered through the torment of losing his wife, and he needed her. He was asking for her.

"Yes," he countered, using his hands to lift her face away from him so he could look at her. Against her will, against her better judgment, her gaze met his. His eyes were filled with such hunger that she all but gasped. Again and again, his thirsty eyes roamed her face, taking in, she was sure, the moisture that glistened from her cheeks, the way her lips trembled and the staggering need she felt to comfort him.

"I'm sorry I upset you."

It was all Carol could do not to beg him to kiss her. The flames of desire and need licked at her, scorching her senses. Unable to resist him a second longer, she trailed her fingertips across the sternly chiseled line of his jaw.

He wove his fingers into her hair and unerringly directed her lips to his. His mouth was warm and moist and unbelievably gentle. No one had ever touched her with such tenderness and care. No kiss had ever affected her so deeply. No kiss had ever showed her such matchless beauty.

When he lifted his face from hers, Alex was breathing hard. Much too hard for such a chaste kiss. It was as though he couldn't bear not to kiss her. He lowered his mouth to the vulnerable hollow of her throat, sliding the tip of his tongue over the exposed flesh. Carol whimpered and arched her neck, thrusting her breast toward him in unconscious need. He lifted her sweater over her head and unsnapped the flimsy opening of her bra until her full breasts spilled into his waiting hands. They both sighed as he dragged his mouth down farther and farther to the peaked softness that seemed to throb with need, waiting impatiently for his touch.

Carol whimpered once more as his moist lips traveled from one nipple to the other, creating a slick trail. She arched her back to give him more of what they both yearned for. His fiery lips closed firmly over her nipple, tugging at her deeply, sucking gently again and again, taking more and more of her into his mouth while the heat built up inside her like a raging inferno.

Tears rained down Carol's face, but these were profound tears of joy. Sliding her fingers through his hair, she pressed him to her. He was solid and muscular and full of strength, both physical and emotional. His touch had filled the hollowness of her life and, she prayed, helped to ease the terrible loneliness he'd exposed.

Alex worked his hands beneath her buttocks, cupping her, lifting her as he pushed the material of her skirt aside, seeking the mound of her femininity. Briefly she struggled, not to hinder him, but to assist him. She could feel the pure sexual power of his arousal that lay just beneath his jeans and instinctively sought release for them both.

"Alex," she pleaded, gripping his shoulders tightly. She couldn't seem to hold her hips still. As if they had a life of their own, her buttocks swayed gently, rhythmically rubbing against him. Her breath came in tiny gasps.

Urgently he sought her mouth and masterfully slid his tongue between her waiting, approving lips. She whimpered, wanting more, seeking more, straining for more and more and more.

Carol was lost, abandoned, and she was certain that only heaven awaited her.

"Ah, Carol," he gasped, his hands pinching into her waist. He buried his mouth in hers as he slid her from his lap, but only long enough to bury his hands in the waistband of her skirt and tug it gently downward.

With her hands braced against his shoulders, she leaned into him, letting him absorb her weakness, borrowing from him his strength. Alex's breath was ragged and guttural, and Carol threw her head back. As she did, her narrowed gaze collided with the woman in the photograph. Carol went stock-still. Alex's wife. The woman he'd loved beyond reason, the mother of his only child. And yet he was holding *her*, kissing *her*, wanting *her*.

"No," she cried, breaking away from him. She nearly stumbled as she whirled around. Her hands shook terribly as she reached for her sweater and did what she could to repair the damage to her clothing. Her fingers worked frantically. The lower half of her body pulsed painfully with the need he'd created. Her hair was completely disheveled, and she was sure her lips were wet and swollen.

"Carol," he breathed, sounding both stunned and dismayed, "what is it? What's wrong?"

"Nothing," she whispered. "Everything."

He was silent for several nerve-shattering seconds while Carol awaited the backlash of his anger. They had both been in a fever-pitch of need and desire. More than once Bruce had warned her that a man couldn't put a hold on his passion. A man was different from a woman, and if a woman refused to give a man what he needed, then she could only expect to suffer the consequences of her folly.

"I'm sorry . . . so sorry," he whispered.

Confused and uncertain, Carol turned to face him. "You are?"

"Yes, of course. I was way ahead of myself." He reached for her, touching the tips of her fingers in abject apology.

Carol frowned. For him to accept the responsibility for what had nearly happened was one thing, but for him to apologize was something else entirely.

"Are you going to be all right?"

She nodded, still too shaken to speak.

He set his hands on the curve of her shoulder and gently kissed the crown of her head. "Thank you."

"For what?" Reluctantly her eyes slid to his.

"For listening, for being here when I needed you, for understanding my grief and not condemning me for rushing you while I tried to bury myself in your softness."

For the remainder of the evening, Alex had been a perfect gentleman. He'd escorted her to the Home Show, where they'd spent several hours wandering from one display to another, discussing the ideas and products represented. They strolled hand in hand, laughing, talking, debating ideas. Carol was more talkative than usual. It helped disguise her uneasiness. She told him of her idea of taking up a portion of her back lawn and turning it into a herb garden. At least when she was talking, her nerve endings weren't left uncovered and she didn't have to deal with what had transpired between them.

After they'd toured the Home Show, Alex had taken her out to eat in a local Greek restaurant. By that time of the evening, Carol should have been famished, but whatever appetite she'd had earlier had long since deserted her.

When Alex dropped her off at the house, he gently kissed her good-night, but if he was expecting an invitation to come inside, she didn't extend it.

Hours later, she lay staring at the ceiling, while shadows of the trees outside her window frolicked around the light fixture like dancing harem girls. Glaring at the clock radio, Carol punched her pillow several times and twisted around so she lay on her abdomen, her arms cradling her head. She should be sleepy. Exhausted. Drained after a long, trying week. Her job demanded its toll in energy, and normally by Friday night, Carol collapsed without a pause, waking refreshed Saturday morning.

She would have liked to convince herself Alex had nothing to do with this restless, trapped feeling. She tried to analyze what was bothering her so much. It wasn't as though Alex had never kissed her before this evening. The impact he had on her senses, on her being, shouldn't come as any shock. She'd known from the first night they'd met that Alex had the power to expose a kaleidoscope of emotions within her. With him, she felt exhilarated, excited, frightened, reborn.

Perhaps it was the shock of passion he'd stroked alive within her when he'd kissed and suckled her breasts. No, she mused, frowning, she'd yearned for him to do exactly that even before they'd arrived at his office. She hadn't been shocked by his need, but convinced of her own.

Squeezing her eyes closed, she tried to force her body to relax. She longed to snap her fingers and demand that she drift into the warm escape of slumber. It was what she wanted, what she yearned for. Maybe in the morning, she would be able to put everything into perspective.

Closing her eyes, however, proved to be a mistake. Instead of being surrounded by peaceful bliss, she was confronted with the image of Alex's tormented features as he told her about Gloria. *I figured you'd understand better than most what it is to lose someone you desperately love.*

Carol's eyes shot open. Fresh tears pooled at the edges as the soft, silent sobs took control. She'd loved Bruce. She'd hated Bruce.

Her life ended with his death, her life began again.

It was the end, it was the beginning.

There hadn't been tears when he'd died—not at first, but later. Plenty of tears, some of profound sadness, and others that spoke of a magnitude of regrets. But there was something more. A release. Bruce died, and at the same moment, she and Peter had been set free from the prison of his sickness and his abuse.

The moisture burned like acid against her face, as she sobbed softly, caught in the horror of those few short years of her marriage.

Bruce shouldn't have died. He was too young to have wasted his life. Knowing he'd been drunk and with another woman hadn't helped her deal with the emotions surrounding his untimely death.

I figured you'd understand better than most what it is to lose someone you desperately love. Only Carol didn't know. Bruce had destroyed any love she'd felt for him long before his death. He'd ravaged all trust and violated any lingering visage of respect. She'd never known love the way Alex had, never shared such a deep and personal commitment with anyone, not the kind Alex had shared with Gloria, not the way her mother had with her father.

And Carol felt guilty. Guilty. Perhaps if she'd been a better wife, a better mother, then Bruce would have stopped drinking. If only she could have been more desirable, more inventive in the kitchen, a spotless housekeeper. Instead, she was guilty. Guilty in every aspect and a terrible failure as a woman, as a wife, as a mother.

"Well?" Peter asked as he let himself in the front door the following morning. He dumped his sleeping bag on the kitchen floor, walked over to Carol and dutifully kissed her cheek.

"Well what?" Carol said, helping herself to a second cup of coffee. She didn't dare look in the mirror, confident there were dark smudges under her eyes. At the most, she'd slept two hours the entire night.

"How did things go with Mr. Preston?"

Carol let the steam rising from her coffee mug revive her. "You never told me James's mother had died."

"I didn't? She had leukemia."

"So I heard," Carol muttered. She wasn't angry with her son, and Alex being a widower didn't make a whole lot of difference—at least it shouldn't—but for reasons she was only beginning to understand, it did.

"James said it took his dad a long time to come to grips with his mother's death."

Carol felt her throat muscles tighten.

"James keeps a picture of her in his room. She was real pretty."

Carol nodded, remembering the bright blue eyes smiling back at her from the framed photograph in Alex's office. Gloria's warmth and gentleness were apparent to all.

"I thought we'd work in the back yard this morning," Carol said, as a means of changing the subject.

"Ah, Mom," Peter groaned. "You know how I feel about yard work."

"But if we tackle everything now, it won't overwhelm us next month."

"Are you going to plant a bunch of silly flowers again? I can't understand it. Every year you spend a fortune on that stuff. If you added everything up, I bet you could buy yourself a sports car if you did away with all those fancy flowers."

"Buy who a sports car?" she challenged, arms akimbo.

"All right, all right," Peter muttered, clearly not wanting to argue. "Just tell me what I have to do."

Peter's attitude could use an overhauling, but Carol wasn't in the best of moods herself. Working with the earth, digging her fingers deep into the rich soil, was basic to her nature and never more than now.

The sun was out when Carol, dressed in her oldest pair of jeans and a University of Oregon sweatshirt, knelt in front of her precious flower beds. She had tied a red bandanna around her head and knotted it at the back of her neck.

Peter brought his radio outside and plugged it into the electrical outlet on the patio. Next, he arranged an assortment of rap tapes in neat piles.

Carol glanced over her shoulder and groaned inwardly. She was about to be serenaded with music of which understanding the words was impossible. In many ways, that in itself was a blessing.

"Just a minute," Peter cried, and started running toward the kitchen.

That was funny. Carol hadn't even heard the phone ring. Ignoring her son, Carol settled back on her haunches and wiped her wrist under her nose. Already the heat was causing her to perspire. Bending forward, she dug with the trowel, cultivating the soil and clearing away a winter's accumulation of weeds.

"'Morning."

At the sound of Alex's voice, Carol froze. "Alex," she whispered, twisting around to confront him. "What are you doing here?"

"I came to see you."

"Why?"

He joined her, kneeling beside her on the lush, green grass. His eyes locked with hers, and the look he held was thirsty and eager, as if it had been aeons since he'd last seen her, instead of a few hours.

"What are you doing here?" she demanded, digging far more vigorously than necessary. She didn't want to have to confront Alex. It was too soon. She hadn't fully recovered from their last encounter and already was being forced to face another.

"I couldn't stay away," he whispered, his voice harsh and husky both at once, and tinged with a thread of anger as if the lack of control bothered him. "You were upset last night, and we both ignored it instead of talking it out the way we should have."

"You were imagining things," she said, offering him a bogus smile.

"No, I wasn't. I felt guilty, too."

"Guilty?" she cried. "Whatever for?"

"Because I told you about Gloria and didn't ask you about your husband. It would have been the perfect time for you to have told me about him."

Carol's stomach lurched. "That was a very long time ago . . . and best forgotten."

"But you loved him and were saddened by his death, and I should have realized that telling you about Gloria would be especially painful for you. I should have been more sensitive to your needs.''

She squeezed her eyes closed. ''There's nothing to feel guilty over. You talked openly and honestly, and I appreciated knowing about your wife.''

''Maybe so,'' Alex conceded, ''but I frightened you, and now you're confused and uncertain.''

''Nothing could be further from the truth.'' She continued working, dragging the pronged tool through the damp soil.

Alex chuckled softly. He gripped her shoulders and turned her toward him as his knowing gaze scanned her features. ''You shouldn't lie, Carol Sommars. You have the uncanny habit of blushing every time you do.''

''That's ridiculous.'' As if on cue, she felt her cheeks grow pink. Carol groaned inwardly, furious with Alex and more so with herself.

''No, it isn't ridiculous.'' He paused, and the edges of his lips quivered as he studied her. ''You're doing it now.''

''Where are the boys?''

Alex's chuckle deepened. ''Don't try changing the subject—it isn't going to work.''

''Alex, please.''

''Hey, Mom, you'll never guess what!''

Grateful for the distraction, Carol dragged her eyes away from Alex and centered her attention on her son, who stood on the patio, looking exceptionally pleased about something.

''What is it, Peter?''

''James and Mr. Preston brought over one of those fancy, heavy-duty tillers. They're going to dig up that garden space you've been talking about for the past two summers.''

Carol's gaze flew back to Alex's, full of unspoken questions.

"You mentioned something last night about wanting to grow an herb garden, didn't you?"

Nodding demanded a supreme effort. "Yes, but why...I mean, you don't have to do this." She felt flustered and surprised, and overwhelmed that he would take a casual comment seriously and go out of his way to see that her wish was fulfilled.

"Of course I don't have to, but I want to. Peter and James and I are your willing servants, isn't that right, boys?" Neither bothered to answer, being far more interested in sorting through the cassette tapes Peter had set out to play.

Two hours later, Carol had been delegated to the kitchen by all three men, who claimed she was a world-class nuisance.

"Mom," Peter claimed, "do something constructive like make lunch. You're in the way here."

Slightly taken aback by her son's assessment of her role, Carol muttered under her breath, and did as he asked. Her ego suffered further when James sent his friend a grateful glance. Even Alex seemed pleased to have her out from under their capable feet.

A few minutes later, Alex strolled into the kitchen. He paused when he noticed her busy stacking sandwiches onto a dinner plate. He walked over to her, casually looped his arms around her trim waist and nuzzled her neck.

"Alex," she protested in a fierce whisper, "the boys will see you."

"So?"

"So, it's bad enough for them to think the things they do without your adding fuel to the fire."

"They're too busy to care."

"I care!"

His growl was low and sexual as he slid his hand from her navel up her midriff, pausing just under her breasts. "I know."

"If you don't stop I'll...I'll...I don't know what I'll do...but it won't be pleasant." Her threat was an empty one, and Alex knew it as well as she did. She was trembling the way she always did when he touched her. The more personal the caress, the more she shivered.

"I told the boys I was coming inside to pester you, and I'm nothing if not a man of my word," Alex delighted in informing her, clearly relishing her uneasiness. Her shyness appeared to please him.

He slipped his hand under her sweatshirt, and Carol bit into her lower lip. With his hands tucked against the sides of her waist, he pulled her back, so her buttocks nestled against the rigid evidence of his need. Her eyes widened with surprise and wonder.

"See," he whispered huskily. His body had hardened even more, and when he spoke, his voice was ragged and breathless. "You do the same thing to me."

"Alex..."

"Don't say it," he grumbled, "I already know—this isn't the time or place, and you're right to put up a fuss, but I don't have to like it." Slowly and with great reluctance, he released her, dragging his fingers across her flat stomach and down the length of her thighs.

Carol was aware of every nuance of this man. He made the most innocent of caresses candy-sweet with sensations. His touch only created a need for more. Much more.

Once he'd released her, Carol sighed with relief...or was it regret, she didn't know anymore. She carried the plate of sandwiches to the table and brought out a pitcher of fresh lemonade.

Alex pulled out a chair, twisted it around and straddled it. "I like watching you move," he whispered.

Her eyes flew to him, and she noticed that he was studying her the way a starving man looks upon a table set for Thanksgiving dinner. "I like touching you even more."

"Alex . . . please don't, you're making me blush."

He laughed lightly. "I like that, too. Dear God, being with you makes me feel alive again. I hadn't realized how desensitized I'd become to life. The first time we kissed I knew what I'd been missing. All those arranged dates, all those wasted evenings . . . and all the time you were right under my nose and I didn't even know it."

"I . . . I think I'll put out two kinds of chips," Carol said, completely unsettled by the way he spoke so openly, so frankly.

"You have fabulous breasts." His eyes were dark, darker than she thought possible, filled with the promise of things to come.

"Alex, please." She braced her hip against the counter, under the onslaught of his words.

"They taste even better than they look. So sweet and full."

Carol closed her eyes and swallowed a moan. "Stop, Alex. Don't say anything more."

"I can't help it. I feel as though I've been granted a second chance at life, as though I was within inches of losing it all and hadn't realized it. Tell me I'm not behaving like an idiot, tell me you feel it, too."

She did feel the things he did, more profoundly than she dared let him know. "I . . . think we've both been alone too long . . . people who are as sexually starved as we are must think these kinds of thoughts all the time."

Her words didn't please him. He frowned and slowly stood. "You may find this difficult to believe, Carol, but there hasn't been anyone since Gloria died that made me feel the things you do. And trust me, there've been plenty who've tried."

Gulping, Carol whirled around and made busy work, opening a bag of potato chips.

Alex joined her, leaning against the counter and facing her so she couldn't ignore him. "You, on the other hand, don't even need to touch me to make me respond. You might not want to admit it, but it's the same for you."

"When you decide to pester someone, you don't do it by half measure, do you?" she muttered.

"Admit it, Carol."

"I . . ."

He slid his lips across hers. "Are you ready to admit it yet?"

"I think you're being ridiculous."

"I know." He leaned forward and kissed her again, briefly, darting his tongue in and out of her mouth with lightning quickness.

Carol's knees buckled and she swayed toward him.

With a masculine growl, Alex reached for her. Without a question, Carol fell into his arms, so hungry for his touch, she felt as if she were on fire. Their mouths mated, each twisting and turning against the other, famished beyond reason.

The sound of someone clearing his throat was followed with, "Hey, we're not interrupting anything, are we?" Peter was standing just inside the kitchen. "In case you two haven't noticed, it's lunchtime."

Chapter Seven

Alex pressed one knee on the green and stretched out his putter, judging the distance to the hole with a sharp eye. He'd been playing golf with Barney every Sunday afternoon for years.

"So when do I get to meet this female dynamo?" Barney pressed after Alex had successfully completed the shot.

"I don't know yet," Alex said as he reached inside the cup for his golf ball. He inserted the putter back inside his bag before striding toward his cart.

"What do you mean, you don't know?" Barney echoed. "What's with you and this woman? I swear you've been a different man since the moment you met her. You stare off into space with this goofy look on your face. I talk to you and you don't hear me, and when I start to ask you about her, you get defensive."

"I'm not defensive, I'm in love."

"Alex, buddy, listen to the wise voice of experience. You're not in love, you're in lust. Trust me, I recognize that gleam in your eye. Ten to one you haven't bedded her yet. I suggest you get her in the sack and be done with it before you end up doing something foolish."

Alex's gaze fired briefly as it scooted to his friend. How Barney knew how far the physical aspect of his relationship had progressed with Carol was anyone's guess.

"I have every intention of, as you put it, bedding her. Only I want her sleeping with me every night for the rest of my life. Carol's not the type of woman to have a fling, and I refuse to insult her by suggesting one."

Barney stared at Alex as if seeing him for the first time. "I don't think I ever realized what an old-fashioned kind of guy you are. Apparently you haven't realized it, but the world is into a casual age. Our clothes are casual, our conversations are casual, and yes, even our sex is casual. In case you hadn't heard, you don't have to marry a woman to take her to bed these days."

"Continue in this vein," Alex concluded, "and you're destined to become a casual friend."

Barney rolled his eyes dramatically. "See what I mean?"

If three wives hadn't been able to set Barney straight, Alex doubted that he could, either. "As I recall, the last time we had this conversation," Alex reminded him, "you insisted my settling down was the thing to do. I'm only following your advice."

"But not yet," Barney contended. "You haven't played the field enough. There are riches out there—female gold nuggets just waiting to be picked up and sampled, then gently set back in place for the next treasure hunter."

"You mean like Bambi and what was the name of the other one?"

"Babette."

"Do all their names start with *B*?"

"Stop being clever," Barney snickered. "I have your best interests at heart, and frankly I'm concerned. Two years after Gloria's gone, you suddenly announce it's time to start dating again. Man, I was jumping up and down for joy. As far as I was concerned it was past time—I was about to suggest grief counseling. Then you go out with a grand total of ten different women, calmly inform me you've met *the one,* and you plan to marry her. Just like that, and worse, you haven't even slept with her yet. How are you going to find out if you're sexually compatible? That's a big issue these days, you know."

"We're compatible, trust me."

"You may think so now, but *bingo*, once she's got a wedding band through your nose, it's an entirely different story."

"Stop worrying, would you?" Alex eased his golf cart into his assigned parking space. From the moment he'd decided to look for another wife, Barney had been a constant source of amusement. The problem was, his most hilarious moments had come in the form of women his friend had insisted he meet.

"I apologize if I'm beating a dead horse, but frankly Alex, I'm worried about you," Barney muttered as he lifted his clubs from the back of the cart. "You don't know women the way I do. They're scheming, conniving, money-hungry, and the only way they can get their clenches into you is by marriage. Don't be so eager to march up the aisle with Carol. I just don't want you to go through what I have."

After three wives, three divorces and child support payments for two separate families, Barney was speaking from experience.

"Gloria was one of a kind," his longtime friend reminded him. "You're not going to find another one like her. So if it's those qualities that attract you to Carol, look again, you may be seeing only what you want to."

"You wanna yell?" Angelina Pasquale shouted from the doorway of the kitchen into the living room where her grandchildren were squabbling. "Then let's have a contest, only I've been doing it longer, I can be heard all the way to Jersey City."

Peter and his younger cousins ceased their shouting match, and with a sharp nod of her head, Angelina returned to the kitchen, satisfied that a single threat from her was enough to force a peace movement that would last through the remainder of the afternoon.

Carol was busy slicing tomatoes for the salad, and her sister-in-law, Paula, was spreading butter over thick slices of French bread.

The sauce was warming on the stove, and the water for the long strands of fresh pasta was just starting to boil. The pungent scent of fresh basil and thyme circled the kitchen like smoke from a camp fire. From earliest memory, Carol's mother had cooked up a fresh pot of spaghetti sauce every Saturday evening. The unused portion from Sunday's dinner was served in a variety of ways throughout the week. Leftover pot roast became something delectable with her mother's sauce served over the top. And chicken with Mama's sauce rivaled even the Colonel's in Carol's mind.

"So, Carol," her mother murmured, wiping her hands dry on the ever-present apron that was tied around her thick waist. She took a large wooden spoon and stirred the kettle of simmering sauce. "I suppose your English friend thinks good spaghetti sauce comes from a jar," she muttered disparagingly. This was her mother's way of letting Carol know the time had come to invite Alex and his son to Sunday dinner.

"Mama, Alex plays golf on Sundays."

"Every Sunday?"

Carol nodded.

"That's because he's never tasted my sauce," her mother returned, shaking her head as though to suggest Alex had wasted a good portion of his life walking from green to green every Sunday afternoon in a futile search for excellent spaghetti sauce.

Adding two serving spoons to the salad, Carol set the wooden bowl on the dining room table.

Tony, Carol's brother, sauntered into the room and slipped his arms around Paula's waist. "How much longer until dinner? The natives are growing restless."

"Eleven minutes," Angelina answered. She tasted the end of the wooden spoon, pressed her fingertips to her lips and murmured her approval in her native language.

Carol returned to the kitchen and noticed that her mother was watching her under the guise of waiting for the water to boil. The question Carol had expected all day finally came.

"You gonna marry this non-Italian?" her mother pressed, then added the noodles and stirred with enough energy to cause a whirlpool inside the large stainless-steel pot.

"Mama," Carol cried. "I barely know Alex. We've only gone out a handful of times."

"Ah, but your eyes are telling me something else."

"The only thing my eyes are interested in is some of that garlic bread Paula's buttering," Carol said, hoping to divert her mother's attention away from the subject of Alex.

"Here." Her sister-in-law handed her a slice. "But it won't taste nearly as good as a man feels." Paula twisted her head back far enough to press a quick kiss upon her husband's cheek.

Tony's hands slipped further around Paula's waist as he whispered in his wife's ear. From the way her sister-in-law's face flooded with warm color, Carol didn't need much of an imagination to guess what Tony had said.

Carol looked away. She wasn't embarrassed by the earthy exchange between her brother and his wife, instead she felt a peculiar twinge of envy. The realization came like an unexpected charge of electricity, shocking her. In all the years she'd been alone, Carol had never once longed for a pair of arms to cuddle her or for a man to make low, suggestive whispers in her ear. Those intimacies were reserved for the happily married members of her family.

Yet, here she was, standing in the middle of her mother's kitchen, yearning for Alex to stroll up behind her, circle her waist and whisper his candy-sweet promises in her ear. The image was so vivid that she hurried into the living room to escape it.

It wasn't until later, when the dishes were washed, that Carol had a chance to be alone and sort through her thoughts. Tony and Peter were puttering around in the garage. Paula was playing a game of Yahtzee with the younger children. And Angelina was rocking in her chair, her nimble fingers working the delicate yarn into a sweater for her youngest grandchild.

"So are you gonna tell your mama what's troubling you?" she asked Carol out of the blue.

"Nothing's wrong," Carol fibbed. She couldn't discuss what she didn't understand. For the first time in her life, she felt distanced from the love and laughter that was so much a part of the Sunday dinners with her family. For years she'd clung to the life she'd built for herself and her son. These few, short weeks with Alex had changed everything. He was really getting to her. The thick, secure walls she'd built around her heart were starting to crack under the force of his persistence, and she felt powerless in dealing with him.

Alex had discovered every chink in her armor and had used it to his own advantage. Digging up the space for her herb garden was a good example. She could have asked her brother to do it for her. Eventually she probably would have. But Tony did so many things to help her already that she didn't want to burden him with another request. It wasn't as if tilling up part of the back yard was of earth-shattering importance. One casual mention to Alex, and before she knew it, there was freshly tilled earth waiting for basil and Italian parsley where there had once been lawn.

"You like this non-Italian, don't you?"

Carol responded with a tiny shake of her head.

A slow, easy smile spread from her mother's mouth to her eyes. "I thought as much. You got the look."

"The look?"

"Of a woman falling in love. Don't fight it so hard, my bambina. It's past time you met a man who brings color to your cheeks and a smile to your lips."

Only Carol wasn't smiling. She felt confused and ambivalent. She was crazy about Alex; she prayed she would never see him again. She couldn't picture her life with him; she couldn't picture her life without him.

"I lit a candle in church for you," her mother whispered. "And said a special prayer to St. Scholastica."

"Mama..."

"God and I had a good talk, and He told me it's predestined."

"What's predestined?"

"You and this non-Italian," her mother returned calmly.

"Mama, that doesn't make the least bit of sense. For years you've been telling me to marry a rich old man with one foot in the grave and the other on a banana peel. You claimed everyone loves a rich widow."

"Keep looking for the rich old man, only when you find him point him out to me. With any luck his first wife made spaghetti sauce with tomato soup and he'll worship my feet."

Carol couldn't keep from smiling. She wasn't so sure about her mother lighting candles in the church on her behalf, or deciding that marrying Alex was predestined, but from experience she'd learned it didn't do any good to argue.

Tony, Paula and their two children left around five. Usually Carol headed for home around the same time, but this afternoon she lingered. The 1940s war movie on television held Peter's attention, and her gaze drifted to it now and again.

It wasn't until she felt the moisture on her cheeks that she realized she was crying. The tears had been dredged up from the bottom of her soul, dusted with doubts and riddled with a multitude of fears.

Doing what she could to wipe the moisture aside so as not to attract attention to herself, she focused her eyes on the television screen. Her dear mother was right, she was falling in love, head over heels in love, and it was frightening her to death. She should be happy, instead she was terrified and weepy.

Silently Angelina set her knitting aside and joined Carol on the sofa. Without a word, she pressed a tissue into Carol's hand. Then she wrapped her arm around her youngest daughter's thin shoulders and pressed her head tenderly to her generous bosom. While gently, tenderly, patting Carol's back, Angelina whispered soothing words of love and encouragement in a language Carol could only partially understand.

Alex didn't see Carol again until Monday afternoon when he pulled into the high school parking lot. He angled his van in front of the track, four spaces down from her. He waited a couple of minutes, hoping she would come and see him of her own free will. He should have known better. The woman wasn't willing to give an inch.

Determined to be as nonchalant, Alex opened his door, walked over to the six-foot-high chain-link fence and pretended to be watching the various groups participate in the field events. Neither James nor Peter were trying out for any of those positions.

Then he casually strolled toward Carol, who was determined, it seemed, to ignore him, hiding behind the pages of a woman's magazine.

"Hello, Carol," he said after a decent interval.

"Alex." She held the magazine in place as if her hands had been cemented in the position.

"Do you mind if I join you?"

"Sure." The hesitation was long enough to relay the message that she would indeed mind. He ignored it, opening the passenger door and sliding inside her car. Only then did Carol bother to close the magazine and set it aside.

By now, Alex told himself, he should be accustomed to Carol's aloof attitude toward him. It was this way nearly every time they were together. It reminded him of swimming in an unheated pool. The initial plunge was enough to set him to shivering, but once he'd been in the water for any length of time, the chill left him and it became downright comfortable.

Carol had never shown any real pleasure in seeing him. He had to break through those chilly barriers each and every encounter. The strangest part was that he knew she was as strongly attracted to him as he was to her. And not just in the physical sense. Their lives were like matching bookends, only Carol refused to see it in those terms.

"Did you have a good day?" he asked.

She nodded and glanced away as though she feared sharing a part of her life with him was akin to admitting she enjoyed his company.

"I suppose it would be too much to ask that you missed me the last couple of days?" he asked hopefully.

"Yes," she ventured.

Alex was almost embarrassed at the way his heart raced into his throat. "You missed me," he repeated, feeling like a kid who had unexpectedly been granted free rein in a candy store.

"No," Carol countered, clearly disconcerted, "it would be too much to ask me to admit as much."

"Oh." Damn, but the woman knew how to deflate his pride!

"It really was thoughtful of you to dig up that area in my backyard Saturday. I'm grateful, Alex."

Crossing his arms over his chest, Alex leaned against the back of the cushioned seat and did a fair job of hiding his injured pride with a lazy shrug. "It wasn't any trouble." Especially since the two boys had done the majority of the work, leaving him free to "pester" Carol in the kitchen. With everything in him, he wished they were

back in that kitchen now. He wanted her warm and willing in his arms the way she'd been Saturday afternoon,
her lips moist and swollen with his kisses, her eyes dark
with passion.

"The boys will be out any minute," Carol said, her gaze
studying the empty field.

Alex guessed that this was his cue to vacate the vehicle,
but he wasn't taking the hint. When it came to dealing
with Carol Sommars, he was learning that his two greatest allies were James and Peter.

The time had come for him to play his ace.

Alex waited until the last possible minute. Both boys
had walked onto the parking lot, their hair damp from a
recent shower. They were chatting and joking and in an
apparent good mood. Climbing outside of Carol's car,
Alex leaned against the fender in a relaxed pose and casually crossed his arms and his ankles.

"Peter, did you mention something about wanting to
go camping?" he said, casting Carol a defiant look.
"James and I were thinking of heading for the Washington coastline this coming weekend and thought you and
your mother might like to go with us."

"We are?" James asked, delighted and surprised.

Peter's eyes darkened with excitement. "Camping?
You're inviting Mom and me to go camping with the two
of you?"

At the mention of the word, Carol opened her car door
and vaulted out in a move so fast a roadrunner would have
been envious. Her gaze narrowed on Alex as if to declare
a foul in this most recent exchange and charge him with a
penalty.

"Are you two free this weekend?" Alex asked with a
practiced look of innocence, formally extending the invi-

tation. The ball was in her court, and he was interested in seeing how she volleyed this one.

"Yes," Peter shouted. "We're interested."

"No," Carol countered at the same moment. "We already have plans."

"We do?" her son cried and moaned. "Come on, Mom, Mr. Preston just offered to take us camping with him and James. What could possibly take precedence over an opportunity like this?"

"I wanted to paint the living room."

"What? Paint the living room? I don't believe it." Peter slapped his hands hard against his thighs and cranked his head back so far it was a wonder he could remain upright. "You know how I feel about camping," he whined.

"Give your mother time to think it over," Alex urged, confident that given time Carol would change her mind or that Peter would do it for her. "We can talk about it tomorrow evening."

James gave Peter the okay signal, and feeling extraordinarily proud of himself, Alex led the way back to his van, automatically giving his son the keys.

"You're going to let me drive?" James asked, sounding more than a little stunned. "Voluntarily?"

"Count your blessings, boy, and drive."

"Yes, sir!"

Carol was furious with Alex. He'd played a faultless game, and she had to congratulate him on his fine closing move. All day she'd primed herself for the way she was going to act when she saw him again. She'd allowed their relationship to progress much further than she'd ever intended, and it was time to cool things down.

With her mother lighting candles in church to St. Scholastica and having heart-to-heart talks with God, matters had gotten completely out of hand. Her mother barely complained anymore that Alex wasn't Catholic, and worse, not Italian. It was as if those two prerequisites no longer mattered.

What Carol hadn't figured on was the rush of adrenaline she'd experienced when Alex pulled into the school parking lot. She swore her heart beat faster and stronger than any of the runners on the track. It had demanded every ounce of determination she possessed not to toss aside the magazine she'd planted in the car and run to him, bury her face in his chest and ask him to explain what was happening to her.

Apparently Alex had read her perfectly. He didn't appear the least bit concerned over her lack of welcome. That hadn't so much as fazed him. All the arguments she'd collected had been for naught. Then at the last possible minute he'd introduced the subject of them taking this camping trip together, in what she had to admire as a brilliant move. Her chain was only as strong as the weakest link. And her weakest link was Peter!

Grudgingly she had to admire Alex for his brilliant strategy.

"Mom," Peter cried, as restless as a first grader in the seat beside her. "We're going to talk about it, aren't we?"

"About the camping trip?"

"It's the opportunity of a lifetime. The Washington coast—I've heard it's fabulous—"

"We've got plans."

"To paint the living room? We could do that any old time."

"Peter, please."

He was silent for only a moment. "Do you remember when I was eleven?" he prompted.

Here it comes, Carol mused darkly. "I remember," she muttered, knowing it would have been too much to expect him not to drag up the lowest point of her life as a mother.

"We were going camping then, too, remember?"

He said *remember* as though it were a dirty word and he expected to be punished for using it so freely.

"You promised me an overnight camping trip and signed us up for an outing through the Y? But when we went to the planning meeting you got cold feet."

"Peter, they gave us a list of things we were supposed to bring, and not only did I not have half the items on the list, I didn't even know what they were."

"You could have asked," Peter cried.

"It was more than that, and you know it."

"Just because we were each going to hike at our own pace? They said we'd get a map. We could have found the camp, Mom, I know we could have."

Carol had had visions of wandering through the woods for days on end with nothing more than a piece of paper that stated she should head east—and she had the world's worst sense of direction. If she could get lost in a shopping mall, how would she ever expect to find her way through dense forest?

"That wasn't the worst part of it," Peter murmured. "Right there in the middle of the meeting you leaned over and asked me what it would cost you to buy your way out of the trip."

"You said you wouldn't leave for anything less than a laser tag set," Carol cried, tormented by the unfairness of it all. The toy had been popular and expensive at the time and had cost her a pretty penny. But her son had conveniently forgotten that part.

"I feel like I sold my soul that day," Peter said with a sigh large enough to unfurl flags.

"Peter, honestly!"

"It wasn't until then that I realized how much I was missing by not having a dad."

The kid was perfecting the art of "guilt."

"Once again," he argued, "I have the rare opportunity to find out what it's like to experience the great out-of-doors, and it's like a nightmare happening all over again. My own, dear, sweet mother is going to pull the rug out from under my feet."

Carol stopped at a red light and pretended to play a violin. "This could possibly warp your tender mind."

"It just might," Peter countered, completely serious.

"Twenty years from now when they lock those prison doors behind you, you can cry out that it's all my fault. If only I'd taken you camping with Alex and James Preston then the entire course of your life would have been different."

A short pause followed her statement.

"Sarcasm doesn't suit you, mother."

Peter was right of course, but Carol was getting desperate. At the rate matters were going, she'd end up spending Saturday night sitting in front of a camp fire, fighting off mosquitoes and the threat of wild beasts.

Because she felt guilty, despite every effort not to, Carol cooked Peter his favorite chicken-fried steak dinner, complete with gravy and mashed potatoes.

After the dishes had been cleared and Peter was supposed to be doing his homework, Carol found him talking on the phone, whispering frantically into the receiver. She didn't need a crystal ball to realize her son was discussing strategies with James. It was clear that the three of them were in cahoots against her.

Carol waited until Peter was in bed before she marched into the kitchen and righteously punched out Alex's phone number. She barely gave him the opportunity to answer when she laid into him with both barrels.

"That was a rotten thing to do."

"What?" he asked, feigning innocence.

"You know damn well what I'm talking about. Peter has pulled every string in the book from the moment you mentioned this stupid camping trip idea."

"Are you going to come or is this war?"

"It's war right now, fellow."

"Good. Do the spoils go to the victor? Because I'm telling you, Carol Sommars, I intend to win."

"Oh, Alex," she said with a sigh, bracing her back against the wall. She slid all the way down to the floor, longing to weep with frustration. "How could you do this to me?"

"Easy. The idea came when you told me it was too much to ask for you to miss me. That was below the belt, love, and fair is fair."

"But I don't know anything about camping. My idea of roughing it is going without valet service."

"It'll be fun, trust me."

Trusting Alex wasn't at the top of her priority list at the moment. He'd pulled a fast one on her, and she wasn't going to give him the opportunity to do it again.

"Is Peter sleeping?" Alex questioned softly.

"If he isn't, he should be." She didn't understand where this conversation was heading.

"James is down, too," he said softly. "After the cold shoulder you gave me this afternoon, I'm in need of something to warm my blood."

"Try a hot water bottle."

"It won't work—keep the door unlocked and I'll be right over."

"Absolutely not. Alex Preston, listen to me, I'm not dressed for company and—"

It was too late, he'd already disconnected the line.

Chapter Eight

Standing in front of her locked screen door, Carol had absolutely no intention of letting Alex inside her home. It was late, nearly eleven, and they both had to go to work in the morning. When his car pulled into the driveway, she braced her feet apart and stiffened her back. She should be furious with him. Should be nothing, she was furious!

But when Alex climbed out of his car, he paused. The porch light was dim, just bright enough to outline his handsome features.

For the longest moment he did nothing but stand in her driveway, his hands buried deep inside his pockets as he stared at her. Staring seemed such an inadequate word to describe the intense way his eyes locked with her own. Not a muscle moved in the hard, chiseled line of his jaw, and his eyes feasted on her with undisguised hunger. Even from the short distance that separated them, Carol noted that his wonderful soul-gray eyes had darkened with need.

He wanted her.

God help her, despite all her arguments to the contrary, she wanted him, too.

Before he had marched two steps toward her, Carol had unlocked the screen door and held it open for him.

"I'm not going camping," she announced, her voice scarcely audible. Her lips felt dry and her hands moist. Once she'd bravely stated her position on the subject, her breath escaped on the end of a ragged sigh. It was in her mind to rant at him, call him a coward and a cheat to have used her own son against her this way, but not a word made it from her mind to her lips.

Alex turned and closed the front door for her.

The only light in the room was a single dim lamp on the other side of the room.

They didn't move, didn't breathe.

"I'm not going to force you to go," Alex whispered. "In fact, I . . ." He paused as he lowered his eyes to her breasts, and whatever he intended to say trailed into nothingness.

Carol felt his eyes on her as keenly as she had his mouth when he'd suckled her breasts. Her breath scattered as her nipples tightened with such hardness they ached. The weighted, restless feeling didn't stop there, but descended to the hollow core hidden between her legs. This was ridiculous. He hadn't so much as touched her. If she hadn't known better, Carol would have thought she was suffering from a fever. She felt hot and moist in all the wrong places. Hot and needy. Hot and barren.

In an effort to break this unnatural spell, she closed her eyes, but that proved to be a mistake. A terrible mistake. Her treacherous mind became filled with the image of Alex poised above her, sliding his sex, slow and deep, all the way inside her. She gasped and bit her lip as her eyes shot open.

Emotion thickened the air.

"Carol?"

She couldn't have answered him had her life depended on it. Her back was pressed to the door, and she flattened her hands there, bracing herself for fear of what would happen next.

Not once in all the years of her married life had Carol felt as she did that moment. So hot. So needy. So empty. If he didn't touch her soon, she would die. It demanded every ounce of strength she possessed to pull her flattened hand from the door and hold it out toward Alex.

He came to her in a single, unbroken movement, his mouth crushing hers, his tongue a savage but welcome invader. Carol wound her arms around him and leaned into his solid strength, craving it as she never had before. Again and again and again he kissed her, until she was melting in his arms.

The molten heat within her spread to every secret part that made up her being. The hot, silken threads circled and tightened her heavy breasts, then slipped lower to her hips, stiffening even more until she slowly started to rotate the lower half of her body against him in a sluggish, gyrating motion. The silken cord glided even further down her body, wrapping its way around her thighs and the hot pulsating center of her femininity, leaving her weak with a need she couldn't define.

"Alex." She tore her lips from his and tossed back her head. "Alex," she breathed again, almost panting. "Something's wrong . . . very wrong."

She could feel his breath against her neck and his fingers in her hair, directing her mouth back to his, kissing her with such heat, Carol thought she would disintegrate. Then his hands were on her buttocks, pressing her so close that she could feel the tortured hardness of his arousal. Instinct led her then, and she started to move against him in hurried, jerky movements.

He closed his hands roughly over her hips and controlled her frenzied thrusts, slowing them and finally coordinating them with his own heated response. With each swirling movement he lifted her higher and higher, pressed into her harder and harder, all the while kissing her with a carnal fever.

The molten threads that had woven their way around her constricted her even more, and the heat of his kiss, of his tongue, of his sex, licked at her senses like raging tongues of fire.

Then it happened. Carol gasped at the intensity of it and wrenched her mouth from his. Her eyes flew open as the snugly coiled tightness within her soared toward sublime relief. One rippling shudder followed another, and she whimpered and bit into her lower lip as the tears flooded her eyes. She clenched Alex's shirt and buried her face into his neck as the delicious tremors went on and on and on.

Aeons passed before they slowly started to abate.

She'd climaxed for the first time in her life.

"Carol." Alex breathed her name close to her ear while gently stroking the back of her head. "Are you all right?"

She nodded wildly, longing to throw back her head and laugh. She'd never felt more "all right" in thirty-four years. Nor more embarrassed. Alex hadn't done anything more than kiss her, and she'd behaved like an...an animal. God only knew what he must think of her. Reality slapped her hard across the face. How could she possibly look him in the eye again?

Alex was everything Bruce had never been. The gentle, unselfish lover. Tender. Concerned.

At the memory of her late husband and the crude, cruel ways in which he'd used her, physically and emotionally, Carol started to weep.

"Sh-h-h, baby," Alex whispered. "It's all right."

"No...no, it isn't," she countered, sobbing. "You don't understand...you couldn't possibly know."

The tears came in earnest then, a great storehouse that had been building up inside her over the years. The long, lonely, barren years.

With the tears came the pain, pain so intense she could barely breath. The agony spilled from her heart and into the moisture that flowed from her eyes. The trauma that had been buried so deep within her stormed out in a torrent of tears that she could no more stop than she could control.

Huge sobs shook her shoulders, giant hiccupping sobs that she felt all the way to her toes. Sobs that ate at her strength. Her breathing was choppy and ragged as she stumbled toward the edge of hysteria.

Alex was speaking to her in soft, reassuring whispers, but Carol couldn't hear him, couldn't understand him. It didn't matter what he said, nothing mattered. Not anymore.

She clenched his shirt tighter and tighter. Soon there were no more tears to shed, no more emotion to be spent. Alex continued to hold her. He put his arms all the way around her, and although she couldn't understand what he was saying, his voice was unbelievably gentle.

Once the desperate crying had started to subside, Carol drew in giant gulps of oxygen in a futile effort to gain control of herself and her senses.

Slowly Alex guided her toward the sofa and sat her down, then he gathered her in his arms and tenderly held her.

Time lost meaning to Carol, until she heard the clock chime midnight. Until then she was satisfied with being held and protected in Alex's arms. He asked no questions, demanded no explanations. He simply held her and allowed the pain to unravel its way out of her.

This newfound contentment in his arms was all too short-lived, however. Acute embarrassment stole through the stillness, coating the room. Fresh tears stung Carol's eyes. Her mind, her thoughts, her memories were steeped in emotions too strong to bear.

"I . . . I'll make some coffee," she whispered, unwinding her arms from him, feeling she had to escape.

"Forget the coffee."

She broke away and stood, though she wasn't sure her feet would support her. Before he had the chance to stop her, she hurried into the kitchen and braced her hands against the counter, uncertain if she could perform the uncomplicated task of making a pot of coffee.

Alex followed her into the darkened room. He placed his hand on her shoulder and gently turned her around, so she had no choice but to face him. "I want to talk about what happened."

"No . . . please." She leveled her eyes at the floor.

"We *need* to talk."

"No." She shook her head emphatically. "Not now. Please not now."

A long, desperate moment passed before he gently kissed the crown of her head. "All right," he whispered. "But soon. Very soon."

Carol doubted she could ever discuss what had happened between them, but she hadn't the strength or the courage to say as much to Alex. To do so would have only invited argument.

"I . . . I think you should go now."

His nod was reluctant. "Will you be all right?"

"Yes." A bold-faced lie if ever there was one. She would never be the same again. She was mortified to the very marrow of her bones by her behavior. First by the sexual release and fulfillment she'd found in Alex's arms when he'd done nothing more than kiss her. And if that wasn't humiliating enough, the tempest of tears that had followed was.

No, she wouldn't be all right, but she would pretend that she was, the same way she'd been pretending from the moment she'd married Bruce.

The message waiting for Alex when he returned to his office the following afternoon didn't come as any surprise. His secretary gave him the pink slip, and the instant he saw Carol's name, he knew. She was working late that evening and asked if it would be possible for him to pick up Peter from track practice and drop him off at the house.

The little coward! He took a seat at his desk, leaned back in his chair and frowned. He hadn't wanted to leave her the night before. Hadn't wanted to walk out of her kitchen without being assured she was all right. Carol, however, had made it clear she wanted him to leave. Equally apparent was the knowledge that his being there was only adding to her distress. Whatever Carol was dealing with, whatever ghosts she'd encountered, were deep and dark and ugly. She'd made it clear she had to face them alone.

And so he'd left her, reluctantly, regretfully. But he hadn't stopped thinking about her all day. The thought of her had filled every waking minute—and every sleeping one, too, for that matter.

Even now, hours later, he could remember in vivid detail the way she'd started to unfold and blossom right before his eyes. It was as if she were a delicate rosebud brought into a hothouse, and little by little, she'd flowered open. Because of him. For him.

The memory of the way she'd gasped with shock and delight and tossed back her head and moved against him was enough to tighten his loins with high-voltage need.

She'd been so honest. So surprised.

If he hadn't known better, Alex would think it was her first time. Then again, maybe it was, but that thought brought several questions with it. His frown deepened. She'd never talked about her marriage. Alex didn't even know her late husband's name. Questions bombarded him from all sides, and he cursed the lack of answers.

And now, his sweet, delectable coward had gone into hiding.

"Will you talk to her, Mr. Preston?" Peter pleaded as he climbed inside the van in the school parking lot. "Mom's never gone camping, and I think she'd probably like it if she gave it half a chance."

"I'll talk to her," Alex promised.

Peter sighed with relief. "Good."

Sounding both confident and proud, James added, "My dad can be persuasive when he wants to be."

Alex intended to be very persuasive!

"I tried to reason with Mom this morning, and you know what she said?" Peter's changing voice pitched between two octaves and sagged with defeat.

"What?"

"She said she didn't want to talk about it. Doesn't that sound just like a woman? And I thought Melody Wohlford was difficult to understand."

Alex stifled a chuckle. "I'll tell you boys what I'm going to do. We'll pick up hamburgers on the way home, and I'll drop you both off at my house. Then I'll drive over to your place, Peter, and wait for your mother there."

"Good idea," James said, sounding more than pleased.

"But while I'm gone, I want you boys to do your homework."

"Of course."

"Naturally," James echoed. "Just do what you can to convince Mrs. Sommars to come along on the camping trip."

"I'll do everything I can," Alex promised.

Carol let herself in the front door, drained from a long, taxing day at the hospital, and exhausted from the long sleepless night that had preceded it. That morning, she'd been tempted to phone in sick, but unfortunately, she knew the schedule, and with two nurses already out due to illness, there wasn't anyone to replace her. So she'd gone to work feeling emotionally and physically hung over.

"Peter, I'm home," she called, letting herself in the front door. "Peter?"

Silence echoed back at her. Walking into the kitchen, she deposited her purse on the counter and strolled toward her son's bedroom. She'd contacted Alex and asked that he bring her son home, with instructions to phone her back if he couldn't. She hadn't gotten the message to the contrary and just assumed he would pick up her son and drop him off at the house.

Peter's room was empty, his bed unmade, with an array of clean and dirty clothes littering his floor. Everything was normal there.

This was what she got for trying to avoid seeing Alex, Carol mused, chastising herself. Peter was probably still waiting at the high school track for her and wondering where she could possibly be.

"Damn," she muttered under her breath as she hurried back into the kitchen and reached for her purse.

The doorbell chimed as she walked through the living room. Impatiently she jerked the door open and her dark eyes collided with Alex's. She gasped.

"Hello again," he said in the warm husky way that never failed to affect her. "I didn't mean to startle you."

"You didn't." He did, but she wasn't about to admit it. "Apparently you didn't get my message...Peter must still be at the school."

"No. He's at my house with James."

"Oh." That was such an inadequate word for the instant dread she felt. They were alone, and there wasn't any means of escape, at least not by the most convenient means—Peter.

Alex stepped into the house and for the first time, she noticed he was carrying a white paper bag. Her gaze settled on it and she frowned.

"Two Big Macs, fries and shakes," he explained.

"For whom?"

Alex arched his thick eyebrows with the question. "Us."

"Oh..." He honestly expected her to sit down and eat with him? It would be impossible. "I'm not hungry."

"I am—very hungry. If you don't want to eat, that's fine. I will, and while I'm downing my dinner, we can talk."

It wouldn't do any good to argue, and Carol knew it. Without another word, she turned and walked to the kitchen. Alex followed her, and his movements, as smooth and agile as always, sounded like a thundering herd of elephants behind her. She was aware of everything about him. When he walked, when he breathed, when he moved.

His eyes bored holes into her back, but she ignored the command to turn and face him. She couldn't bear to look him in the eye. Just the thought of what had happened between them the night before was enough to set her cheeks flaming.

"How are you?" he asked in that husky, caring way of his.

"Fine," she answered cheerfully. "And you?"

"Not so good."

"Oh." Her heart was pounding, clamoring like jungle drums in her ears. "I'm...sorry to hear that."

"You should be, since you're the cause."

"Me? I'm...sure you're mistaken." She brought two plates down from the cupboard and set them on the table.

As she scooted past him, Alex captured her hand. "I don't want to play word games with you. We've come too far for this, and we're going a good deal further."

Unable to bear listening to his words, she closed her eyes.

"Look at me, Carol."

She couldn't do it. She lowered her head, squeezed her eyes closed and shook her head.

"There's no need to be embarrassed by what happened."

Naturally he could afford to be generous, it wasn't him who'd acted like a...a love-starved hussy. Nor had he been the one to dissolve into a frenzy of violent tears and emotion afterward. It was something of a minor miracle that Peter had slept through the episode. Thank God the track coach worked him so hard that he fell into bed exhausted each night and didn't budge until morning.

"We need to talk."

"No..." she cried and broke away. "Couldn't you have just ignored what happened? Why do you have to drag it up now?" she demanded. "Does it delight you to embarrass me this way? Do you get a kick out of seeing me this miserable?" She paused, breathless, her chest heaving. "Please, just go away and leave me alone."

Her fierce words gave birth to a brief, tension-filled silence.

Using his thumb and forefinger, Alex gripped her chin and lifted her head. Fresh emotion filled her chest, knotting in her throat as her eyes slid reluctantly to his.

"I don't know what happened last night," Alex growled, "at least not entirely. All I know is we shared an incredible closeness that surpasses anything I've ever known. Yes, it was sexy as hell, but it was more than that." His voice was gruff, angry, soft, emotional. "I've never felt closer to anyone than I did to you last night, and dammit all, I don't want to lose that. We've got something special, Carol, and I refuse to let you throw it away. Understand?"

She bit into her lower lip, sniffled, then slowly nodded.

The tension eased from Alex, and he reached for her, gently drawing her into his arms. She went without question, burying her face into the thick column of his neck.

Long, lazy moments passed before he spoke. "I want you to tell me about your marriage."

"No," she cried and frantically shook her head.

He was silent again, tense, and she could feel him withdrawing from her—or maybe she was the one withdrawing. She wanted to ask him to be patient with her, to give her breathing room, space to analyze what was happening between them.

Just when she was ready to speak, she felt him relax against her. He chuckled softly, his warm breath mussing her hair. "All right, I'll strike a bargain with you. If you go camping with me this weekend, I'll drop the subject— not forever, mind you, but until you're comfortable enough to voluntarily tell me on your own."

Carol lifted her head, her dark eyes meeting his. "You've got a black heart, Alex Preston."

He chuckled and kissed the tip of her nose. "When it comes to courting you, I've learned I need one."

"I can't believe I'm doing this," Carol muttered as she headed up the steep trail into the thick foliage. The surf pounded the Washington beach far below. But directly in front of her was a narrow path that led straight into the heart of the celebrated Rain Forest.

"We don't have to wait for you guys, do we?" James whined, obviously eager for him and his friend to do some exploring on their own.

Carol was about to ask a long list of questions when Alex spoke. "Feel free," he told the two youths. "Carol and I will be back down to camp in time for dinner. We'll expect you to be there then."

"Great."

"All right."

Within two minutes both boys were out of sight, and Carol was left to deal with the increasingly difficult climb on a path a mountain goat would have had trouble manipulating.

"You're doing fine," Alex said from behind her. Breathless with the physical exertion demanded to march up the steep incline, Carol paused and pressed her back against the edge of the embankment and took a couple of minutes to catch her breath.

"I love it when you get all hot and sweaty for me."

"Will you stop," she cried, embarrassed and amused by his words.

"Never."

To complicate things, Alex moved with the grace and skill of an elk even while carting a backpack. Thus far, he hadn't even worked up a good sweat. Carol, on the other hand, was practically panting. She hadn't realized how out of shape she was until now.

"This view had better be worth all this effort," she said with a moan, five minutes later. The muscles in her calves were beginning to protest, and her heart was pounding so hard it echoed in her ears like a Chinese gong.

To make matters worse, Carol had worn the worst possible combination of clothes. Not knowing what to expect weatherwise, she'd donned heavy boots, jeans and a thick sweatshirt, plus a jacket. Her head was covered with a bright pink cap her mother had knitted for her last Christmas. Should they happen upon a snowstorm, Carol was prepared.

"It is worth the climb," Alex promised. "Do you want me to lead?"

"No way, fellow," she said, instantly dismissing his offer, "I'd probably never be able to keep up with you."

A few minutes later, Carol staggered into a clearing. She stopped abruptly, caught breathless by the beauty that surrounded her. The forest was thick with a variety of trees and budding wild flowers. Huge tree limbs were draped with mossy green blankets that hung down so far they danced against the spongy ground. A series of moss-coated stumps dotted the area, some sprouting huge white mushroom caps. A gentle breeze drifted through the meadow and, catching her breath, Carol removed the hat from her head in an abstract form of worship.

"You're right," she murmured. "This is wonderful...I feel like I'm standing in a cathedral...this makes me want to pray."

"This isn't what I wanted you to see," Alex said, resting his hand on the curve of her shoulder.

"It isn't?" she whispered in disbelief. "You mean there's something better than this?"

"Follow me."

Carol removed her jacket, stuffed her hat into the armhole and tied the sleeves around her waist. Her movements were eager as she followed Alex across the winding narrow pathway.

"There's a freshwater cove about a mile from here," he explained, turning back to look at her. "Are you up to the trek?"

"I think so." She felt wonderful. Apparently she'd gotten a second wind, because she'd rarely felt more alive or more physically fit.

"You're being a good sport about all this," Alex said, smiling back at her.

"I knew I was going to be all right when I saw that you'd pitched the tents close to the public rest rooms. I'm not comfortable unless I'm around something that goes flush in the night."

Alex chuckled. They hiked for another twenty minutes and came to the edge of a cliff that fell sharply into the water. The view of bright green waters, contrasted by brilliant blue skies, was beautiful enough to bring tears to Carol's eyes. The park department had set up a chain-link fence along the edge to ward off the chance of anyone falling. A roughly hewn bench had been carved out of an old tree trunk.

Alex gestured for her to sit down. Spreading out her coat, Carol sat down and gazed out at the beauty before her.

"You hungry?"

It didn't take her more than a moment to decide. "Starving."

"I thought you would be." He slipped the pack off his back and set it down in front of them. Peeling back the zipper, he removed a silver plastic bag that resembled the thirty-three-gallon ones Carol used to line her garbage cans.

"What's that?" she asked.

"A plastic garbage bag."

"Oh." Well, that was what it looked like.

Following the plastic bag, he removed a fat whistle. He held it up for her inspection. "A whistle," he announced before she could ask. Finally he found what he was searching for and set a thick chocolate bar on the bench and pulled out two apples.

"Without appearing completely stupid," Carol said, taking a bite of her apple, "may I ask why you hauled a garbage bag all the way up here? I didn't see a single piece of litter."

"In case we get lost."

"What?" she cried, alarmed. She'd assumed Alex knew his way back to their campsite. He'd certainly implied as much.

"The best of hikers have been known to get lost. This is just a precaution."

"When . . . I mean, I thought you were experienced."

He wiggled his eyebrows suggestively. "I am."

"Alex, this isn't any time to joke."

"I'm not joking. The garbage bag, the whistle and the candy bars are all part of the hug-a-tree project."

"Hug-a-tree?"

"It's a way of preparing children, or anyone else for that matter, in case they get lost in the forest. The idea is to stay in one place—to literally hug a tree. The garbage bag is for warmth. If a person slips inside it, feet first, and crouches down, gathering the opening around the neck, he or she can keep warm in near-freezing temperatures. It weighs practically nothing. The whistle aids rescuers in locating whoever's lost, and the candy is for the obvious."

"Do you mean to tell me we're chowing down on our limited supply of food rations?" Carol took another bite of her apple before Alex could change his mind and take it away from her.

"Indeed we are, but then we're practically within sight of the campground, so I don't think we're in any danger of getting lost."

"Good." Too hungry to care, Carol peeled aside the paper from the chocolate bar and took a generous bite.

"I was waiting for that," Alex murmured, setting aside his apple.

Carol paused, the candy bar angled in front of her mouth. "Why?"

"So I could kiss you and taste the chocolate on your lips." He reached for her, dragging the upper part of her body toward him. Their chests collided. Meshed. Breast to breast.

His mouth found hers with such need, such hunger, that Carol groaned. Alex hadn't touched her in days, hadn't pressed anything physical on her, patiently giving her time to determine the boundaries of their relationship. Now she was starving for him, eager for his kiss and eager for his touch.

His kiss was slow, so slow and deliberate. His mouth and tongue drew lazy circles around hers, then mated with hers in age-old tradition.

Carol moaned and sagged against him.

"Dear God, you taste sweet," he whispered, tugging at her lower lip with his teeth. "But then again, you should."

Chapter Nine

Her sleeping bag and air mattress didn't look as comfortable as a bed at the Hilton, but they appeared adequate, Carol decided later that night. At least Alex had enough equipment for the four of them. All Carol and Peter owned was one GI Joe sleeping bag, decorated with little green army men, and Carol wasn't particularly excited about having to sleep inside that.

They'd hiked and explored most of the afternoon. By the time everything was cleared away after dinner, dusk had settled over Salt Creek Park. Carol was all out of energy by then, but Peter and James insisted they couldn't officially call it camping unless everyone sat around the camp fire, roasted marshmallows and sang silly songs. And so a lengthy songfest had ensued.

Carol was yawning when she scooted inside the small tent she was sharing with Peter. Alex's and James's larger tent was pitched next to their own. By the dim light of the lantern hanging from the middle of the tent, Carol undressed, creamed her face and then slipped inside the sleeping bag.

"Is it safe yet?" Peter yelled impatiently from outside the tent.

"Safe and sound," Carol returned. She'd just finished zipping up the bag when Peter pulled back the flap and stuck his head inside.

Smiling, he withdrew, and she heard him whisper something to James about how unreasonable women could be. Carol didn't know what she'd done that could be considered irrational, and she was too drained to inquire.

"Good night, everyone," Carol called out when Peter dimmed the lantern.

A mixed chorus of "good nights" was returned, and content, she rolled onto her stomach, pressed her cheek onto the thick pillow and closed her eyes.

Within minutes Carol was sound asleep.

"Carol."

She woke sometime later, as her name was whispered close to her ear. Jerking her head up, she encountered Alex, kneeling just inside the tent, fully dressed. He pressed his finger to his lips, indicating she should be quiet.

"What is it?"

"I want to show you something."

"Now?"

He grinned at her lack of enthusiasm and nodded.

"It can't wait until morning?" she said, yawning.

"It'll be gone by morning," he informed her in a whisper. "Get dressed and meet me in five minutes."

Personally she couldn't understand what he found so important that she couldn't see by the light of day.

"If you're not out here in five minutes," he warned in a husky whisper as he stood outside her tent, "I'm coming in after you."

Carol grumbled as she scurried around looking for her clothes. It was difficult to slip into her jeans in the cramped space, but with a few acrobatic moves, she managed. Before she crawled out, she tapped Peter's shoulder and told him she would be back in a few minutes.

Peter didn't seem to care one way or the other.

Alex was waiting for her, hands buried in his pockets to ward off the chill air. His lazy smile wrapped its way around her heart and squeezed tight. For all her moaning and complaining about this camping trip, Carol was having the time of her life.

"This had better be good," she warned, and ingloriously yawned.

"It is," he promised. He held a flashlight and a blanket in one hand and reached for hers with the other. Then he led the way toward the beach. Although she was wearing her jacket, the wind nipped at her and she shivered. Alex must have noticed, because he slipped his arm around her shoulder and pulled her closer into the protective shelter of his arms.

"Where are we going?" She whispered the question, not sure why she felt the need to do so.

"To a rock."

"A rock," she repeated, incredulous. "You woke me from a sound sleep so I could view a *rock*?"

"No, to sit on one."

"I couldn't do this at noon in the warm sun?" she muttered disparagingly, laughing at him.

"Not if you're going to look at the stars."

Carol's step faltered. "Do you mean to tell me, you forced me from a warm, cozy sleeping bag in the middle of the night to show me a few measly stars? The very same ones I could view from my own bedroom window any night of the week?"

Alex chuckled. "Are you always this testy when you just wake up?"

"Always," she told him. Yawning loudly, she placed the back of her hand over her mouth.

Although they were only a few feet from the campsite, it was hidden behind a clump of trees. Carol could hear the ocean, but she couldn't see it.

"I suppose I should choose a tree now. Which one looks the most friendly to you?" Carol asked.

"A tree? Whatever for?"

"To hug. Didn't you tell me this afternoon that if I ever get lost in the woods that a tree is my friend? If we get separated, there's no way in heaven I'd ever find my way back to camp."

Alex chuckled and dropped a kiss on the crown of her head. "I won't let you out of my sight for a minute, I promise."

"The last time I trusted a guy, I was eighteen and I turned up pregnant three weeks later." She meant it as a joke, but once the words were out they hung in the air like a thick mist between them.

"You were only eighteen when you married?"

Carol nodded, pulled her hand free from his and stuffed it in the pocket of her jacket. She could feel herself withdrawing from him. She pulled a little more inside herself where it was safe and comfortable.

They walked in silence for several minutes.

Alex aimed the flashlight at the pathway and a few moments later, paused. "This way."

"Over there?" Carol asked. She squinted, but she couldn't see any rock.

"Just follow me," Alex urged. "And no more wisecracks about what happened the last time you listened to a guy. I'm not your first husband, and it would serve us both well if you remembered that." His words were light, teasing, but they were packed with a punch that sent Carol reeling.

He reached for her hand, lacing his fingers through hers, holding on tight. Carol could almost hear the endless litany of questions as they paraded through Alex's mind. He wanted her to tell him about Bruce of her own free will. No one fully knew what a nightmare it had been. Not even her mother. And Carol wasn't about to drag out all the pain for Alex to examine.

Within a couple of minutes, Alex had located "his" rock. Carol couldn't see what all the fuss was about, it looked like an ordinary rock to her, silhouetted against the beach.

He climbed up the side first, seemingly familiar with its shape and size, and then offered Carol his hand to assist her. Once they were perched atop the smooth, round surface, he spread out the blanket and motioned for her to sit down.

Carol did as he asked, and gathered her knees under her chin.

Alex settled down beside her. "Now," he said, pointing toward the heavens, "Can you see *that* outside your bedroom window?"

Having forgotten the purpose of this outing, Carol cast her gaze toward the dark sky and then straightened with wonder and surprise. The stars were out in force, hundreds...thousands, littered the black velvet night. The sky was so heavy with the glittering treasures that it seemed to sag down and touch the earth. "Oh, Alex," she breathed.

"Was it worth waking up for?" he pressed.

"It was well worth it," she returned, thanking him with a smile.

"I thought you'd think so." His returning smile sailed straight into her heart.

She'd been struck by so much extraordinary beauty in such a short while that she felt ready to burst. Turning her head slightly, she smiled at this man who had opened her eyes to life, to beauty, to love, and whispered fervently, "Thank you, Alex."

"For what?"

"For the hike in the rain forest, for the view of the cove, for ignoring my complaints and showing me the stars, for...everything." For coming into her life. For leading her by the hand. For being incredibly patient with her.

"You're most welcome."

Lost in the magic, Carol closed her eyes and inhaled the fragrant scent of the wind, the ocean and the night. Rarely had she experienced contentment or this level of uncomplicated happiness. Her blood sang with discovery and joy.

The breeze came, and combined with the sounds of pounding surf, it sounded like the playful chatter of children. Throwing back her head, Carol tried to take it all inside her, hold it to her breast and savor the moment.

"I don't think I've ever appreciated how truly beautiful you are until now," Alex murmured. His face was carved in severe, but sensual, lines, and his eyes had darkened with emotion.

Carol turned, and when she did, he brushed back the dark curls from the smoothness of her cheek with his fingers. His hand lingered on her face, and Carol covered it with her own, closing her eyes to the wealth of sensation that came with his touch.

He brought his free hand to her hair, threaded its length through his fingers as though the texture were pure silk. He traced her lower lip with the calloused pad of his index finger. Unable to resist, Carol circled it in moist forays with the tip of her tongue, drawing it into her mouth, sucking on it lightly.

It seemed time stood still as Alex's eyes sought and held hers.

He kissed her, and it was excruciatingly slow, and his touch was so hot it scorched her senses. When he lifted his head, her breath staggered from her lungs. It never failed. Alex's touch reduced her to a mindless, witless mass of hot need. This incredible weakness he invoked terrorized her, and yet she wouldn't have it any other way.

With every other man she'd met since she'd become a widow, she'd been the one in control, the one to set the limits. But when Alex held her, there was no doubt in either of their minds who was in charge. Despite herself, whatever he asked of her, she willingly complied. Whatever he needed, she gave.

He pressed warm kisses in the hollow of her neck and slipped his hands inside her jacket, circling her waist and bringing her closer.

"Open up to me," he whispered. "Give me your mouth...all of it." He urged her lips wider and wider apart. His tongue filled her, met her own in a swirling erotic game that left them both breathless. Alex dragged his mouth from hers. "Dear God...the things you do to me."

"The things I do to you?" she whispered, pressing her forehead to his own. "They can't be compared to what you do...have always done to me."

His lips quivered with the beginning of a smile, and Carol leaned forward just enough to kiss him again, employing the techniques he'd taught her, darting the tip of her tongue between his lips. Restless, Carol shifted positions, kneeling in front of him. Silently she leaned forward and slanted her mouth over his.

Under her jacket Alex slid his hands up and down her back. He stopped abruptly, went stone-still and tore his mouth from hers.

"What's wrong?" Carol asked, lifting her head. Her hands were planted on his shoulders.

"You're not wearing a bra, are you?"

"No. You said I had only five minutes to dress, so I hurried."

His eyes burned into hers, then skidded lower to the snap at her jeans. "Did you...take any other shortcuts?"

"Wanna find out?"

He sucked in a giant breath. "I don't think I heard you right."

"You heard me," she told him softly and peeled off her jacket. Although her fingers were trembling, she managed to unbutton the front of her shirt, spreading it open.

For the first time since they'd met, Carol discovered that Alex was at a complete and utter loss of words.

"I...I promised myself when you agreed to go camping that I was going to do everything I could to keep my hands off you." His voice was so low and weak that Carol had to strain to hear him.

"I think that was a wise decision," she murmured, and paused, looking up at him. Alex's eyes were filled with surprise. An inner happiness she had banished from her life so long ago she hadn't known it was missing, pulsed through her now. Once her own shirt was open, she brought her hands to his, peeling open the buttons and lifting it free from his waistband.

"Carol?" He stopped her, holding her at her wrists. "I . . . be good, will you? I'm only human. . . ."

"I'm only human, too," she whispered. Leaning forward, she gently rubbed her lips across his, creating a moist, delectable friction. Gently her tongue played over his lips, sliding back and forth again and again, teasing him, testing him, loving him.

He was moaning by the time she finished. "That's being good?" he demanded in a husky murmur.

"Oh, yes," she countered. "It's very good."

"Two can play this game." He claimed her mouth in an urgent kiss that drove the oxygen from her lungs. His hands were in her hair as he ground his lips over hers as though to make her suffer for the torment she'd put him through. Gradually the forcefulness left him, and his kiss softened until it was slow, easy and relaxed.

By the time he freed her, Carol was so weak with longing that she clung to him, drooped her head and breathed deeply.

"You don't play fair," she chastised him. If he was declaring war, then she wasn't going to take it lying down. She smiled at the unintended pun.

"Carol," he said, watching her closely as she shifted positions once more. Only this time she climbed onto his lap, wrapped her long legs around his waist and looped her arms around his neck.

"Oh...Carol." Alex moaned and closed his eyes as she slowly rubbed her bare breasts against the tight muscular wall of his chest.

"Sh-h-h," she whispered, kissing him once more, using her tongue in all the ways he'd taught her.

Tightening his hands around her shoulders he lowered his mouth to the pebbled summit of her breast. He repeatedly lapped the beaded flesh with velvet strokes of his tongue. Then his lips curled around it and carefully brought the nipple into his mouth. He suckled at it gently, then surprised her by greedily feasting. Almost immediately, he gentled the action again.

Carol's hands were in his hair, and her teeth marked her lower lip at the slow, thorough way in which he made love to her.

"Such...beautiful breasts," he whispered, lifting them in his hands, then bunching them together. He used his tongue to make a slippery trail between the valley, sliding his mouth from one pulsing nipple to the next.

Carol's hips started to move, rubbing against his hardness. She wanted to stop, but she couldn't help it, she couldn't seem to hold still. The fire was returning, the hot need coursed through her blood like wildfire.

"Oh, baby..." he whispered, easing his hands between her legs to stroke her inner thighs.

She started to protest when he reached for the snap of her jeans, but he silenced her with a deep kiss that drained away her strength. When he slipped his mouth from hers, their eyes locked.

"Do you remember what happened the other night?" he asked.

It wasn't something she was likely to forget. Just having him mention it was enough to flood her face with the hottest of colors.

"Do you?" he repeated.

She looked away and nodded, embarrassed beyond belief.

"I want to see that joy on your face again. Tonight." He punctuated his words with a lengthy kiss. "Now." He lifted her just enough to ease open her zipper.

Her hand stopped him. "Alex . . . no."

He wrapped his hand around her neck and drew her mouth back to his. "I want to give you more pleasure than you've ever known."

Her eyes drifted closed, and she whimpered softly. He didn't know, he didn't realize, that he already *had* shown her more sensual pleasure than she'd dared believe existed. He'd shaken awake a deep part of her that she believed was long dead and buried.

"Let me give it to you . . ." he pleaded. He clasped her around the waist and in one swift, smooth motion repositioned their bodies so they were lying side by side, breast to breast, abdomen to abdomen. Their breaths mingled, their moist lips scant inches apart. With his eyes locked with hers, he pushed aside the fabric of her jeans and eased his hand into the elastic waistband of her bikini underwear.

A deep rush of air escaped her lungs. She moaned and closed her eyes when Alex slowly, methodically eased his hand between her parted thighs.

"Open your eyes," he whispered fervently. "I want to see you."

It demanded everything in her to do as he asked. He thanked her with a wet, hot kiss. When he released her mouth, Carol sighed into the hollow of his throat.

He eased his hand further down and slid his finger inside the dewy folds that were the most intimate part of her womanhood. Almost against her will she grew hot . . . hotter than she'd ever been before . . . searing hot . . . scalding hot . . . incredibly hot. She arched her back and swallowed a cry as the purest form of sensation hit her as hard and strong as a runaway train. Wave upon luscious wave of fiery excitement lapped over her, and she was hurled into the brightest, most blinding light, felt its warmth and its brilliance in every part of her body. She felt whole, complete, well.

Alex's mouth sought and found hers, swallowing her moans and blocking out her cries. Wrapping her arms around his neck she buried her face in the hollow of his throat, kissing him, hugging him, thanking him. Alex had done things to her that no man, not even her husband, had ever dreamed of doing. Alex had led her to the very reaches of paradise, thrown open the gate and escorted her inside.

"Sweet heaven," he said, his breathing as ragged as her own. "If this feels this good, I hate to think what will happen when we decide to really let loose."

Thursday afternoon, with a stethoscope secured around her neck, Carol walked down the wide hospital corridor toward the nurses' station. Her steps were clipped and her heart heavy. She hadn't talked to Alex since late Sunday when he'd dropped Peter and her at the house following their camping trip. There could be a variety of excellent reasons why he hadn't called or why she hadn't seen him. Maybe he was simply too busy—that made sense. Maybe he simply didn't want to see her again—perhaps he'd decided to start dating other women. Younger women. Prettier women. Lord knew he was handsome enough to have a harem. Perhaps aliens had captured him, and he was trapped in some spaceship circling uncharted universes.

Whatever the reason, it translated into one glaring, inescapable fact. She hadn't seen or heard from Alex in four long days. However, she reminded herself, she didn't need a man to make her happy. She didn't need a relationship.

"There's a call for you on line one," Betty Mills told her. "Do you want me to take a message?"

"Did the person give a name?"

"Alex Preston. He sounds sexy, too," Betty added succulently. "I don't suppose he's that handsome guy you were having lunch with not so long ago."

Carol's heart slammed against her chest first with alarm and then with relief. All week she'd done everything she could to ignore the gaping hole left in her life without Alex there. She'd pulled deeper inside herself. All it would have taken was a simple phone call—she could have contacted him. She could have asked Peter to talk to James. She could have driven over to his house. But she'd done none of those things.

"Carol? Do you want me to take a message or not?" Betty pressed.

"No, I'll get it."

Betty chuckled. "I would, too, if I were you." With that, she turned and marched away.

Carol moved to the nurses' station and was grateful no one else was around to overhear her conversation. "This is Carol Sommars," she said, with as professional a tone as she could manage.

"Carol, it's Alex."

His words burned into her ears. "Hello, Alex," she said, hoping she didn't sound terribly stiff. Her pulse broke into a wild, absurd rhythm at the sound of his voice, and despite her best efforts, a warm, sluggish gladness settled over her.

"I'm sorry to contact you at the hospital, but I haven't been able to reach you at home the past several nights."

"I've been busy every night." Busy trying to escape the loneliness. Busy ignoring questions she didn't want to answer. Busy hiding.

"Yes, I know," Alex returned, impatiently. "Are you purposely avoiding me?"

"I...I thought you...if you want the truth, I assumed you'd decided not to see me again."

"Not see you," he repeated loudly, stunned. "Are you crazy, woman? I'm nuts about you."

"Oh." Her mouth twitched, but whether it was from irritation or sheer blessed relief, Carol didn't know. If he was so crazy about her, why had he neglected her all week? If he was nuts about her, why hadn't she heard from him for days on end?

"You honestly haven't figured out the way I feel about you yet?"

"You haven't been at the school in the past few days, and since I didn't hear from you it made sense—at least to me—that you wanted to cool things, and honestly, I don't blame you. Matters are getting much too hot and much too... well, fast, and personally I thought that... well, that it was for the best."

"You thought *what*?" he demanded, his voice exploding over the wire. He sounded a good distance away. It might have been the telephone connection, but the hum that rang over the line had a distinct long-distance sound to it. "When I get home the first thing I'm going to do is kiss some sense into you."

"When you get home?"

"I'm in Houston."

"Texas?"

"Is there any other?"

Carol didn't know. "What are you doing there?"

"Wishing I was in Portland, mostly. A friend of mine, another contractor, is involved in a huge project here and ran into problems. There must have been five messages on my recorder from him when we returned from the camping trip. He needed some help and fast."

"What about James? He isn't with you, is he?"

"He's staying with another friend of mine. I've probably mentioned him before, his name is Barney."

Vaguely Carol *did* remember either Alex or James mentioning the man, but she couldn't remember where or when she'd heard it. "How...long will you be gone?" She hated the way her voice dipped slightly, and the telltale need she felt for him was all too evident.

"Another week at the least."

Her heart zoomed to her feet, and then gradually righted itself. "A week?"

"I don't like it any better than you. Lord, I can't believe how much I miss you. How much I needed to hear your voice."

Carol felt the same things, only she hadn't been willing to admit it, even to herself.

There was a slight commotion coming from Alex's end of the line, and when it cleared, he said, "I'll try and phone you again, but we're working day and night and this is the first real break I've had in three days. I'm glad I got through to you."

Her grip tightened on the receiver. "I'm glad, too."

"I've got to go. Bye, Carol, I'll see you Thursday or so of next week."

"Goodbye, Alex...thanks for phoning." She was about to hang up when she realized there was something more she had to say. She cried his name, almost desperate to catch him before he hung up.

"I'm here. What is it?"

"Alex," she said, sighing with relief. "I've . . . I want you to know I . . . I've missed you, too."

The sound of his chuckle was as warm and melodious as a hundred-voice choir. "It's not much, but it's something. Keep next Thursday open for me. Understand?"

"You've got yourself a date."

Tuesday evening of the following week, Carol was teaching her birthing class. Ten couples were sprawled on thick pillows on the carpet in front of her as she led them through a series of prescribed exercises. Carol enjoyed this work almost as much as she did her daytime job at the hospital.

"Everyone is doing exceptionally well tonight," she said, praising the teams. "Okay, partners, I have a question for you. I want you to tell me, in seconds, how long you think a labor pain lasts."

"Thirty seconds," one young man shouted out.

"Longer," Carol said.

"Sixty seconds," yelled another.

Carol shook her head.

"Ninety?"

"You don't sound any too sure about that," Carol said, smiling. "Let's stick with ninety seconds. That's a nice round number, although in the last stages of labor it wouldn't be unusual for a contraction to last much longer."

The pregnant women eyed each other wearily.

"All right, partners, I want you to show me your biceps. Tighten them up as hard as you can. Good. Good," she said as she surveyed the room, watching as several of the men brought up their fists until the muscles of their upper arms bulged. "Make it as tight and as painful as you can," she continued. Many of the men were already gritting their teeth.

"Very good," she went on to say. "Now hold that until I tell you to relax." She walked to the other side of the room. "As far back as 1913 it was accepted that fear and tension could interfere with the birthing process. Many believed even then that deep breathing exercises and relaxation could and would aid labor." She paused and glanced at her watch. "That's five seconds."

The look of astonishment that crossed the men's faces was downright comical.

"Keep those muscles tightly clenched," Carol instructed. She strolled around the room, chatting amiably as the men held their arms as tight as possible. Some were already showing the strain.

"Thirty seconds," she announced.

Her words were followed by a low groan. Carol couldn't help smiling. She hated to admit how much she enjoyed their discomfort, but the exercise was an excellent illustration. The smile remained on her lips as the door in the back of the room opened to admit a latecomer. Carol opened her mouth to welcome the person, but the words never made it to her lips.

There, framed just inside the door, stood Alex Preston.

Chapter Ten

Carol's eyes burned into Alex's. Alex's eyes burned into Carol's.

The room went completely still with the kind of calm that usually precedes a storm. The air felt heavy, and the quiet seemed eerie and unnatural. It wasn't until Carol realized that several taut faces were staring up at her anxiously that she pulled her attention away from Alex and back to her class.

"Now where were we?" she asked, flustered and nervous.

"Ninety seconds," one of the men shouted out.

"Oh. Right." She glanced at the second hand on her watch and nodded. "Ninety seconds."

A huge wave of relief could be felt all the way across the room.

A few minutes later Carol dismissed everyone for a fifteen-minute break. Her friend and teaching partner, Joyce

Mandle, strolled over to Carol, paused, and eyed the back of the room where Alex was patiently waiting. He was leaning against the back wall, his ankles crossed and his thumb hooked in the belt loop of his jeans.

"He's gorgeous."

Carol felt too distracted and tongue-tied to respond, although her thoughts had been traveling along those same lines. Alex was the most sexy man Carol had ever known. Unabashedly wonderful, too.

"He's . . . been out of town," she said. Her eyes were magnetically drawn to Alex's. She drank in the tall, lean sight of him.

Joyce draped her arm across Carol's shoulders. "Since your portion of tonight's class is finished, why don't you go ahead and leave?"

"I couldn't." Carol tore her eyes from Alex long enough to study her co-teacher. They were a team, and although they'd divided the class into two distinct sections, they stayed and lent each other emotional support.

"Yes, you can. I insist. Only . . ."

"Only what?" Carol pressed.

"Only promise me that if another gorgeous hunk walks in off the street and looks at me the way your friend is looking at you, you'll return the favor."

"Of course," Carol answered automatically.

Joyce's voice dipped to a whisper. "Good. Then we'll consider this our little secret."

Carol frowned. "I don't understand—what do you mean by our little secret?"

"Well, if my husband found out about this agreement, there could be definite problems."

Carol laughed. Joyce was happily married and had been for fifteen years.

"If I were you I wouldn't be hanging around here talk-ing," Joyce murmured, pressing her hand in the small of Carol's back. "Don't keep him waiting any longer."

"Okay...thanks." Feeling unaccountably shy, Carol retrieved her purse and her briefcase and walked toward Alex. With each step that drew her nearer, her heart felt less weighted. By the time she made her way to the back of the room, she felt nearly airborne.

He straightened, his eyes warm and caressing. "Hello."

"Hi."

"Peter told me you were teaching tonight and where. I hope you don't mind that I dropped in unexpectedly this way."

"I don't mind." *Mind?* Her heart was soaring with such gladness that she could have walked on water. She wouldn't even need an airplane to fly. No, she didn't mind that he'd dropped in—not in the least.

For the longest moment all they did was gaze at each other like starry-eyed lovers.

A noise in the front of the room distracted Carol. She glanced over her shoulder and discovered several couples watching them with a good deal of undisguised curiosity.

"Joyce said she could finish up here, and I could...should leave now."

Alex grinned, and with the boyish action, Carol could feel whole sections of the sturdy wall around her heart start to crumble. This man's smile was nothing short of lethal.

"Remind me to thank her later," Alex said. He re-moved the briefcase from her unresisting fingers and opened the door, letting her precede him outside.

They weren't two steps out the door when Alex paused. Carol felt his hesitation and stopped, turning to face him. It was in that moment she knew Alex was going to kiss her. It was at that moment that she knew she would die if he didn't. It didn't matter that they were standing in front of a public building. It didn't matter that it was still light enough for any number of curious passersby to see them. It didn't matter that they were both respected professionals.

Alex scooped her into his arms, and with a lavish sigh he lowered his head and covered her lips with the sweetest, wildest kiss of her life. His lips played over hers the way a musician tests a rare, delicate instrument. He coaxed her lips apart and swept her mouth with his tongue. Then he nipped at her lower lip, brought it into his mouth and sucked gently. He claimed her mouth again and again, tenderly, greedily, gently.

"Dear God in heaven, I've missed you," he whispered. "The hours felt like years, the days like decades."

Carol felt tears pool in the corners of her eyes. She hadn't thought about how empty her life had felt without him, how bleak and alone she was with him out of town. Now it poured out of her in a litany of sighs and kisses. "I . . . I missed you, too . . . so much."

For years she'd been content in her own secure world, the one she'd created for herself and her son. The borders had been narrow and confining, but she'd made peace with herself and found serenity. Then she'd met Alex, and he'd forced her to notice how cramped and limited her existence was. If that weren't enough, he pointed toward the horizon into the land of shared dreams and honeyed promises.

Alex's hands were in her hair, and his tongue was caressing hers in slow, sultry circles. By the time he dragged his mouth from hers, she felt as though she were melting.

When he spoke, his voice was heavy with need. "Come on, let's get out of here."

She nodded and followed him to his car, ready to abandon her own with little more than a second thought and follow him to the ends of the earth if he suggested it.

He unlocked the passenger door, hesitated and turned around to face her. His eyes were bright and dancing. "Let's dispense with formalities and elope. Now. Tonight. This minute."

The words hit her as hard as a prizefighter's fist. She blinked at the unexpectedness of his suggestion, ready to laugh it off as a joke.

But Alex was serious. Dead serious. He looked as shocked as Carol felt, but she noted that once he'd said it, the idea was gaining momentum. The mischievous spark was gone, replaced by a solemn, needy look.

"I love you, Carol. I love you so damn much that my buddy in Texas practically threw me on the plane and told me to get home before I died of it. He claimed he'd never seen anyone more lovesick and made me promise we'd name one of our children after him."

The mention of a child was an unexpected right cross to the jaw that followed his punch to her solar plexus, and she flinched involuntarily.

Alex set his hands on her shoulders, and the beginnings of a smile touched his eyes and then his sensuous mouth. He smiled so endearingly, so captivatingly, that all Carol's arguments fled like a fine layer of dust in a whirlwind.

"Say something."

"Ah . . . my car is parked over there." She pointed over her shoulder in the general vicinity of her Ford. Her throat was tight and was constricting more each moment.

He laughed and hugged her. "I know this is sudden for you. I'm a fool not to have done this properly. I swear I'll do it again over champagne and a rare steak and offer you a diamond so large you'll sink in a swimming pool, but God help me, I can't hold the way I feel inside any longer."

"Alex . . ."

He silenced her with a swift kiss. "Believe me, blurting out a proposal like this is as much of a surprise to me as it is to you. I had no idea I was going to ask you tonight. The entire flight home I kept thinking about how I could make it as romantic as possible. The last thing I expected to do was impulsively shout it out in a parking lot. But something happened tonight, something wonderful and unexplainable." He reached for her limp hands and brought them to his lips. He kissed her knuckles with an endearing reverence. "I walked into your class, hoping to surprise you, and saw you with all those pregnant women, and I was hit with the most powerful punch of my life." His voice grew quiet and serious as his eyes melted into hers. "All of a sudden, from out of the blue, my mind conjured up the image of you heavy with our child, and I swear to you it was all I could do not to break down and weep." He paused long enough to run his fingers through his hair. "Children, Carol . . . our children. We're going to have the most incredibly beautiful babies." He closed his eyes, and a deep sigh rumbled through his chest.

Carol felt frozen. The chill worked its way from her heart, the icy circles rippling first over her abdomen, then growing larger and more encompassing until the cold extended down her arms and legs and into her fingertips and toes.

"I know this is abrupt, and I'm probably ruining the moment, but say something," Alex urged anxiously. "Anything."

Carol's mind refused to function properly. Panic was closing in, and her chest went tight with a hundred misgivings. "I...don't know what to tell you."

Alex threw back his head and laughed. "Dear God, I don't blame you. All right," he said, his eyes flashing, "repeat after me. I, Carol Sommars." He paused, and glanced expectantly at her.

"I...Carol Sommars..."

"Am crazy in love with Alex Preston." Once more he paused, waiting for her to echo his words.

"Am crazy in love with Alex Preston."

"Good," he whispered and leaned forward just enough to brush his mouth over hers. His arms made their way around her, locking at the small of her back and dragging her unresistingly toward him. Their bodies melded together, thigh to thigh, womanhood pressing against manhood, his hard chest cushioning her soft breasts. Briefly he closed his eyes and sighed, and when he spoke, his voice was husky and warm. "You know the best part about those babies is going to be making them."

A deep blush worked its way up her neck, coloring her cheeks with what she was sure was a highly uncomplimentary shade of pink. Her eyes darted away from his.

"Now all you need to do is say yes," Alex said, his eyes and his heart laughing.

"I can't, I...don't know," she cried, and to her horror, she started to sob. Not the delicate, dainty cry of a confused woman, but the harsh mournful cries of one in anguish.

Alex had apparently expected anything but tears. "Carol? What's wrong? What did I say?" He wrapped his arms around her and pressed her head to his shoulder.

Carol thought to resist his touch, but she so desperately needed it that she buried her face in the curve of his strong neck and silently wept. Alex's arms were warm and safe, his hands gentle on the crown of her head. She did love Alex. Somewhere between the rescue the night her car broke down and the camping trip, her well-guarded heart had succumbed to his formidable appeal. But falling in love was one thing—marriage and children were something else entirely.

"Come on," Alex said after a long moment. He opened the car door for her.

"Where are we going?" she asked between sniffles.

"My house. James isn't there yet, and we can talk without being disturbed."

Carol wasn't sure what more he could say, but she agreed with a short nod of her head and climbed inside. He closed the door for her, then paused and ran a hand over his weary eyes.

Neither of them said much during the ten-minute drive to Alex's home. He helped her out of his car and then unlocked the front door to his house. His suitcases had been haphazardly dumped onto the living room carpet. When he noticed Carol's gaze resting on them, he said, "I was in something of a hurry to find you." With that, he led the way into the kitchen and automatically started making a pot of coffee.

Carol pulled out a tall stool at the counter and seated herself. His kitchen, in fact his home, wasn't the least bit the way she expected. A woman's touch could be seen and felt in every room. The kitchen was yellow and cheery. What remained of the evening light shone through the window above the sink, sending warm shadows dancing across the polished tile floor. Matching mushroom-shaped ceramic canisters lined the counter, along with a row of well-used cookbooks.

"Okay, love, tell me what's on your mind," Alex urged, facing her from behind the barrier of the tile counter. Even then Carol wasn't safe from his magnetism.

"That's the problem," she said, swallowing tightly. "I don't *know* what's on my mind. I'm so confused and unsure."

"I know I hit you with the idea out of the blue, but once you start thinking about it, you'll realize how perfect we are for each other. Surely you've thought along those lines yourself."

"No," she said quickly, and for emphasis, shook her head. "I hadn't...not once. The thought of marriage hadn't so much as crossed my mind."

"I see." He braced his hands against the edge of the counter, then raised his right one to rub his eyes.

Carol realized he must be exhausted and immediately was overcome with a surge of remorsefulness. She *did* love Alex, although having to admit as much openly—to him and, perhaps more emotionally demanding, to herself— had sapped the strength from her.

"What do you want to do?" he asked softly.

"I don't know that, either," she whispered, diverting her gaze to her hands, which were tightly clenched in her lap.

"Would some time to think matters through help?"
She nodded eagerly.

"How long?" Alex asked.

"A year, several months, or at the very least three or four weeks."

"How about two weeks?" Alex suggested.

"Two weeks," she echoed feebly. That wasn't nearly long enough. She couldn't possibly reach such an important decision in so little time, especially when there were other factors to consider. Her mind was flooded with excuses, but she wasn't allowed to voice a single one before Alex pressed his finger to her lips and silenced her.

"If you can't decide in that amount of time, then I sincerely doubt that you ever will."

A protest came and went in a single breath. There were so many other factors that he hadn't mentioned. It seemed he'd conveniently forgotten about their sons! Peter and James may well have something to say about them becoming a family.

She was about to mention this when Alex stated, "I don't think we should draw the boys into this until we know our own minds. The last thing we need is pressure from them."

Carol couldn't have agreed more.

The coffee had finished perking, and Alex poured them each a cup. "How about dinner Friday night? Just the two of us." At her hesitation, he added, "I'll make a point of giving you what remains of this week to sort through your thoughts, and on Friday if you have any questions or doubts we can discuss them then."

"But not a final decision?" Carol pressed, uneasy with the time limitation. He said two weeks, and she was going to need every minute of that time to determine what would be best.

Carol woke around three with her stomach muscles in hard, painful knots. She flattened her hands over her abdomen, and at a breath-stopping cramp, she tucked her knees under her chin. A wave of nausea hit her equally hard, and she wasn't able to stifle a groan. The last thing she wanted to deal with now was a bout of the flu.

She lay perfectly still, taking in several deep breaths with the fervent hope that this would ward off her growing need to vomit. It didn't work, and within a couple of minutes, she was racing into the bathroom.

A few moments later, sitting on the floor, her elbow braced against the edge of the toilet, she breathed deeply.

"Are you all right?" Peter asked from behind her.

"I will be—just give me a couple of more minutes."

"What's wrong?" Peter pressed. He handed her a warm washcloth, and followed that with a cup of water.

"The flu, I guess."

He helped her to her feet and walked her back into her bedroom. "I'm fine, Peter, really. I appreciate the help, but it would be better if you went back to bed. I'll be well by morning."

"I'll call work for you and explain that you're too sick to come in."

She shook her head. "No...I'll need to talk to them myself." Her son dutifully tucked the blankets around her and gave her a worried look before he silently slipped out of her bedroom.

Peter must have turned off her alarm when she wasn't looking, because the next thing Carol knew it was eight-thirty and the house was filled with an eerie silence.

Sitting up, she waited for the attack of nausea to hit her. It didn't come, and she brushed the hair away from her face. She'd slept like the dead. It astonished her that she hadn't heard Peter roaming about. He generally was as noisy as a rampaging herd of buffalo. Perhaps he'd over-slept as well.

In case he had, she shoved the sheets back, sat on the edge of the bed and stuffed her feet into her slippers, be-fore wandering into the kitchen. The minute she stepped inside, it was apparent her son had been up and about. A box of cold cereal was resting in the middle of the kitchen table, along with a bowl half filled with milk and crusts from several pieces of toast.

Posted on the refrigerator door was a note from Peter, informing her that he'd phoned the hospital and talked to her supervisor, who'd said Carol didn't need to worry about coming in. He proudly added that he'd made his own lunch and that he would find a ride home from track practice, so she should stay in bed and drink lots of fluids. In a brief postscript he casually mentioned that he'd also phoned Grandma Pasquale.

Carol's groan had little to do with the way she was feeling. All she needed was her mother, God bless her dear heart, hovering over her and driving her slowly but surely crazy. No sooner had the thought formed in her mind when the doorbell chimed, followed by the front door flying open. Her mother burst into the house as though Carol lay on her deathbed and was calling out to God to spare her long enough to talk to her mother.

"Carol," Angelina cried, walking through the living room. "What are you doing out of bed?"

"I'm feeling much better, Mama."

"You look like death. Get back in bed before the undertaker gets wind of how you look."

"Ma, please, I'm just a little under the weather."

"That's what my Uncle Giuseppe said when he had the flu, God rest his soul. His wife never even got the chicken stewed, he went that fast." She pressed her hands together, raised her eyes to the ceiling and murmured a silent prayer.

"Peter shouldn't have phoned," Carol grumbled. The last thing she wanted was her mother fussing at her bedside, spooning chicken soup down her throat every time she opened her mouth.

"Peter did the right thing. He's a good boy."

At the moment Carol considered that point debatable.

"Now back to bed with you before you get a dizzy spell." Her mother made a shooing motion with her hands as though she were herding brainless sheep toward green pasture.

Mumbling under her breath, Carol did as Angelina asked. Not because she felt especially ill, but because it expended too much energy to argue. Carol might as well try and talk her mother into sampling canned spaghetti sauce as convince her she wasn't on her deathbed and desperately in need of mothering.

Once Carol was lying down, Angelina pushed the rocking chair into Carol's bedroom and sat herself down. Before another minute passed, her nimble fingers were working the knitting needles. Several balls of yarn were lying at her feet in case she wanted to start a second or third project within the next couple of hours.

"According to Peter you were sick in the middle of the night," Angelina murmured. With her eyes narrowed, she studied Carol, as if a good stare would reveal the exact nature of her daughter's illness. She shook her head and then paused to count the neat row of stitches before glancing back to Carol, clearly expecting an answer.

"It must have been something I ate for dinner," she suggested lamely.

"Peter said you were looking at parts of a toilet that no one should see that close up."

Her teenage son certainly had a way with words, Carol would grant him that much.

"I'm feeling better."

"Your face is paler than bleached sheets. Uncle Giuseppe has more color than you, and he's thirty years in the grave."

Carol leaned her head back against the pillows and closed her eyes. She might be able to fool just about anyone else, but her mother knew her far too well.

Several tense moments passed. Angelina said not a word, patient to a fault. Her mother knew, Carol swore she knew. Carol kept her eyes closed, fearing another searching look would reveal everything. Oh, what the hell, Angelina would find out sooner or later.

"Alex asked me to marry him last night." The words were scarcely more than a whisper. Carol tried to keep her voice even, but it pitched and heaved like a tiny boat tossed about in a squall.

"Ah," her mother said softly. "That explains everything. From the time you were a little girl, you got an upset stomach whenever something troubled you, although why you should be troubled when this man tells you he loves you is something else again."

Carol didn't need her mother to repeat stories from her childhood about the times she was queasy for her to know it was the truth.

"So what did you say to him?"

"Nothing," she whispered.

"This man brings color to your cheeks and a smile to your eyes and you said *nothing*?"

"I . . . need time to think things through," Carol cried. "This is an important decision . . . I've got more than myself and my life to consider. Alex has a son and I have a son . . . it isn't as simple as it sounds."

Her mother made a small negative sound and shook her head. Her rocker was going ninety miles an hour, and Carol was certain the older woman's thoughts were churning at equal speed.

"Don't be angry with me, Mama," she whispered. "I'm so frightened."

Angelina stopped abruptly and set her knitting aside. She reached for Carol, holding out her hands and closing them gently around her daughter. A soft smile lit up her eyes. "You'll make the right decision."

"How can you be so sure? I've been wrong about so many things—I've made so many expensive mistakes in my life. I don't trust my own judgment anymore."

Her mother pressed Carol's head against her ample bosom. "Follow your heart," she urged.

The words were of little comfort. She'd followed her heart when she'd married Bruce, convinced their love would see them through every difficulty. The marriage had been a disaster from the honeymoon onward, growing more painful and more difficult with each passing day. The horror of those years with Bruce was like a tight fist gripping her heart and squeezing the last drop of confidence from her soul. She'd offered her husband everything she knew to give, relinquished her pride and self-respect, and to what end? Bruce hadn't appreciated her sacrifices. He hadn't cherished her love, but turned it into something cheap and expendable.

"Whatever you decide will be right," her mother said once again. "In my heart I know it will be."

Carol closed her eyes to mull over her mother's confidence in her, which she was sure was completely unfounded. Angelina seemed to trust Carol's judgment more than Carol did herself.

A few minutes later, her mother started to sing softly, and her sweet, melodious voice was harmonized with the click of the knitting needles.

The next thing Carol knew, it was early afternoon and she could smell the chicken soup simmering in the kitchen.

Angelina left a brief note for her that was filled with warmth and wisdom. Feeling worlds better, Carol dished herself up a bowl of the thick broth and noodles and leisurely enjoyed her first nourishment of the day.

By the time Peter slammed into the house several hours later, she was almost back to normal.

"Mom," he said rushing into the room. His face was pink and his eyes bright. It looked as though he'd run the entire way home. His chest was heaving as he shoved his books on the table. His arms started waving in different directions as he anxiously waited while he caught his breath.

"What is it?" Carol asked, humored by the sight her son made. He was seldom this excited.

"Why didn't you say anything?" he demanded, kissing her cheeks the way her mother did when she was this pleased about something. "This is great, Mom, really great. Now we can go fishing and camping and hiking all the time."

"Say anything about what? And what's this about fishing?"

"Marrying Mr. Preston."

Carol was halfway out of her seat before she realized that she'd moved. "Who told you . . . who so much as mentioned our getting married as a possibility?"

"A possibility?" Peter countered. "I thought it was for real. At least that's what James said."

"James told you?"

Peter gave her a perplexed look. "Who else would have? He told me about it first thing when I arrived at school this morning." He stopped and studied her, his gaze narrowed and cautious. "Hey, Mom, don't look so put out—I'm sorry if you were keeping it a secret. Don't worry, both James and I think it's a great idea. I've always wanted a brother, and having one the same age who happens to be my best friend is even better."

Carol was so outraged she could barely think straight. "He had no business saying a word."

"Who? James?"

"Not James," Carol cried. "Alex." If he thought to use the boys to influence her decision one way or the other, then he had another think coming.

Carol marched into her bedroom with all the authority of a conquering army. Throwing on a pair of jeans and an old sweatshirt, she hurried into the living room without so much as bothering to run a brush through her tousled hair.

"Where are you going?" Peter demanded. He'd dished himself up a bowl of soup and was following her around the house like a lost puppy while she searched for her purse and car keys.

"Out," Carol stormed.

"Looking like that?" He sounded aghast.

Carol whirled around, hands on her hips, and glared at him.

Peter raised one hand. "Sorry. Only please don't let Mr. Preston see you, all right?"

"Why not?"

Peter rolled his shoulder with a delicate shrug. "If he gets a look at you, he might withdraw his proposal. Honestly, Mom, this is the best thing that's happened to us in years. Don't go ruining it."

Chapter Eleven

James answered the door, and a smile automatically came to his lips when he saw it was Carol. Then his eyes narrowed as though he wasn't completely sure it was her after all. Without his saying as much, Carol realized he was taken aback by her appearance. Normally she was well-dressed and well-groomed, but what Alex had done— had tried to do, demanded swift and decisive action. She didn't feel it was necessary to don pantyhose for this confrontation.

"Where is he?" Carol demanded, arms akimbo.

"Who? Dad?" James asked and frowned. "He's watching the news." The teenager pointed toward the family room, which was adjacent to the kitchen.

Without waiting for James to escort her inside, Carol burst past him, intent on giving Alex a thick slice of her mind. She was furious. More than furious. If he'd honestly believed that involving the boys would affect her decision, then he knew absolutely nothing about her. In fact, he knew so little, they had no business even considering getting married.

She refused to be pressured, tricked, cajoled or anything else, and before this day was over Alex would know that in no uncertain terms.

"Carol?" Alex met her halfway into the kitchen. His eyes softened perceptibly as he reached for her.

Carol stopped just short of his embrace. "How dare you," she jeered between clenched teeth.

"How dare I?" Alex repeated. His eyes grew round with surprise, but he remained infuriatingly calm. "Would you mind elaborating, because I'm afraid I don't know what you're talking about."

"In a pig's eye."

"Dad?" James ventured into the kitchen, keeping his back close to the counter as he circled closer to his father, giving Carol a wide berth. "Something must be really wrong," the teenager said, and then his voice dropped to a whisper as he pointed to Carol's feet. "Mrs. Sommars is wearing two entirely different shoes."

Carol's gaze shot downward, and she mentally groaned. But if either of the Preston men thought to throw her off her guard with the fact she wore a blue tennis shoe on her right foot and a hot pink slipper on her left, then she had news for them both.

"I have the feeling Mrs. Sommars was in something of a hurry to talk to me," Alex explained. The smile that jiggled at the corners of his mouth did little to quell her brewing temper.

James nodded. "Do you want me to disappear for a few minutes?"

"That might be a good idea," Alex replied with an appreciative shake of his head.

James shared a knowing look with his father before discreetly vacating the room. As soon as Carol heard James's bedroom door close, she ground her fists into her hips, determined to confront Alex.

"How dare you bring the boys into this," she flared.

"Into what?" Alex walked over to the coffeepot and brought down two mugs. He held one up to her, but she refused the offer with a hard shake of her head. "I'm sorry, Carol, but I don't know what you're talking about."

Jabbing her index finger at him, she circled the kitchen. "Don't give me that, Alex Preston. You know damn good and well what I mean. We agreed to wait, and you saw an advantage and without the least bit of compunction, you took it! Did you honestly think dragging Peter and James into this would help matters? How could you be so foolish?" Her voice wobbled, but her eyes were as cutting as she could make them.

"I didn't mention the possibility of our getting married to James, and I certainly didn't say anything to Peter." He braced his forearms against the kitchen counter and returned her disbelieving glare with maddening composure.

Carol tossed back her head and angled her chin at a proud tilt. "I don't believe you."

His eyes flared briefly with that, but he didn't argue with her. "Ask James then. If he heard that I'd proposed marriage to you, then the information didn't come from me."

"You don't honestly expect me to believe that, do you?" she cried, not nearly as confident as she had been earlier. The fight had gone out of her voice, and she lowered her hands to her sides, less certain each minute. The ground that supported her outrage started to shift and crumble with doubts.

"I told you I wouldn't bring the boys into this," he reminded her smoothly. "And I didn't." He looked over his shoulder and shouted for James, who threw open his bedroom door immediately. Carol didn't doubt for an instant that the youth had had his ear pressed to it the entire time they'd been talking.

With his hands buried deep in his jean pockets, James casually strolled into the room. "Yes, Dad?"

"Do you want to tell me about it?"

"About what?" James wore a look of innocence that few would question.

"Apparently you said something to Peter about the relationship between Mrs. Sommars and myself. I want to know what it was and where you found out about it." Alex hadn't so much as raised his voice, but Carol knew without a doubt that he expected the truth and wouldn't let up until he got it.

"Oh...that," James muttered. "I sort of overheard you saying something to Uncle Barn."

"Uncle Barn?" Carol asked.

"A good friend of mine. He was the one I was telling you about who kept Jim while I was out of town."

"Please call me *James*," his son reminded him.

Alex raised both hands. "Sorry."

"Anyway," James went on to say, "you were on the phone last night talking to him about the basketball game that's playing tonight, and I heard you tell Uncle Barn that you'd popped the question to Carol—Mrs. Sommars. I'm not stupid, Dad. I knew you were talking about the two of you getting married, and I thought that as your sons both Peter and I had a right to know. You should have said something to us first, don't you think, instead of to an old college buddy?''

"First of all, this marriage business is up in the air—when and if anything's decided, you two boys will be the first to find out about it."

"What do you mean the wedding is up in the air?" This piece of information clearly took James by surprise. "Why? What's the holdup? Personally Peter and I think it's a great idea. We'd like it if you two got married. For one thing, it'd be great to have a woman around the house. You try, Dad, but when you hemmed my jeans they looked terrible. And frankly your cooking could be improved. But if you married Mrs. Sommars all that would be fixed."

"James," Alex returned with barely restrained impatience, "I think it's time for you to go back into your room before Carol decides the last thing she ever wants to do is get involved with the likes of us."

James wore an affronted look, but without question, he sharply pivoted and marched back into his bedroom.

Alex waited until his son was out of sight. He sighed expressively and rammed his fingers through his hair hard enough to uproot a handful. "I'm sorry, Carol. I had no idea James overheard my conversation with Barney. I thought he was asleep, but I obviously should have been more careful."

"I . . . understand," Carol whispered, mollified.

"Contrary to what James just said," Alex continued, the line of his mouth tight and unyielding, "I don't want to marry you for your sewing or your cooking skills. I could give a tinker's damn if you do either. I love you, and I'm hoping that we can make a good life together."

James tossed open his bedroom door and stuck out his head. "Peter says she's as good a cook as his grandmother, and she can sew up a storm. The problem is, with her working full-time and teaching on the side, she doesn't have the time she needs to do either properly. If she were to decide to marry us that would all change, too."

Alex sent his son a look hot enough to melt tar.

James quickly withdrew his head and just as promptly closed his bedroom door.

"I'll talk to Peter and explain the mix-up, if you'd like," Alex offered.

"No...I'll say something to him." Suddenly feeling self-conscious, Carol swung her arms at her sides and retreated a couple of steps backward. "I suppose I should think about getting home."

"You were sick last night?" Alex asked, his eyes warm and tender. "James said something about it when I picked him up after school. I would have gladly given Peter a ride home, but he'd apparently found another way because he was gone before James could find him."

"Peter decided to run home."

"But you had been ill?"

She nodded. "I...must have caught a twenty-four-hour bug." Her eyes darted around the room. She felt so foolish, standing there with her hair looking like God knew what, dressed in the oldest clothes she owned, wearing mismatched shoes.

"You're better today?"

"Worlds better. Thank you." She was slowly but surely edging her way toward the front door. The sooner she escaped, the better it would be for everyone involved. If Alex were merciful, he would never mention this visit again.

She was all the way across the living room, and had her back pressed against the front door, when Alex flattened his hands on either side of her head.

"Have you come to a decision?" he asked softly. His gaze dropped to her mouth. "Do you need any help?"

"The only thing I've managed to come up with is the flu," she murmured in a feeble attempt at humor. Unfortunately Alex wasn't amused, and she rushed to add, "Obviously you want to know which way I'm leaning, but I haven't had time to give your proposal much thought. I will, I promise I will...soon. Real soon." She realized she was chattering, but she couldn't seem to stop. "We're still on for Friday night, aren't we? I'm sure I'll have some issues to discuss with you then."

The doorbell chimed, frightening Carol half out of her wits. She gasped and automatically catapulted herself into Alex's arms. He apparently didn't need an excuse to press her close. When he released her several awkward seconds later, he smiled at her and then kissed the tip of her upturned nose.

"That'll be Barney now. It's time the two of you met."

"That was Carol Sommars?" Barney asked for the third time in as many minutes. He scratched the underside of his jaw and continued to frown. "It isn't any wonder Bambi mistook her for a bag lady. I'm sorry, man, you're my best friend and we've been buddies for a lot of years, but I've got to tell you, you can do better than that."

Chuckling, Alex dismissed his friend's statement with a grain of salt and led the way into the family room. If he lived to be a hundred, he would never forget the mortified look Carol wore as she raced from the house. He didn't need to be a prophet to know she'd wanted to crawl in a hole and die.

Barney certainly hadn't helped matters any. Doing his best to keep a straight face, Alex had introduced the two.

Barney had taken one look at Carol, his eyes had widened and his mouth had slowly dropped open in disbelief. His Adam's apple had wobbled up and down a couple of times before he had the presence of mind to step forward and accept Carol's outstretched hand. Barney had mumbled something about what a pleasure it was to finally meet her, but his eyes had said something else entirely.

"Trust me," Alex felt obliged to explain, "she doesn't always look like that."

Barney walked over to the refrigerator and opened it. He stared inside for a long time before he reached for a cold beer. "What time do the Trail Blazers play?"

Alex checked his watch. Both he and Barney were keen fans of Portland's professional basketball team. The team had been doing well this year and were into the first round of the play-offs. "The *TV Guide* said seven."

"So," Barney said, making himself comfortable in the overstuffed chair. He crossed his legs and took a long, slow swig of beer. "What happened to her foot?" he asked casually. "Did she sprain it?"

"Whose foot?" Alex hadn't a clue what his buddy was talking about. It must be his night for wandering around in a fog. First Carol had come in madder than hops, and he hadn't a clue why, and now Barney was asking him abstract questions.

"Carol's," Barney said, casting Alex a questioning glance. "She was wearing a slipper—you mean you didn't notice? Did she fall and twist her ankle?"

"Naw," James answered for Alex, wandering into the family room holding a bag of pretzels. He plopped himself down on the sofa, brought up his legs and crossed them on the coffee table. "She does weird stuff like wearing two different shoes all the time, according to Peter. Once she wore Peter's swimming goggles in the shower.''

Barney's eyes widened expressively with that tidbit of knowledge. ''Do I dare ask why?''

''It made perfect sense once Peter explained what happened. Apparently his mother had gone to one of those cosmetics stores and they put some fancy stuff on her eyes, and she didn't want to ruin it when she took a shower, so she wore Peter's rubber goggles.''

''Why didn't she just take a bath?'' Barney asked. He was casting Alex looks that suggested his friend have his head examined. Barney didn't have to say anything more for Alex to know he viewed Carol as a real fruitcake.

''She couldn't take a bath because the faucet was broken,'' James explained, ''and her brother hadn't gotten around to fixing it yet.''

''That makes sense,'' Alex said in Carol's defense.

Barney rolled his eyes and tipped the beer bottle toward his lips.

To his credit, Barney didn't say anything more about Carol until James was out of the room. ''You're really serious about *this* woman?'' His question suggested that Alex may have inadvertently introduced Barney to the wrong one, and that the whole meeting was a setup to some kind of joke that was to follow.

''I couldn't be more serious. I told you that I've asked her to marry me—I don't get any more serious than that.''

''And she's thinking about it?'' Barney asked mockingly. Being the true, blue buddy that he was, Barn clearly couldn't understand why Carol wouldn't automatically leap at his friend's offer. Barney's eyes told Alex that there couldn't possibly be that much to consider. What more could a woman want?

To be perfectly frank, Alex had wondered the same thing himself. True, he'd blurted out the proposal in a parking lot. He still had trouble believing he'd done anything so crazy. As a contractor, he'd sold himself and his company a hundred times. He'd prepared bids, presented them with polish and professionalism along with solid arguments that made his proposals sound attractive and intelligent. Carol deserved nothing less.

But something had happened to him when he'd visited her birthing class. Something enigmatic and profound. Even now he had to struggle not to get choked up when he thought about it.

After nearly two weeks in Texas, Alex had been starving for the sight of her, and he'd barely noticed the others in the class. In afterthought, he was sure what happened could be attributed to the sight of all those soon-to-be mothers.

In fifteen years Alex hadn't given babies more than a passing thought. He had a son and was grateful for the one child. He may have suffered a twinge of regret at the news that there would be no more, but he'd been more concerned about his wife's well-being than the fact they wouldn't be adding to their family.

Then he'd watched Carol strolling among those pregnant couples, and the desire for another child, a daughter, had seared through his heart like a branding iron. He'd decided while he was in Texas that he loved her and wanted to marry her, but the idea of them starting a family of their own hadn't so much as crossed his mind. But why not? They were both young enough and healthy enough to raise a houseful of children.

He'd been standing at the back of her class, waiting for her when it happened. Out of the blue, yet as clear as anything he'd ever seen or felt, Alex saw Carol heavy with a child—with *his* child. He'd realized at the time that this—he used the word vision for lack of a better one—was probably due to physical and emotional exhaustion. Wanting to hold on to the image as long as he could, he'd slowly closed his eyes and clung to it. Her breasts were full, and when she smiled at him, her eyes had filled with a radiance that couldn't be described with words. With a luminous joy, she'd taken his hand and settled it over her protruding stomach. In his mind's eye, he'd experienced the movement of their child and had been so emotionally impacted that he'd had to struggle with his composure for several moments afterward.

The fantasy was what had prompted the abrupt marriage proposal. He wanted to kick himself now. If he'd taken her in his arms, kissed her and said all the things she deserved to hear, then matters might have gone differently. He hadn't meant to rush her, hadn't meant to be so damn pushy, but once he realized how resistant she was to the idea, he'd more or less panicked. This two week ultimatum to decide one way or the other was unfair. He would tell her that on Friday night when they went for dinner.

Then again, maybe he wouldn't. He would wait to hear what she was thinking, which way she was leaning, before he put his foot any farther down his throat.

A slow, lazy smile moved over his mouth. Perhaps it wasn't too late for that after all.

"Alex?"

His name seemed to be coming from a good distance away.

"What?" he said, pulling himself out of his thoughts.

"The game's started. Are you interested or not?" Barney's look suggested someone should check Alex to see if he had a fever. He did, and there was only one cure. Carol Sommars.

Carol dressed carefully for her dinner date with Alex Friday evening. After sorting through her closet and laying half of everything she owned across the bed, she chose a demure, high-necked dress of soft pink that buttoned down the back. That seemed safe enough.

She could rarely remember feeling this awkward. For all the emotional trauma she'd endured this week, one would think the fate of the free world rested on whether she had decided to marry Alex Preston or not. Like sitting on a teeter-totter, she'd swayed back and forth with her decision most of the week. One day she decided she would be a fool not to marry him, and the next, she'd been equally convinced she would be crazy to trust a man a second time.

Marrying Alex meant relinquishing her independence. It meant surrendering, and placing herself and her son at the mercy of another human being. Memories of her marriage to Bruce viciously swiped at her soul, and each time she contemplated ceremoniously handing her well-ordered life over to another man, she broke into a cold sweat.

Jagged edges, like those from a broken mirror, jabbed at her consciousness, reminding her of the nightmare she'd escaped with Bruce's death.

Years ago, when she was little more than a teenager, someone had told her it took a hell of a man to replace no man. It wasn't until Carol graduated from college with her nursing degree and was completely on her own that she fully understood that statement. Her life was good, too good to tamper with, and yet . . .

Her thoughts were more confused and tangled than two fishing lines when the doorbell chimed. She paused, took a calming breath and headed across the room.

"Hello, Alex," she said, smiling.

"Carol."

He looked too good to be true in a three-piece suit. Her eyes took him in, and she felt some of the stiff resolve leave her tense muscles. It was when her gaze reached his eyes that she realized he was chuckling.

"We're going to dinner," he said, eyeing her dress, "not to a baptism."

She blinked, not sure she understood.

"If that collar went any higher up your neck, it'd reach your nose."

"I . . . I was removing temptation," she said, cursing herself for the heated blush that broke out over her face like a crimson tide.

"Honey, at this rate, the only thing we'll be removing is that dress."

Carol decided the best thing she could do was ignore his remark. "Did you say where we're going for dinner?"

"No," he answered cryptically, and his warm eyes caressed her with maddening purposefulness. "I didn't mention where. It's a surprise."

"Oh." After all the time they'd been together, after all the moments she'd spent in his arms, after all the dreams she'd dreamed about Alex, she shouldn't feel nearly this uncomfortable. But her heart was galloping, her hands felt damp, and her breath was coming in soft, fluctuating gasps, and dear God, they hadn't even left her house yet.

"Are you ready?"

It was a question he shouldn't have asked. *No*, her mind screamed. *Yes*, her heart countered. "I guess so," her lips answered, not in the least bit sure.

Alex led her outside and held open his car door for her.

"It was certainly thoughtful of you to drop the boys off at the theater. Personally I don't think they were that keen on seeing the Walt Disney version of *Peter Pan*," she said, slipping inside his car.

"I gave them a choice of things to do this evening."

"I don't think attending a movie on the other side of town or being sent adrift in the Columbia River without paddles is their idea of a choice."

Alex chuckled at his own wit. "I don't want anyone disturbing us tonight."

Their gazes merged. Alex's was hot and hazy and so damn suggestive, Carol's heart skipped a beat. For sanity's sake, she quickly looked away.

"I hope you like steak."

"I love it."

"The champagne's cooling."

"You must have ordered in advance," she murmured, having a difficult time finding something to do with her hands. Her fingers itched to touch him...it was more than an itch, it was a need. A need that only served to confuse and trouble her more each minute. She'd never felt this restless, this needy.

"I...hope you explained to Barney...your friend, that I...that I don't normally look the way I did the evening we met. When I got home and looked in the mirror...well, I could just imagine what he must have thought." Carol cursed the madness that had sent her rushing out of her house that evening to confront Alex.

"Barney understood."

"Oh, good."

A couple of minutes later, Alex eased his car into his own driveway. Carol turned to him somewhat surprised. "Did you forget something?"

"No," he said enigmatically.

A moment later, he was leading her into the house. She paused in the doorway, and her heart gave a sudden, sharp lurch. They weren't going to any restaurant. Alex had planned to bring her back to his house from the first.

The drapes were drawn, and the lights had been lowered. Carol noted that the dining room table was set with china and crystal. Two tapered candles rested in the middle of the table, waiting to be lit.

Alex walked over to the stereo and pushed a single button. Immediately the room was drenched with the strains of violins.

Carol was still trying to assimilate what was happening when he walked over to the table and lit the candles. Tiny flames licked out at the night, sprang to life and sent a golden glow shimmering across the room.

"Shall we?" Alex said, holding his hands out to her.

Carol was too numb to reply one way or the other. He removed the lacy shawl from her shoulders and draped it over the back of the sofa. Then he took her purse from her unresisting fingers and set it next to her shawl. When he'd finished, he turned and slowly eased her into his arms.

Their bodies gently came together, and an electrified shudder went through her. She wasn't a complete fool— she knew what Alex was planning. She lowered her eyelids. Dear God, her heart was on the warpath, but she wanted this, too.

For one tense moment, she battled the feeling, then with a deep sigh, she surrendered.

Alex wrapped his arms around her. "Oh, baby," he whispered in her ear. "You feel so damn good." He moved suggestively against her.

The instant flash of need that sprang to life inside her was palpable. Never in her life had she ever wanted to be held this much. Never had she wanted to be touched this much. Or kissed. Or loved.

She emptied her lungs of air as his hands slowly slid from her waist, over the small of her back, down the rounded curve of her buttocks, to settle on the back of her thighs. He lifted her then, ever so slightly, ever so subtly.

There was music, such beautiful music, and then Carol remembered that they were supposed to be dancing. She pressed her fingertips to the curve of his shoulder. His mouth edged toward hers. Carol felt the sigh work its way through her lungs. Alex's breath was moist and warm, his hands gentle as they pressed her closer and closer.

When he kissed her and buried his tongue in her mouth, Carol felt a tremendous sense of relief. He groaned. She groaned. She ached in ways she'd never known a woman could ache.

Pressed as she was, the lower half of her body in intimate contact with his lower half, Carol couldn't help being aware of him. He was hard, so hard, and aroused and wanting. His mouth ate at hers with fire and demand.

Need and want warred within her, finally arriving at a stalemate. She slipped her hands all the way around his neck and offered him her tongue in an erotic game of cat and mouse.

He brought his hands to her back, blindly fiddling with the buttons. He dragged his mouth away from hers long enough to mumble a curse about her choice of clothes.

That all too brief moment helped Carol to collect her scattered senses. "Alex," she whispered, "what are you doing?"

"Undressing you."

"Why?" she asked breathlessly, knowing the moment she asked, what a stupid question it was.

"Why?" he repeated, coating the word with amusement. "Because we're going to make love."

Her pulse went wild.

"I love you. You love me. Right?"

"Oh . . . yes."

"Good." He kissed her, slowly rubbing his open mouth over hers with such demand that Carol feared they would both disintegrate if she didn't do something fast. She broke away from him with what little strength she'd managed to garner.

Alex didn't seem to notice that she was resisting him. He'd opened her dress enough to draw it down the length of her arms, which severely constricted her movements. When he encountered the silk teddy, he ground out his frustration in a hard kiss that was designed to rob her of reason. He succeeded despite her best efforts.

"Alex . . . please don't," she begged, struggling to keep her head clear of the sensual fog.

"Tonight's a new beginning for us. I'm crazy in love with you. I need you so much that I can't think straight anymore."

"You brought me here to make love to me, didn't you?" she cried.

"You mean it isn't obvious?" he asked as he nibbled kisses along the side of her neck.

"Why now? Why not that night we were stargazing at the Washington coast . . . why tonight?"

"Carol, do we need to go through this blasted evaluation?"

"I have to know," she cried, pushing herself away from him. Her hands trembled, and it was with some difficulty that she righted her dress. "The truth, Alex. I want the truth."

"All right," he murmured, obviously having a problem cooling his passion. "I'll tell you what you seem to find so important to know. I thought . . . I believed that if we made love, it would help you decide you wanted to marry me."

Carol felt as though he'd tossed a bucket of ice water in her face. The sting of his words felt like a thousand needles. Her hand covered her pounding heart. "Oh, God . . ." she whispered. "Not again."

"Carol? What's wrong?"

"Bruce did this to me, too . . . pressured me into giving in to him . . . then he hated me . . . punished me. . . ." Blindly she reached for her purse and headed for the front door.

Alex caught up with her before she made it outside. His hand bit into her shoulder as he whirled her around. By then she was sobbing, her whole body trembling, but there were no tears. Only stark terror—stark memories.

Alex took one look at her and hauled her into his arms. "Carol, dear God." He plowed his fingers into her hair. "It's all right, baby, it's all right. I would never have forced you."

Chapter Twelve

All Carol could do was cry, and the pile of used tissues was mounting more each minute. Alex tried every way he knew to comfort her, to help her, but everything he did only seemed to make matters worse. One thing he'd gleaned—she definitely didn't want him to touch her.

She'd curled herself up in a tight ball on his sofa and covered her face as she wept. She wouldn't talk to him. She wouldn't look at him. The only understandable statement she'd made in the last fifteen minutes had been a demand that he take her home.

Fear knotted his stomach. He had the unexplainable feeling that if he were to do as she asked, he would never see her again. He had tonight and only tonight to repair the trust he'd unwittingly destroyed.

"Carol, I'm sorry." He must have told her that twenty times. God knew it was true enough. Everything he did with this woman was wrong. This evening was the perfect example. He couldn't have blown it any more had he tried. For days he'd been searching for a way to prove to Carol how much he loved her and how right they were for each other.

This evening had seemed the perfect place and time. He'd planned to give her the wine, the music, the flowery words and the diamond ring she deserved.

To his way of thinking, if everything went right, he would make love to her, and afterward, they could discuss the details of their wedding and their lives. He wanted her warm and willing in his bed, and although it was more than a little arrogant of him, he didn't think he would have any problem getting her there.

He'd also come to the conclusion that once they made love, she would recognize that their being together had been predestined from the first, and their marriage would naturally follow.

His plan had worked flawlessly—like a dream. Carol had walked into the house, had seen that the table was set and the candles ready to light. She'd looked at him with those huge chocolate-brown eyes of hers and given him a seductive smile that suggested he was a naughty boy. Then, with barely a pause, she'd willingly waltzed into his arms.

From there everything had gone downhill. An Olympic skier couldn't have made a swifter decline.

One minute he was kissing her, marveling at the power she had over his body, and the next, she was cold and trembling, demanding answers to questions that should have been more than obvious.

"Would you like some coffee?" he asked her gently for the second—or was it the third?—time. It demanded every ounce of restraint he possessed not to pull her into his embrace. His arms ached with the need to hold her.

"No," she whispered starkly. "I want to go home."

"We need to talk first."

"Not now. I *need* to go home." She rubbed her hands down her face, and reached for a clean tissue. Apparently she was gaining some resolve because she stood, wrapped her shawl around her like a shield of armor and headed for the door. "If you won't drive me, then I'll walk."

Alex heard the desperation in her voice and was helpless to do anything but what she asked. He stood, and the regret swept through him like a brushfire. If there was anything he could do to ease her pain, he would have done it. If there were any words he could have uttered to help her, he would have said them gladly. But all she wanted was for him to take her back to her own home. Back to her own bed. Back to her own life.

Good Lord, who did he think he was? Some Don Juan who could sweep this beautiful, sensitive woman into his bed and make mad, passionate love to her? He felt sick to his stomach with the way he had plotted and planned to use her own body against her, to exploit the magnetic attraction between them to serve his own means.

Now he was losing her, and there wasn't anyone he could blame but himself. He'd known his chances weren't good the night he'd asked her to marry him. He'd hoped to see joy flash from her eyes when he suggested they intertwine their lives. He'd longed to see happiness flare from her and have her hurl herself into his arms, excited and overcome with emotion.

He should have known he'd been watching too many 1940s movies.

He'd asked Carol to marry him, and none of the things he'd wanted had happened. Instead, her eyes had reflected fear. And tonight . . . tonight he'd witnessed stark terror.

Alex was astute enough to realize the problem lay in Carol's brief marriage. Whatever had happened in the past had left deep emotional scars. Even when he'd felt the closest to her, Alex had gleaned damn little about her relationship with her late husband. She'd let tidbits of information drop every now and again, but rarely, and every time she did, Alex had the feeling she had regretted it.

On her way out the door, Carol grabbed a handful of fresh tissues, and with nothing more he could say or do, Alex led the way to his car.

He opened the passenger door for her, noticing how she avoided any possibility of their accidentally touching as she slipped inside.

The tension inside the close confines of the compact car was as thick as an Irish stew. Alex could barely breathe in it. He didn't know how Carol could tolerate the tautness that was more binding than cords. God knew he couldn't deal with it.

When he braked at a stop sign, he decided to try one last time.

"Carol, please, how many times do I have to tell you how sorry I am? I made a mistake. I behaved like a bastard. What do you want me to do, because I'll do it. Anything you say. I love you! You've got to believe I'd never intentionally do anything to hurt you."

His pleas were met with more of the same strained, intolerable silence.

In frustration he pressed his foot to the gas, and they abruptly surged ahead. The seat belts were the only things that kept the two of them from slamming forward with the car. Alex was about to apologize, but he would be damned before he'd tell her he was sorry one more time that evening.

The fiercest argument of their courtship now ensued, and the crazy part was, neither of them uttered a word. Every now and again, Alex could hear Carol drag a rickety breath through her lungs, and he knew she was doing everything within her power not to cry. Each tear she shed, each sob she inhaled, felt like a self-inflicted knife wound.

He was losing her, and there wasn't a damn thing he could do about it. It wouldn't be nearly so tragic if he hadn't cared for her so damn much. After Gloria had died, Alex had never truly believed he would fall in love again. Even when he'd made the decision to find another wife, he hadn't expected to stumble upon the depth of emotion that he'd experienced with Carol.

And now it might well be too late.

"Hey, Mom, did you and Mr. Preston have a fight or something last night?" Peter asked the first thing the following morning.

"W-why do you ask?"

Peter popped two frozen waffles into the toaster, then stood guard over them as though he expected Carol to run and snatch them out of his hands.

"I don't know. Mr. Preston was acting strange last night when he picked us up from the movie."

"Strange?"

"I think the word James used was melancholy. Mr. Preston's usually a real kick. I like him, I mean, he's about the neatest adult I know. He doesn't treat me like I'm a kid, and he likes the same things I like and—I don't know—I just think he's an all around great guy. He's about the best one you've ever gone out with. Fact is, Mom, men don't come much better than James's dad.''

''He is . . . nice, isn't he?'' she agreed. She locked her fingers around the handle of her coffee mug and cast her gaze anywhere but where her son might catch it.

Peter leaned toward her and squinted. ''Have you been crying?''

''What makes you ask anything that silly?'' She tried to make a joke out of the question.

''Your eyes are all puffy and red like you have an allergy or something.''

''Pollen sometimes affects me this way.'' That was the truth. It didn't happen to be affecting her eyes at that particular moment, but what Peter didn't know wouldn't hurt anything.

The waffles popped up, and Peter reached for them, muttering under his breath when he burned his finger. He spread a thin layer of margarine across and topped them off with a thick line of syrup. Once that task was complete, he added two more waffles to the toaster, then he sat across the table from Carol.

''I kind of thought you and Mr. Preston might have had a fight or something,'' Peter said earnestly, obviously feeling it was safe to probe some more. ''That would have been sad, because on the way to the movie he was telling us that he wanted to make this dinner the most romantic one of your life. Was it?''

''He . . . tried.''

''How did the Baked Alaska taste?''

''The Baked Alaska?'' Carol's mind was a blank. ''Oh . . . it was great.''

''Mr. Preston made everything himself. Right down to the salad dressing. James told me he'd been shopping for this dinner for days. It would have been terrible if you'd had a fight and ruined it.... You love Mr. Preston, don't you?'' Peter asked after a pregnant pause.

Carol closed her eyes to the waves of emotion that assaulted her from all sides. She would be a fool not to admit it. And her heart refused to allow her to lie. But what no one seemed to understand was that love isn't a cure-all. She'd loved Bruce, too—or thought she did—and look where that had gotten her.

''Yes,'' she whispered. Her gaze was averted from her son, but she could hear his sigh of relief.

''I knew you did,'' he said cheerfully, slicing into his breakfast. ''I told James you were wild about his dad and that whatever happened between you two at dinner would take care of itself in the morning.''

''I'm sure you're right,'' Carol murmured.

An hour later, Carol was working in the garden space Alex had tilled for her several weeks earlier. She was cultivating the lush rich soil, preparing it to plant several varieties of herbs that same afternoon. She'd done her homework and discovered a wide variety that grew well in the moist climate of the Pacific Northwest.

Her back was to the kitchen, and she hadn't heard the doorbell. Nor was there the usual commotion when Peter let someone in the house.

Yet without a doubt, she knew Alex was standing in the doorway watching her. She felt his presence in the same way she experienced his absence.

Running her forearm across her brow, she leaned back on her haunches and removed her gloves. ''I know what you want to say,'' she said plainly, ''and I think it would be better if we dropped the issue entirely.''

''Unfortunately that's a luxury neither of us can afford.''

"Oh, damn, I knew you were going to say that," she muttered, awkwardly struggling to an upright position. Her knees were caked with mud and the sweat was pouring down both sides of her flushed face.

There'd probably been only two other times in her life that she'd looked worse, and Alex had seen her on both occasions.

With the hand cultivator gripped tightly in her fist, she walked over to the patio furniture and plopped herself down. "All right, say what you have to say and be done with it."

Alex grinned. "Such resignation!"

"I'd rather be working in my garden."

"I know." He flexed his hands a couple of times while he apparently sorted through his thoughts. "I suppose I should start at the beginning."

"Oh, Alex, this isn't necessary, it really isn't. I overreacted last night. All right, you made a mistake, you're only human—I forgive you. Your intentions weren't the least bit honorable, but given the circumstances they were understandable. You wanted to lead me into your bed and afterward make an honest woman of me. Right?"

"Something like that," he admitted. Although it went without saying that the issue was much more complicated than that.

"The thing is, I've been made an honest woman once and it was the worst mistake of my life. I'm not looking to repeat it."

"What was your husband's name?" Alex demanded without preamble.

"Bruce...why?"

"Do you realize you've never told me?"

She shrugged, not the least bit surprised. She never talked about Bruce unless it was unavoidable.

"Tell me about him, Carol," Alex pleaded, "tell me everything. Start with the first minute you noticed each other and then lead me through your relationship to the day you buried him."

"I can't see how that would solve anything."

"Tell me, Carol," he demanded.

"No." She vaulted to her feet, her heart in a panic. "There's nothing to say."

"Then why do you close up tighter than a miser's fist anytime someone mentions him?"

"Because!" She paced the patio. Standing still was impossible. Stopping abruptly, she whirled around and glared at him, angry all over again for his pushy attitude. "All right, you want to know, I'll tell you. We were teenagers—young, stupid, naive. We made love in the back seat of a car...and when I got pregnant with Peter we got married. Bruce died three years later in a car accident."

Her words were followed by a stark silence.

An eternity passed before Alex spoke again. "That's only a summary. Tell me what really happened in those three years you were married." His voice was soft and insistent.

Her chest tightened painfully, squeezing the air from her lungs. Would nothing satisfy him short of blood? How could she ever hope to describe three years of living in hell? She couldn't, and she didn't even want to try.

Alex wouldn't possibly understand, and nothing she could ever say would help him. What purpose would it serve to dredge up all that misery? None that she could see.

Slowly she lowered herself onto the deck chair, trying with everything in her to still her churning thoughts. The memories spit and coughed in her mind like boiling oil.

The pain was so distinct, so acute, that she opted for the only sane solution. She backed away.

Alex reached for her hand, holding it loosely, not applying any pressure. "I know this is difficult."

He hadn't a clue. He couldn't have or he would never ask this of her.

"Bruce and I were married a long time ago. Suffice it to say that the marriage wasn't a good one. We were much too young . . . and Bruce had problems." She bit into her bottom lip, not willing to continue. "I don't want to drag up the past. I don't see where it would do any good."

"Carol, please."

"No," she said sharply. "I'm not about to dissect a marriage that ended thirteen years ago simply because you're curious."

"We *need* to talk about it," he insisted.

"Why? Because I get a little panicky when you start pressuring me into bed? Trust me, any woman who's gotten pregnant without a wedding band on her finger would react the same way I did. You know the old saying about once burned, twice shy." She tried to make light of it and failed. Miserably.

For the longest time Alex said nothing. He did nothing. He stared into the distance, and Carol hadn't a clue which path his thoughts were taking.

"I never expected to fall in love again," he said.

Carol frowned at the way his words were filled with self-derision.

"Gloria knew, but then she always *did* know me better than I did myself." He paused for a moment, and a sad, almost bitter smile tweaked at the junction of his lips. "I'll never forget the last time we were able to talk, really talk. The following day she slipped into a coma, and soon afterward, she slipped gracefully into death. She knew she was dying and had accepted death, welcomed it as a friend. The hospital staff knew it was only a matter of time. But at the time I couldn't, I wouldn't, let go of her. I had such faith God would heal her. Such unquestionable trust. He did, of course, but not the way I wanted.''

''Alex...'' Tears were beginning to clog her eyes. She didn't want to hear about Gloria and the wonderful marriage he'd shared with her. The contrast was too painful. Too bleak.

''Gloria took my hand and raised her eyes to mine and thanked me for staying at her side through the end. She apologized because she'd been ill. Can you imagine anyone doing that?''

''No.'' Carol's voice was the faintest of whispers.

''Then she told me that God would send another woman into my life, someone healthy and whole who would love me the way I deserved to be loved. Someone who would share my success and who would love our son as much as she did.'' He paused and smiled again, but it was the same sad smile he'd used before. ''Trust me, this was the last thing I wanted to hear from my wife. First of all, I was in the denial stage, and I refused to believe she was dying, and second, nothing could ever have convinced me I could ever love another woman as much as I loved Gloria.''

Carol squeezed her eyes closed and took in deep breaths to keep from weeping openly.

''She told me when I met this other woman and decided to marry her that I shouldn't feel guilty for having fallen in love again. She must have known that would be something powerful I'd be dealing with later. Her hand, connected to all those tubes, reached for mine. She squeezed my fingers—she was so damn weak, and so incredibly strong. And wise, so very wise. Within a few hours she was gone from me forever.'' He rubbed his hand over his eyes and hesitated before continuing. ''I didn't believe her. I didn't think it would be possible for me to love anyone as much as I loved her.

''Then I met you, and before I knew how it happened, I was falling head over heels in love all over again.'' Once more he pressed a weary hand over his face. His expression was blank, his eyes revealed so little emotion. ''And again I'm learning the lesson of relinquishing the woman I love. I'll give you the two weeks to make your decision, Carol. In fact, I'll make it easy for you. I won't call or contact you until the seventh—that's exactly two weeks. You can tell me your decision then. All right?''

''All right,'' she agreed, feeling almost numb.

Slowly he nodded, then stood and walked out of her house, and out of her life.

''The way I see it,'' Peter said, holding a red Delicious apple in one hand and staring at his mother, ''James's dad can adopt me.''

Carol's heart constricted with a fleeting pain that scooted through her every time Peter not-so-casually mentioned Alex's name. He seemed to plan these times with precision care. Just when she least expected it. Just when she was certain she knew her own mind. Just when she was feeling overly confident. Then *pow*, right between the eyes, Peter would toss some unexpected remark her way. The explosion was generally preceded with some bit of information about Alex or a comment about how wonderful it would be when they were one big, happy family.

''I'd have to marry Alex first, and I'm not sure that's going to happen,'' she said reproachfully. One challenging look defied him to contradict her.

"Well, it makes sense, doesn't it? *If* you marry, naturally." Peter took a huge bite of the apple. A thin line of juice dripped down the side of his chin, and he wiped it away with the back of his hand. "I haven't heard from Dad's family in years, and they wouldn't care if someone adopted me. That way we'd all share the same last name. Peter Preston has a cool sound to it, don't you think?"

"Peter," she ground out, frustrated and angered by the way he chose to turn a deaf ear to everything she said. "If this is another tactic to manipulate me into marrying Alex so you can go fishing, then I want you to know right now that I don't appreciate it."

She was under enough pressure—mainly from herself—and she didn't need her son applying any more.

"But, Mom, think about how good our lives would be if you married Mr. Preston. He's rich...not Donald Trump wealthy, but—"

"I think I've heard all of this conversation that I want. Now sit down and eat your dinner." She dished up the crispy fried pork chop and a serving of rice and set the plate on the table.

"You're not eating?" Peter asked, looking mildly disappointed. "This is the third night this week that you've skipped dinner."

Carol's appetite had been nil for the entire two weeks. "No time, I've got to get ready for class."

"When will these sessions be over?"

"Two more weeks," she said on her way into her bedroom. Two weeks seemed to be the magical, mystical time period of late. Alex had given her two weeks to decide if she would accept his proposal. He'd granted her the adequate breathing space she needed to come to a sensible decision. Only "sensible" was the last thing Carol felt. It shouldn't be this damn difficult. She couldn't understand why she was teetering with such massive doubts. Carol knew the answer to that question almost immediately.

Alex's marriage had been wonderful.

Hers had been a disaster.

He was looking to repeat what he'd shared with Gloria.

She was looking to avoid the pain Bruce had brought into her life.

"Mom . . . phone."

Carol froze. Her two weeks were up that day, and she'd been on tenterhooks waiting for Alex to contact her. Her entire day had been filled with a growing sense of dread. She'd looked for Alex to come strolling out from behind every closed door, to pop out like a jack-in-the-box when she least expected him. That he'd waited until after dinner was cruel and unusual punishment.

The last thing she'd anticipated was that he would phone.

Wrestling one shoe on, she hobbled over to her nightstand and picked up the telephone receiver, wondering as she did so what she was going to say.

"Hello."

"Carol, it's your mother."

"Hello, Ma, what can I do for you?" Relief coated her voice like warm honey.

Angelina Pasquale paused. "There's something important you should know. I was in the church this morning, lighting a candle to St. Scholastica, and a funny thing happened to my heart."

"Did you see a doctor?" Carol's own heart abruptly switched gears, slipping into overdrive. Her greatest fear was losing her mother to heart disease the way she'd lost her father.

"Why should I see a doctor?" her mother protested. "I was in church. God was talking to me, and He said I should have a heart-to-heart talk with my daughter, Carol, who is making up her mind if she's going to marry this rich non-Italian or if she's going to walk away from the best thing that's happened since the invention of padded insoles."

"Mama, I've got a class—I don't have time to talk."

"You've seen Alex?"

"Not . . . yet."

"What are you going to tell him?"

Her mother was being as difficult as Peter. Everyone wanted to make up her mind for her. Everyone knew what she should do. Everyone, that is, except Carol.

"You know he's not Catholic, don't you?" she reminded her mother, who had once considered that an all-important factor in choosing a husband. Religion and, equally vital—if her potential husband was allergic to tomatoes. That was another sure sign of trouble.

Her mother snickered. "I know he's not Catholic! But don't worry, I've got all that worked out with God."

"Mama, I'm sorry, but I have to leave now or I'll be late for my class."

"So be late for once in your life. Who's it going to hurt? All day I waited, all day I said to myself, my bambina's going to call and tell me she's going to marry again. I want to do the cooking myself, you tell him that."

"Mama, what are you talking about?"

"At the wedding. No caterers, understand? I got the menu all planned. We'll serve . . ."

"Ma, please."

Even at that it took Carol another five minutes to extract herself from the phone. One look at her watch and she groaned. Rushing from room to room, she grabbed her purse, her other shoe and her briefcase. She paused on her way out the door to kiss Peter on the cheek and remind him to do his homework. With that she was out of the house.

Her breathing was labored and uneven by the time she raced through traffic and pulled into the parking lot at the community building where the birthing classes were held.

She'd piled everything she needed into her arms, including her umbrella, when she realized she'd left her lecture notes at the house.

"Damn," she muttered. She took two steps before she remembered she was carrying one shoe.

"It might help if you slip that on instead of carrying it under your arm."

Carol froze, and a thousand fears crystalized around her heart. She whirled around, angry and upset, directing the emotion at Alex. "This is all your fault," she muttered, dropping her shoe to the ground and working it with her big toe until it was positioned correctly for her to slip her foot inside. "First Peter's on my case, and now my mother's claiming she received a message directly from the lips of St. Scholastica and that God's worked out a deal with her, being that you're not Catholic, and frankly, Alex—don't you dare laugh." She finished on a huge breath and severely waved her index finger at him. "I swear if you laugh I wouldn't marry you if you were the last living male in the state of Oregon."

"I'm sorry," he said, holding up both hands as if she were placing him under arrest.

"I should hope so. You don't know what I've been through this past week."

"Your two weeks are up, Carol."

"You don't need to tell me that. I know."

"And you've decided?"

Her eyes drifted shut, and the walls she'd felt closing in on her all day came to an abrupt halt. "I have," she whispered tightly.

Chapter Thirteen

Before you tell me what you've decided," Alex said, moving toward Carol, his eyes smoky gray and filled with tender concern, "let me hold you."

"Hold me?" she echoed meekly. Alex looked one-hundred-percent male, and the lazy smile he wore was potent enough to tear through her solar plexus.

"I'm going to do much more than simply hold you, love," he whispered, inching his way toward her.

"Here? In a parking lot?"

Alex chuckled and slipped his arms around her waist and tugged her closer. Carol hadn't an ounce of resistance left in her. She'd been so lonely, so lost without him. So confused.

His mouth brushed hers. Much too briefly. Much too lightly. His kiss was as gentle and undemanding as mist caressing rose petals.

Carol didn't want him to be so gentle. Not when she was this hungry for his touch. Her lips parted, blossoming into a firm and wanting kiss. Alex sighed his pleasure and sank his mouth into hers. Rippling emotions wrapped their way around Carol's heart, and she clung to him, needing him.

When they drew apart, they rested their foreheads against each other. Alex brushed his nose against hers. "Okay," he said, his breath warm and heavy. "Tell me, I'm ready now."

"Oh, Alex," she murmured, and her throat constricted with ready tears. "I can't decide. I've tried and tried and tried, and the only thing I really know is I need more time."

"Time," he repeated. Briefly he slammed his eyes closed. His wide shoulders sagged with defeat. "You need more time. How much longer? A week? A month? Six months? Would a year fit into your schedule?" He broke away from her and forcefully rubbed his hand along the back of his neck. "If you haven't made up your mind by now, then my guess is that you never will. I love you, Carol, but you're driving me insane with this waiting business."

"Can't you see things from my point of view?" she protested.

"No, I can't," he said and continued with silk-smooth sarcasm. "I'm grateful for this time we've had, because it's taught me something I hadn't been willing to recognize before. I'm lonely, damn lonely. I want someone in my life—someone permanent. I want you as my wife. I *need* you as my wife. But if you don't want what I'm offering, then it's time I cut my losses and looked elsewhere."

A strangled cry erupted from her lips. He was being so unfair to pressure her this way. Everything had to be decided in his time frame, without allowances for doubts or questions. Something broke in Carol. Something she'd been battling with for years. Control. She couldn't—wouldn't—allow another man to control her the way Bruce had. An ice age passed before she finally spoke.

"I think you're right, Alex. Find yourself someone else."

The shock of her words hit him like a blow to the head. He actually flinched, but the whole while his piercing eyes continued to hold hers. Carol saw the regret and the pain flash through his burning gaze, as bright as any sun. Then he buried his hands in his pockets, turned and marched away from her.

It was all Carol could do not to run after him, but she knew if she did that she would be giving up an important part of her self-respect, and her soul.

Joyce Mandle stuck her head out the door and scanned the parking lot. She looked relieved when she found Carol, and waved.

Carol motioned back. Although she wanted nothing more than to be alone, she didn't have any choice but to teach her class.

Joyce called, mentioning the time.

Still Carol couldn't seem to tear her gaze from Alex, holding on to him for as long as she could. He made her feel things she'd never known a woman was capable of experiencing. When he kissed her, she felt hot and quivery, as though she'd just awakened from a long, deep sleep. Spending time with him was fun and exciting. There had been adventures waiting to happen with this man. Escapades in the making. Whole new worlds just awaiting exploration. Yet something was holding her back.

Something powerful and profound that she couldn't put a name to. She wanted everything that Alex was offering her, and at the same time her freedom was too precious, too important.

Carol didn't see Alex again until the end of the week when the boys were participating in the district track meet. James was running in the four-hundred- and eight-hundred-meter races, and Peter was scheduled for the 1500-meter. On their own, the two friends had decided to choose events in which they weren't in direct competition. Carol had been impressed with their insight into each other's competitive personalities.

Carol's mother had decided to attend the meet with her. Angelina was as excited as a kid at the circus. They'd just gotten themselves settled in the bleachers when out of the corner of her eye, Carol saw Alex. She paused at the unexpected blow. Since they both had sons involved in sports, she knew avoiding him would be nearly impossible, but she hadn't expected to see him quite so soon. Although in retrospect, she should have realized he would be attending this important meet.

Preparing herself, she sat stiffly on the bleachers when Alex strolled past. Instantly her heart started to thunder. His friend was with him, the one she'd met briefly . . . was it Barney or Bernie . . . Barney, she decided. Her hands were tightly clenched in her lap, and she was prepared to exchange a polite, if not stiff, greeting with him.

To her consternation, Alex didn't so much as look in her direction. Carol knew that it would have been nearly impossible for him to have missed seeing her. If he'd thought to hurt her, it was amazing how easily he'd done so.

"So when does the man running with the torch come out?" Angelina asked.

"That's in the Olympics, Mama," Carol answered, shocked by how weak her voice sounded.

Her mother turned to look in Carol's direction, and her frown deepened. "What's the matter with you?" her mother demanded. "You look as white as bleached flour."

"It's nothing."

"You look like someone just hit you in the stomach. What is it?"

"Alex . . . just strolled past us."

"Not *the* Alex?"

Carol nodded. Before she could stop her mother, Angelina rose to her feet and reached for Carol's binoculars. "Where is he? I want to get a good look at this man who broke my daughter's heart."

"Ma, please, let's not get into that again." The way her mother had defended her had touched Carol to the core. However, the older woman hadn't wasted any time berating her daughter's foolishness, either. She'd spent most of Sunday muttering things at Carol in Italian. Carol wasn't fluent enough in the language to understand everything, but she got the gist. Angelina thought Carol was a first-class fool to let a man like Alex slip through her fingers. Carol didn't know what she was anymore. A fool or a genius.

"I want one look at this Alex," Angelina insisted. She pressed the binoculars to her eyes and twisted the dials until she had them focused correctly. "I'm gonna give this man the eye. Now tell me where he's sitting."

Carol knew it would be easier to try to bend a tire iron than persuade her mother to remove the binoculars and sit down before she made a scene.

"He's on your left, about halfway up the bleachers in the pale blue sweater," she muttered. If he glanced in her direction, she would be mortified. God only knew what interpretation he'd put on her mother glaring at him through a set of field glasses, giving him what she so quaintly called "the eye."

Her mother apparently found him, because she started speaking in her mother tongue. Only this time what she was saying was perfectly understandable. She was using succulent, suggestive phrases about Alex's sexual talents and how he would bring Carol such pleasure in bed.

"Ma, please," Carol muttered, mortified. "You're embarrassing me."

Angelina sat down and rested the glasses on her lap. Once more she was muttering in her mother tongue, leaning her head close enough to Carol so she couldn't help but hear her.

"Ma," she cried, distressed with the vivid language her mother was using. "You should have your mouth washed out with soap."

Angelina folded her hands and stared at the sky. "Such beautiful bambinos you'd have with this man."

Carol closed her eyes, battling down the mental image of her with more children—Alex's and her children. The emotion that rocked through her drained her of strength.

Her mother took the opportunity to make a few more succinct remarks, but Carol did her best to ignore them. It seemed the track meet was never going to start. Carol was convinced she was going to be forced to spend the afternoon listening to her mother whispering in her ear. Just when she couldn't endure it any longer, the youths involved in the hurdle events walked over to the starting line. They wiggled their arms at their sides and did a couple of stretching exercises. Carol was so grateful to have her mother's attention diverted to the field that it was all she could do not to rush out and kiss the coach.

The four-hundred-meter race followed several hurdle events. Carol watched as James approached the starting line. He looked both confident and eager. Just as they were to take their position, he glanced into the stands and cocked his head just slightly, acknowledging his father's presence. When his gaze slid to Carol's, his eyes sobered before he smiled.

At the gun, the eight youths leapt forward. Before Carol realized what she was doing, she'd vaulted to her feet and was shouting at the top of her lungs.

James crossed the finish line and placed second. Carol's heart felt as though it would burst with pride. Without conscious thought her gaze flew to Alex, and she noted that he looked equally pleased by his son's performance. He must have sensed her eyes on him because he turned his head slightly and their gazes clashed. He held on to hers for just a moment, and then with obvious reluctance pulled it away.

Carol sagged to her seat.

"So who is this boy you scream for like a son?" her mother demanded, giving her an odd look.

"James Preston is the boy who finished second."

"So that was Alex's son?" Angelina asked slowly, as she lifted the binoculars to her eyes once more. She was apparently pleased with what she saw, because she grinned and murmured. "He's a fine-looking boy, but he's a little on the thin side. He needs some of my spaghetti to put some meat on those bones."

Carol didn't comment. Her mother made her cooking sound as important to James as insulin was to a diabetic. Conflicting emotions warred inside Carol. She *did* love James like a son. The realization forced a lump into her throat. And her heart...her poor, unsuspecting heart, was pounding hard enough to drive a freight train.

Feeling someone's eyes on her, she glanced over her shoulder. Instantly Alex looked away. Carol's hands began to tremble, and all he'd done was glance in her direction. God forbid that he should talk to her. At the rate matters were going, her mother would have to send for an ambulance to carry her out of the stadium.

James raced again shortly afterward, placing third in the eight-hundred-meter. As a high school sophomore, he was showing a good deal of potential, Carol mused, feeling exceptionally proud of the teenager.

When her own son approached the starting line for his race, Carol felt as nervous as a bride. The mind, she decided, had a sadistic streak...why else would she compare herself to a bride?

Since the 1500-meter meant almost four long turns around the track, it didn't have the immediacy of the previous races. By the time Peter was entering the final lap, Carol and her mother, too, were on their feet shouting their encouragement. Carol in English. Angelina in Italian. From a distance, Carol heard a loud male voice joining theirs. Alex.

When Peter crossed the finish line in a solid third position, Carol heaved a sigh of pride and relief. Silly tears dampened her lashes, and she raised her fingertips to her mouth. Both the first and second place winners were seniors. As a sophomore, Peter had done exceptionally well.

Again, without any conscious decision on her part, Carol found herself turning to look at Alex. This time he was waiting for her. Their gazes meshed, and they exchanged the faintest of smiles. Sad smiles. Lonely smiles. Proud smiles.

Carol's shoulders sagged with defeat. It was as if the worlds of two fools were about to collide.

He was pushy. She was stubborn.

He wanted a wife. She wanted time.

He refused to wait. She refused to give in.

Still their gazes held, each unwilling to pull away from the other. So many concerns weighted Carol's heart. So many memories. She remembered how they'd strolled through the lush green foliage of the Washington Rain Forest. Alex had linked his fingers with hers, and nothing had ever felt more right. That same night they'd sat around the camp fire and sung silly songs with the boys, and fed each other roasted marshmallows.

The memories glided straight through Carol's heart.

"Carol?"

Dragging her gaze away from Alex, Carol turned her attention to her mother.

"It's time to leave," Angelina said, casting a glance into the stands toward Alex and his friend. "Didn't you notice? The stadium's emptying, and weren't we supposed to meet Peter?"

"Yes..." Carol murmured, "we were...we are."

Peter and James strolled out of the locker room and onto the field together. Each was carrying a sports bag and their school books. The two had apparently just gotten out of the shower.

Carol and her mother were waiting where Peter had suggested. It seemed to be important to him that they keep as far away from the school building as possible for fear any of his friends would realize he had a family.

Alex didn't appear to be around, and for that Carol was grateful. And if it made any sense whatsoever, and it didn't, she was also regretful. She wanted to be as close to him as she could. She was considering moving to Outer Slabobia to escape him. Her life, her thoughts, her desires, were in direct contrast to each other and growing more muddled every second.

Peter and James split company about halfway across the field. Before they parted they shared a brief look, apparently having agreed or decided upon something. Whatever it was, Peter didn't mention it.

He seemed unusually quiet on the ride home. Carol waited until after they dropped her mother off at her house to question her son. "Is something bothering you?"

"Not really." But he kept his gaze focused straight ahead.

"You sure?"

His left shoulder went up and down in an indecisive action.

"I see."

"Mr. Preston was at the meet today. Did you see him?"

"Ah..." Carol hedged. There wasn't any reason to lie. "Yeah. He was sitting with his friend."

"Mr. Miller and Mr. Preston are good friends and have been since they went to college."

Carol wasn't exactly sure what significance that bit of information held, if any.

"According to James, Mr. Miller's been single for the past couple of years, and he dates beautiful women all the time. He's the one who arranges all those hot dates for James's dad... and apparently he's doing it again."

"That's none of our business." Her heart reacted to that, but then what else could she expect? She was in love with the man. It wasn't as if Alex hadn't told her. He'd said if she wasn't willing to accept what he was offering, then it was time to cut his losses and look elsewhere. She just hadn't expected him to start so soon.

"James was telling me that his dad's been going out every night this week."

"Peter," she said softly, "I think it would be best if we made it a rule not to discuss Alex or his dating practices again. You know, and, I hope, have accepted, the fact the relationship between James's dad and myself is over...by mutual agreement."

"But, Mom, you really love this guy."

She arched her eyebrows at that, questioning him.

"You try to fool me, but I can see how miserable you've been all week. And Mr. Preston's been just as unhappy, according to James, and we both think that he's going to do something foolish on the rebound, like marry this Babette girl."

"Peter, I thought I just said I don't want to talk about this subject again."

"Fine," he muttered, crossing his arms over his chest and beginning to sulk. Five minutes passed before he heaved a giant sigh and mentioned, "Babette was a beauty queen. She's not the usual run-of-the-mill bimbo Barney usually meets. Mom, you've got to do something fast. This woman is real competition."

"Peter," she cried.

"All right. All right." He raised both hands in surrender. "I won't say another word."

That proved to be a slight exaggeration. Peter had ways of letting Carol know what was going on between Alex and his newfound friend without ever having to mention either's name.

Saturday, after playing basketball with James in the local park, Peter returned home, hot and sweaty. He walked straight to the refrigerator and took out a cold can of soda, opening it and taking the first three swallows while standing in front of the open refrigerator.

Carol had her sewing machine set up on the kitchen table. Pins were pressed between her lips as she waved her hand, instructing her son to close the door.

"Oh, sorry," Peter muttered. He did as she asked, pressed his back to the cold door and wiped a hand down his face. "Ever hear of a thirty-six-year-old man falling head over heels in love with a twenty-three-year-old girl?" Peter asked disdainfully.

Stepping on a nail couldn't have been more painfully direct than her son's question. "No, I can't say that I have," she said, so flustered she sewed a seam directly up the middle of the sleeve of the blouse she was making. With disgust, she tossed it aside, and when her son had left the room, she trembled and buried her face in her hands.

On Sunday morning, Peter had stayed a few extra minutes in church after mass, walking up to the altar. When he joined Carol a few moments later in the vestibule, she placed her hand on his shoulder and studied him carefully. She'd never seen her son quite so serious.

"Is something troubling you, honey?"

He gave her another of his one-shoulder rolls that was intended to suffice as an answer. "I thought if Grandma could talk to God, then I'd give it a try. While I was up there, I lit a candle to St. Scholastica." His eyes and his words couldn't have been more pointed.

Following mass, Carol and her son drove over to her mother's house. The tears started when she was in the kitchen helping her mother with dinner. The first one rolled down the corner of her eye. A single tear followed by another, and then another. It surprised Carol because she had nothing to cry about. But that didn't seem to matter. Soon the moisture was flowing from her eyes so fast and furious that it was dripping from her chin and running down onto her neck and the top of her dress.

Standing at the sink washing vegetables helped hide the fact she was weeping, but that wouldn't last long. Soon someone would discover the fact she was crying, and for no apparent reason. She struggled desperately to stop, but to no avail. If anything, her efforts only caused her to cry more intensely.

She must have made more noise than she realized, because when she turned to reach for a hand towel to wipe her face dry, she found her mother and her sister-in-law both staring at her.

Her mother was murmuring something to Paula in Italian, which was interesting since the other woman didn't understand a word of the language. But Carol understood each and every one. Her mother was telling Paula that Carol looked like a woman in love who was in danger of losing her man.

With her hand around Carol's shoulder, Angelina led her into her own bedroom. When Carol was a little girl and ill, her mother had always placed her in her own bed and nursed her from there.

Without resistance, Carol followed her mother. By now the tears had become soft sobs. Everyone in the living room stopped whatever they were doing and stared at her. Angelina fended off questions and directed Carol to her bed, pulling back the blankets. Sniffling, Carol lay down. The sheets felt cool against her cheeks, and she closed her eyes. Almost immediately she was asleep.

She woke an hour later and sat bolt upright. Immediately she knew what she had to do. Sitting on the edge of the mattress, she held her hands to her face and breathed in a deep, steadying breath. Merciful heavens, it wouldn't be easy.

Her family was busy in the living room. The conversation came to an abrupt halt when Carol moved into the room. She reached for her purse, avoiding their curious stares. "I...have to go out for a while. I don't know when I'll be back."

Angelina and Peter walked to the front door with her, both looking anxious.

"Where are you going?" her son asked.

She smiled softly, kissed his cheek and announced, "St. Scholastica must have heard your prayers."

Her mother immediately folded her hands and raised her eyes to heaven, looking more pleased than Carol could remember. Peter, on the other hand, blinked, his gaze wide and uncertain. Understanding apparently dawned on him, and with a shout, he threw his arms around Carol's neck and squeezed tight. "Hot damn."

Chapter Fourteen

Alex was in the kitchen fixing himself a sandwich when the doorbell chimed. From experience, he knew better than to answer it before James did. Pressing himself against the counter, Alex waited until his son vaulted from the family room, passed him and raced toward the front door.

Alex supposed he should at least show some interest in who had chosen to drop in unannounced, but frankly he didn't care unless it was one stubborn Italian miss, and the chances of that were more remote than winning the lottery.

"Dad," James shouted. "Come quick."

Muttering under his breath, Alex dropped his turkey sandwich on the plate and headed toward the living room. He was halfway through the door when he jerked his head up. It was Carol. Through a fog of disbelief, he saw her, dressed in a navy skirt and white silk blouse beneath a thick rose-colored sweater.

At least the woman strongly resembled Carol. His eyes must be playing tricks on him, because he was certain the woman who was standing just inside his home was the very one who'd been occupying his thoughts every minute of every hour for days on end.

"Hello, Alex," she said softly.

It sounded like her. Or could it be that he needed her so much that his troubled mind had conjured up her image to taunt him?

"Aren't you going to say anything?" James demanded. "This is Carol, Dad, Carol! Are you just going to stand there like a bump on a log?"

"Hello," he said finally, having some trouble getting his mouth and tongue to work together simultaneously.

"Hello? That's it? You aren't saying anything more than that?" James cried, clearly disgusted.

"How are you?" Carol asked him, and he noticed that her soft voice was husky and filled with emotion.

Someday he would tell her how the best foreman he ever hoped to find had threatened to walk off the job if Alex's foul mood didn't improve. Someday he would let her know he hadn't eaten a decent meal or slept through an entire night since they had parted. Someday he would tell her he'd have gladly given a king's ransom to have found a way to make her his wife. In time, he would tell her all that, but for now, all he wanted to do was enjoy the luxury of looking at her.

"Carol just asked you a question. The least you could do is answer her," James muttered.

"I'm fine."

"Good," she whispered.

"How are you?" From somewhere deep inside he found the strength to dredge up the polite inquiry.

"Not so good."

"Not so good?" he echoed.

She drew her shoulders up straight, and her eyes held his as she seemed to be preparing herself for something. "Do you . . . are you in love with her, because if you are, I'll . . . I'll understand and get out of your life right now, but I have to know that much before I say anything more."

"In love with her?" Alex felt as if he were an echo. "Who?"

"Babette . . . the beauty queen you've been dating."

James cleared his throat, and, looking anxious, glanced toward his father. "I . . . you two obviously need some time alone. I'll leave."

"James, what the hell is Carol talking about?"

His son wore an injured look, as if to suggest Alex was doing him a terrible injustice to suspect he had anything to do with Carol believing Alex was dating Babette.

"James?" He made his son's name a threat in itself.

"Well," the teenager admitted with some reluctance, "Mrs. Sommars might have gotten the impression that you were dating someone else, from something I said to Peter. But I'm sure whatever I said was all very nebulous." His shoulders sagged just a little, and when Alex continued to glare at him, James continued. "All right, all right, Peter and I got to talking the situation over, and the two of us agreed you guys were wasting a whole lot of precious time arguing over nothing.

"Mrs. Sommars is a hundred times better than any of the other women you've dated, and although sometimes she dresses a little funny, I don't mind. I also know that Peter would really like a dad, and he claims you're better than anyone his mom's ever dated. So when Uncle Barn started pressuring you to date that Babette girl, we...Peter and I, came up with the idea of...you know..."

"I don't know," Alex said sternly, lacing his words with steel. "Exactly what did you say to Carol?"

"I didn't," James was quick to inform him. "Not directly, anyway...Peter did all the talking, and he just casually let it drop that you were dating again and..."

"And had fallen head over heels in love with someone else," Carol supplied.

"In the space of less than a week?" Alex demanded. Did she honestly believe his love was so fickle he could forget her in a few short days? Sweet heaven, he'd only retreated to fortify himself with ideas before he approached her again.

"You said it was time to cut your losses and look elsewhere," she reminded him.

"You didn't honestly believe that, did you?"

"Yes...I thought you must have, especially when Peter started telling me about you and the beauty queen. What else was I to believe?"

"I'll just go to my room now," James inserted smoothly. "You two go ahead and talk things out without having to worry about a kid hanging around." He quietly vacated the room, leaving only the two of them.

"I'm not in love with anyone else, Carol," Alex said, his eyes holding hers. "If you came because you feared I was seeing another woman, then rest assured it isn't true. I'll talk to James later and make sure this sort of thing doesn't happen again."

"It won't be necessary."

"It won't?" he asked, frowning. They stood across the room from each other, neither of them making any effort to bridge the distance. The way Alex felt, they might as well have been standing on opposite ends of a football field...playing for opposing teams.

Her eyes drifted shut, and now that one bridge had been crossed, she seemed to be gathering her courage to face another. When she spoke, her voice was low and trembling. "Don't be angry with James..."

"He had no right involving himself in our business."

"It worked, Alex. It...worked. When I believed I was losing you, when I thought of you holding another woman in your arms, I...I wanted to die. I think maybe I did, just a little, because I realized how much I love you and what a fool I've been to think I could go on with my humdrum life without you. I needed time, I demanded time, and you wouldn't give it to me..."

"I was wrong—I realized that later."

"No," she countered, "you were right. I would never have made up my mind, because...because of what happened in my marriage with Bruce."

The whole world seemed to go still as comprehension flooded Alex's soul. "Are you saying...does this mean you're willing to marry me?" he asked, barely able to believe what she was saying. Barely able to trust himself to stand where he was a second longer.

Alex didn't know who moved first, not that it mattered. All that did matter was that Carol was in his arms, kissing him with a hunger that threatened to consume them both.

"Yes....yes, I'll marry you," she cried in between kisses. "When...oh, Alex, I'm so anxious to be your wife."

Alex stifled the sudden urge to laugh, and the equally powerful urge to weep. He buried his face in the soft curve of her neck and swallowed hard before dragging several deep, stabilizing breaths through his lungs. He slid his hands into her hair as he moved his mouth to hers, exploring her lips in all the ways he'd dreamed of doing for so many sleepless nights. His mouth rolled over hers, deepening the kiss to a slow, wild meeting of their lips, of their bodies, of their hearts.

Her purse fell to the floor, and she wound her arms around him, moved against him, whispering over and over again how much she loved him.

"I missed you so damn much," he told her while he moved his hands restlessly down her spine. He lifted her from the carpet and blindly carried her. Even while he was walking across the room, his lips ate at hers. He was so famished for her love that he doubted he would ever be satisfied.

"I thought I'd never kiss you again," she moaned. "I couldn't bear the thought of not having you in my life."

By sheer luck, Alex made his way to the sofa, plopping himself down on the thick cushions and keeping her in his lap. He cupped her hair away from her face as he gazed into her beautiful dark eyes. What fabulous eyes this woman possessed. Alex swore they could eat through a man's soul.

Unable to resist, he kissed her again, and when they drew apart, their lower lips clung in reluctance, as if neither of them were willing to let anything this good end. Alex rested his forehead against hers and closed his eyes to the wealth of warm sensation that bubbled up inside him. The temptation was strong to tilt his head and take her mouth again and again. He didn't want to stop, didn't want to talk, didn't want to do anything but hold her and love her.

"Alex," she whispered, resting her head against his shoulder. "You asked me once about Bruce, and I didn't want to tell you. I was wrong to hold back, wrong not to have explained before—you have a right to know."

"It's all right, love, I won't force you."

She gently stroked his face. "For both our sakes, I need to tell you."

"You're sure?"

She didn't look the least bit certain, but she nodded, and when she started speaking, her soft voice trembled with emotional pain. "I was incredibly young and naive when I met Bruce. He was the most fun-loving, daring boy I'd ever dated. The crazy things he did excited me, but deep in my heart I know I'd never have married him if I hadn't gotten pregnant with Peter."

Alex kissed her brow and continued to stroke her hair as she spoke.

"Although Bruce seemed willing enough to marry me, I don't honestly know how much pressure my father applied." Her voice was gaining strength as she spoke. "It was a bad situation that grew worse after Peter was born. It was then that Bruce started drinking heavily and drifted from one job to another. It seemed each month he grew more depressed and more angry. He claimed I'd trapped him into the marriage, and he was going to be damn sure I paid for what I did to him." She paused and closed her eyes as a wobbly sigh rumbled through her chest. "I did pay, and so did Peter. My life became a living nightmare."

Alex suspected things had been bad for her, but he had no idea how ugly. "Did he beat you, love?"

Her eyes remained closed, and she nodded. "I once heard alcohol referred to as a demon, and after living with Bruce, I believe it. He'd drink, and the demon inside him would give birth to unreasonable fits of jealousy, fear, depression and hatred. The more he drank, the more the anger burst out in violent episodes. There were times when I was sure if I didn't escape, he would have killed me.''

"Didn't your family know? Surely they guessed?''

"I was only able to see them rarely—Bruce didn't approve of me visiting my family. In retrospect, I realize he feared my father. Had Dad or Tony known what was happening, they would have taken matters into their own hands. I must have realized it, too, because I never told them, never said a word for fear of involving them. It was more than that...I was too humiliated. I didn't want anyone to realize the terrible problems we were having, and so I didn't say anything—not even to my mother.''

"But surely there was someone?''

"Once...once Bruce punched me so hard he dislocated my jaw, and I had to see a doctor. She refused to believe all my bruises were due to a fall. She tried to help me, tried to get me to press charges against him, but I didn't dare for fear of what Bruce would do to Peter.''

"Dear God, Carol.'' The anger Alex was experiencing was so profound that he knotted his hands into fists. The image of someone beating the warm, vibrant woman in his arms filled him with impotent rage.

"I'd lost any respect I ever had for Bruce shortly after we were married. Over the next three years I lost respect for myself. What kind of woman allows a man to abuse her mentally and physically, day after day, week after week, year after year? Surely there was something terribly wrong with me. In some ways I can't even begin to understand—all the hurtful, hateful things Bruce accused me of seemed valid after a while.''

"Oh, baby.'' Alex's chest heaved under the weight of her pain.

"Then Bruce didn't come home one night. It wasn't unusual—I knew he'd come back when he was ready, usually in a foul mood. I'd braced myself for it when the police officer came to tell me Bruce had been killed in an automobile accident. I remember I stared up at the man and didn't say anything. I didn't feel anything.

"I was hanging clothes on the line, and I thanked him for letting me know and returned to the backyard and finished with the task. I didn't phone anyone, I didn't even cry."

"You were in shock."

"I suppose, but even later when I was able to cry and grieve, mingled in with all the pain was an overwhelming sense of relief."

"No one could blame you for that, love," Alex answered, wanting with everything in him to wipe away the memory of those years with her husband.

"Now...now do you understand why I couldn't tell you about Bruce?" she pleaded. "Your and Gloria's marriage was so wonderful...it was what a marriage was meant to be. When she died, your and James's love surrounded her. When Bruce died—" she hesitated, and her lips were trembling "—he was with another woman. It was the final rejection, the final humiliation." She drew in a ragged breath and turned, her eyes burning into his. "I don't know what kind of wife I'll be to you, Alex. Over the years I've thought about those three nightmarish years and have wondered what would have happened had I done things differently. Maybe the fault was my own...maybe Bruce was right all along, and if I'd only been the right kind of woman, then he wouldn't need to drink. If I'd done things differently then he might have been happy."

"Carol, you don't honestly believe that, do you?"

"I...I don't know anymore."

"Oh, love, my sweet, sweet love. You've got to realize any problems Bruce had were of his own making. The answers to his misery lay buried within himself from the first. Nothing you could have ever done would have been enough." He cupped her face in his hands, and his eyes held hers. "Do you understand what I'm saying?"

"I . . . I can't make myself fully believe that, and at the same time I know it's true. Only Alex, this time I want everything to be right." Her eyes were clouded and uncertain, as if she suspected he would be angry with her.

"It will be," he promised her, and there wasn't a single doubt in his heart.

Carol awoke when the first fingers of dawn silently parted, then optimistically slipped, through the lush drapes of the honeymoon suite. She closed her eyes and sighed, replete, sated, unbelievably happy. Deliriously happy.

From the moment Carol had agreed to become Alex's wife to this very morning, exactly one month had transpired. One month. It boggled her mind that so much could have happened in so short a time.

In one month, they'd planned, arranged and staged a large wedding, complete with reception, dinner and dance.

True to her word, Carol's mother had insisted upon preparing a reception dinner that would have been impossible to surpass. Carol swore Angelina had started cooking the Sunday afternoon she brought Alex back to the house with her to introduce him to the family.

No sooner had Angelina started dragging out her largest set of pots and pans when Carol's sisters and their families had all arrived. The wedding became a celebration of love, a family reunion, a blending of families, all rolled into one.

At the wedding reception, Alex had surprised her with the honeymoon trip to Hawaii. The boys were mildly put out that they hadn't been included. Hawaii would have been the perfect place to "check out the chicks," as Peter put it. To appease them, Alex promised a family vacation over the Thanksgiving holiday. Peter and James had promptly started talking about a Mexican cruise.

Carol smiled as she savored the thoughts of her wedding day. Peter and James had circulated among the guests, accepting full credit for getting their parents together.

Alex stirred briefly and rolled onto his side, slipping his hand around her waist and tucking his body against hers as naturally as if they'd been married several years instead of three marvelous days.

Carol had been crazy in love with Alex before she married him, but the depth of emotion that filled her breast following the wedding ceremony made what she experienced earlier weak by comparison.

Never had she been more in love. Never had she felt so desirable. As she'd known it would be, Alex's lovemaking was completely unselfish and gentle while at the same time fierce and demanding. Just thinking of how often and well he'd loved her in the last days was enough to increase the tempo of her heart. Scooting just a tad closer, she snuggled her buttocks against his lower half.

Alex stirred immediately. He slid his hand from her waist to cup the fullness of her breast that lay beneath the bodice of her pearl-white lace-and-silk gown. Her mother had given it to her before she had left for the wedding trip, but this was the first night that she'd actually been able to wear it. Every time she put it on, Alex had taken one look at her, and before she knew what was happening, he'd promptly removed it. Not that Carol was complaining.

The gown made her feel like a temptress, a seductress, a woman. Then again, it quite possibly had nothing to do with the gown, but everything to do with the man.

The thick pad of his thumb stroked her nipple, which responded instantly. Carol sighed and rolled onto her opposite side, so they were facing each other.

"Good morning," she whispered.

"Good morning."

Their eyes met and spoke in silent messages.

He was telling her he loved her. She was saying she loved him back. He was saying he needed her. She echoed that need.

Slowly he pulled open the ties at the front of the bodice. Her breasts sprang forward and Alex brought his eyes to them for just an instant before he dragged his hungry gaze back to hers.

The question was in his look, and she smiled joyously, wondering why he felt the need to ask.

He cupped the lush heaviness of her breasts, and she sighed when he lowered his mouth to love her first with a series of kisses to her neck and shoulders, steadily descending to the sweet cleft between her breasts. His touch was tender and daring as he slipped the silk gown up to her waist. Gently he parted her thighs, and his pleasure-giving exploration continued.

Knowing what was coming, Carol bit into her lower lip as he agilely slipped his finger inside the moist folds of her womanhood. At the precise moment his finger entered her, his mouth greedily closed over the already hard peak of her breast. The coupling of pleasure was almost too much for Carol, and she gasped. Smoothing her palms over his shoulders, she arched back her head and moaned his name.

"I'm hurting you?" he paused long enough to ask.

"No...no, don't stop."

"I have no intention of stopping for a very long time." To prove his point, he feasted on the opposite breast, alternating between the two. Lapping, stroking, sucking. All the while he administered to her breasts, his fingers were busy with her lower half. Soon Carol was a churning mass of need. She lifted and rotated her hips against him, marveling at his strength and power. His hard strength and his hard need.

His mouth found hers as he moved against her. Carol's sanity had long since been destroyed, and she whimpered an urgent plea, not even realizing she'd made a sound until it met her own ears.

Alex rolled her onto her back, and once more his eyes met hers. Once more they exchanged silent messages.

He said, I love you so damned much.

She said, I know—please don't make me wait much longer.

Alex kissed her again, lightly, his lips as weightless as the creeping sunlight.

"Carol, oh, love," he murmured, rotating his hips against her. "I want you so much."

"I can tell," she said almost shyly.

Gently he parted her thighs. "I can't believe how good it feels to make love to...you," he said slowly, as slowly as he sank his body into hers, entering her with a gentleness that went beyond words. Inch by inch he joined his body to hers until they were both panting with a pleasure so profound neither of them had the strength to move.

Carol tossed her head to one side. Alex was so velvet-smooth and velvet-hot. He filled her to capacity, but it was more than her body that he occupied. Emotionally and spiritually he satisfied every need she'd ever experienced. Nothing was lacking, nothing had been left wanting.

Yearning to repay him for all he'd given her, Carol raised her hips, bringing their bodies into an even more intimate contact.

Alex groaned. "You're so hot...so incredibly hot." With that, he started to move, making love to her with his whole body. His mouth clung to hers, his tongue mated with hers, his hands were in her hair. Each part of him was buried as deep inside her as his sex.

Her completion came only seconds before his own, and with their arms wrapped around each other, with their legs entwined and their bodies connected, Alex rolled over, reversing their positions.

"Oh, love," he whispered reverently, spreading a short series of moist kisses over her face. "I don't think I'll ever grow tired of making love with you."

"I certainly hope not." She smiled down on him, brushing a stray curl from his brow. She battled down the ready tears that moistened her lashes each time they made love. But the joy in her heart demanded them, and restraining their flow would have been impossible. Alex didn't understand her tears, and Carol could find no way to explain them.

He tenderly wiped the moisture from the edge of her face and kissed her eyes. "I can't bear to see you cry. Please tell me if I'm hurting you."

"Oh, no...never that." After all the times they'd made love, learned and explored each other's bodies in the past three days, he still didn't completely accept her tears, fearing he was the cause and the source. Once again, Carol tried to explain. "I...I didn't realize making love could be this wonderful...this good."

Alex momentarily closed his eyes, his look full of chagrin and something else she couldn't name. "We didn't take any precautions. Last night, either."

His words triggered a slow easy smile. "I know, and I'm glad."

"Why? I thought we decided to wait a few months before we even considered starting."

"We did, only I didn't take into account certain things." She pressed her face to the firm strength of his shoulder and kissed his neck, still shy about talking so freely with him. She hadn't been able to start on the pill, and so they'd agreed that until she could, Alex would be the one to take precautions.

"Not take into account things?" he repeated. "What things?"

Her fingers tightened at his shoulders as she struggled to explain. "The need to feel you close...only you...with nothing separating us—with nothing between us."

"Oh, love," he breathed, threading his fingers into her hair. Forehead to forehead, lips to lips, he kissed her again and again.

"What do you think your chances of getting pregnant are?" he asked after several moments of kissing and touching.

Her tongue circled the circumference of his mouth. "About a hundred percent."

The room went motionless. Noiseless. When Alex spoke again, his voice was strangled. "How would you feel about that?"

"Unbelievably happy. I want your child, Alex."

He hesitated for an instant and then asked, "How can you be so sure?"

"About wanting a baby?" she asked with a small laugh to hide the fact her voice was wavering.

"No, not that, I mean about me getting you pregnant."

Carol raised her head, her lips scant inches from his own and their breaths mingled and merged. "When the lovemaking is this good...this beautiful, then there can't help but be an equally wonderful, beautiful result."

His mouth found hers again for a kiss that grew wilder and wilder, then less urgent, less demanding. Nestling her head in his strong shoulder once more, Carol sighed and closed her eyes. She was warm, satisfied and utterly happy. For the first time in more years than she cared to count, she felt like a woman. A seductive, beautiful woman. A complete woman. A total woman. A woman loved by a man.

It was more than enough.

Epilogue

After all the years that Carol had worked in the labor room, after all the birthing classes she'd taught, she should know by now what was and what wasn't a labor contraction. Still, she wasn't sure and had delayed contacting Alex until she was several hours into her labor.

Resting her hands on her distended abdomen, she gently rubbed her constricting belly while taking in several relaxing breaths. Knowing she shouldn't delay much longer, she reached for the telephone and called Alex at the office.

"Yes," he cried impatiently across the wire. The last week he'd been as nervous as . . . as a soon-to-be father.

"It's Carol."

She heard his soft intake of breath. "Are you all right?"

"I'm fine."

"You wouldn't be calling me at the office if you were fine," he countered sharply. "Is something going on that I should know about?"

"Not really. At least not yet, but I think it might be a good idea if you took the rest of the afternoon off and came home."

"Oh, God."

Carol could nearly hear the blood draining out of his face.

"Now?" he asked.

"If you're in the middle of something, I can wait," she assured him, but she sincerely hoped he wasn't going to keep her twiddling her thumbs much longer, otherwise she was going to end up driving herself to the hospital.

"I'm not worried about me," he cried. "Is the baby coming now? Isn't it early... I mean we're not due for another eight days, and sweet heaven, Carol, I don't know if I'm ready for this."

"Don't worry, I am."

Alex expelled his breath forcefully. "I'll be there in five minutes."

"Alex," she cried. "Don't speed."

She knew her words were for naught the instant she replaced the receiver. Alex hadn't suffered this pregnancy well. When she was nauseous those first few mornings in the first trimester, Alex was nauseous. When her feet swelled up, he was the one who limped. For the entire nine months, Alex had craved pickles and peanut butter. Twice he'd wakened in the middle of the night moaning, and when Carol had asked him what was wrong, he'd murmured something about having false labor pains.

Carol hadn't known what her husband's reaction would be once he learned what the doctor had told her. He'd first suspected when she was four months. At six months, his suspicions were confirmed. For the past three months she'd kept the secret to herself. Alex was so concerned, so worried about her, and she didn't want to add to his burden.

From a block away, Carol could hear the roar of Alex's truck as he sped toward the house. The sound of him hitting the brakes was followed by the car door slamming. Immediately afterward, Alex vaulted into the house, breathless and as pale as a hospital sheet.

Swaying gently in the rocking chair, Carol held out her hands to him. "Settle down, big daddy."

He flew to her side and knelt in front of her, taking her hands in his and pressing soft kisses to her knuckles. It took him a moment to compose himself, but Carol could plainly see how difficult it was. His eyes were closed, and his shoulders were heaving as he breathed deeply.

"This is it, isn't it? We're in labor?" he asked, once he found his voice. He looked for a moment as though he were experiencing a contraction himself.

"We're in labor," Carol told him and gently patted his head, resisting the urge to remind him to practice his breathing techniques.

"How can you be so calm about this?"

She smiled and bent forward enough to brush her lips over his. "One of us has to be."

"I know...I know...you need me to be strong for you now, but look at me," he said, holding out his hands for her to inspect. "I'm trembling so hard I can barely keep my wits about me." Gently he laid those same shaking hands over Carol's abdomen, and when he glanced up at her, his eyes were bright with unshed moisture. "I love this baby so much. I dreamed of her long before you even agreed to marry me, and now that she's about to be born, I feel so humble, so unworthy."

"Alex . . . there's something you should know."

He silenced her with a kiss. "If you have anything to tell me, it'll have to wait until we get to the hospital."

On second thought, Carol realized he was right. Once he heard her news, she feared she would be the one driving *him* to the hospital.

"I've phoned my mother and the doctor, and my suitcase is by the door." She did her best to disguise the intensity of the contraction from him by closing her eyes and breathing slowly and deeply until it passed. When she opened her eyes, she discovered Alex watching her intently. If possible, he looked even paler than he had before.

"Are you going to be all right?" she asked.

"I . . . I don't know. I love our baby, but I love you even more. Honest to God, Carol, I don't know if I can stand to see you in pain. I feel all mushy inside and—"

His words were interrupted by the sound of another car pulling into the driveway and two doors slamming. James burst into the door first, followed by Peter, both looking as excited as if it were Christmas morning.

"What are you two doing home from school?" Carol demanded.

"Word just came that you were in labor. You don't honestly think we'd miss this, do you?"

"Word just came?" Carol echoed. "From whom?"

The two boys eyed each other. "We've got our sources," James supplied.

This wasn't the time or the place to quiz them. "All right, boys, we won't discuss this now. James, take care of your father. Peter, load up the car. I think it might be best if you drove me yourself. James, bring your father—he's in no condition to drive."

The boys leaped into action. "Come on, Dad, we're going to deliver a baby," James said, urging his father toward the late-model sedan the two boys shared.

By the time they arrived at Ford Memorial, Carol's pains had increased dramatically. She was wheeled to the labor room and prepped while Alex, James and Peter were left to fend for themselves in the waiting room.

Fifteen minutes later, Alex joined her. He was more composed by now, more in control. He smiled shyly and reached for her hand, clenching it between both of his. "How are you doing?"

"I'm more concerned about you." The delivery room was being readied, and now was as good a time as any for her to tell him her big news.

"You're concerned about me. Why?"

"Because you're about to receive something of a shock." She couldn't help smiling.

His eyes widened. He must have realized how serious she was because he lowered himself into the chair and for an instant it looked as if he'd stopped breathing.

"Alex, I'm going to be fine and so are our daughters."

He stared at her blankly for several seconds. She assumed for a moment that she was going to have to spell it out for him, but her news hit him and his entire face said as much. "Our *daughters*?"

"Yes, love, we're having twins. Two perfect little girls."

"How do you know that? When did you find out? Why wasn't I told? Oh, God," he pressed his arm around his stomach and doubled over. "You're having a pain, aren't you?" he gritted between clenched teeth.

Laughing, Carol brushed his face with her lips. "No, darling, you are."

Joyce Mandle came into the room, looking pleased. She handed Alex a hospital gown and suggested he change his clothes. Carol was ready to be wheeled down to delivery by the time he finished. The pains were strong and hard, but she managed to smile up at Alex.

"Don't worry, love."

"Twins," he repeated, as though in a daze. "Twin girls?"

"Twin girls," she repeated.

Alex reached for her hand and they met, palm to palm, heart to heart.

"Grandma, can I have seconds on the zabaglione?" James called from inside the large family kitchen.

Angelina Pasquale's smile widened at the request. Her eyes squarely met those of her daughter. "I told you my cooking would put some meat on his bones."

"That you did, Mama," Carol said, sharing a special smile with her husband. She'd only been home from the hospital a week. Royalty couldn't have been treated any better than she had in the last several days. James and Peter were crazy about their sisters, and thus far the only task allotted Carol had been diaper changing and breast feeding. She was well aware that the novelty would wear off, but she didn't expect it to be any time soon. Angie and Alison had stolen two teenage hearts without even trying.

"I brought you some tea," Alex said, scooting onto the cushion next to her. His eyes were filled with a wealth of love. From the moment Carol had been rolled into the delivery room, the light in Alex's eyes hadn't changed. It was filled with an indescribable tenderness and a love that went beyond words. His hand had gripped hers and when her body had brought forth two perfect identical daughters, there had been tears in both parent's eyes. Tears of joy. Tears of gratitude. They each had been granted so much more than they'd ever dreamed. A new life. A new love. A new appreciation for all the good things in store for them and their combined families.

The soft lilting words of an Italian lullaby drifted toward Carol and Alex. Carol's mother rocked gently in the chair, a sleeping infant cradled in each arm. Angelina's eyes were partly closed as she sang. The words were familiar to Carol; she'd heard her mother sing them to her as a child and she'd heard Angelina sing them often to her grandchildren.

When she'd finished, Angelina Pasquale paused and murmured a soft, emotional prayer in her native language.

"What did she say?" Alex asked, leaning close to Carol.

A smile tugged at the edges of Carol's mouth. Her fingers were twined with Alex's and she raised his knuckles to her lips and kissed them gently. "She was thanking St. Scholastica for a job well done."

* * * * *

Silhouette Special Edition

COMING NEXT MONTH

#607 BEST MAN—Jo Ann Algermissen
Sylas Kincaid detected the pain masked by Alana Benton's brittle poise, and he sensed that masculine cruelty had put it there. But surely the love of a better man would bring her heart out of hiding...

#608 A WOMAN'S WORK—Laura Leone
Hardworking Marla Foster stunned her firm by capturing Brent Ventura's account. But Brent's dangerously unprofessional mix of irreverence and relentless sex appeal soon proved Marla's job had only just begun!

#609 THE OTHER MOTHER—Pamela Jerrold
Her suddenly widowed sister left pregnant surrogate mother Caitlin O'Shea high and dry. But prodigal brother-in-law Sam Ellison seemed oddly eager to keep Caitlin's bundle of joy all in the family.

#610 MY FIRST LOVE, MY LAST—Pat Warren
Rafe Sloan's motives for helping Nora Maddox find her missing son weren't entirely altruistic. The abrupt ending to their old affair had left burning questions, and Rafe was prepared to probe deeply for the answers....

#611 WITH NO REGRETS—Lisa Jackson
Jaded attorney Jake McGowan rationalized that he was helping beautiful, desperate Kimberly Bennett with her child-custody suit merely to win *him* sweet revenge on Kimberly's shady ex-husband. So why was his trademark cynicism beginning to feel like caring?

#612 WALK UPON THE WIND—Christine Flynn
A hurricane blew sheltered Nicole Stewart into Aaron Wilde's untamed world. Their island idyll couldn't last, but could she return to privileged society once she'd tasted primitive passion, once she'd walked upon the wind?

AVAILABLE THIS MONTH:

You'll flip . . . your pages won't!
Read paperbacks *hands-free* with

Book Mate • I

The perfect "mate" for all your romance paperbacks

Traveling • Vacationing • At Work • In Bed • Studying • Cooking • Eating

Perfect size for all standard paperbacks, this wonderful invention makes reading a pure pleasure! Ingenious design holds paperback books OPEN and FLAT so even wind can't ruffle pages — leaves your hands free to do other things. Reinforced, wipe-clean vinyl-covered holder flexes to let you turn pages without undoing the strap . . . supports paperbacks so well, they have the strength of hardcovers!

Pages turn WITHOUT opening the strap.

SEE-THROUGH STRAP

Reinforced back stays flat.

Built in bookmark

BOOK MARK

BACK COVER HOLDING STRIP

10" x 7¼", opened.
Snaps closed for easy carrying, too

Available now. Send your name, address, and zip code, along with a check or money order for just $5.95 + .75¢ for postage & handling (for a total of $6.70) payable to Reader Service to:

Reader Service
Bookmate Offer
901 Fuhrmann Blvd.
P.O. Box 1396
Buffalo, N.Y. 14269-1396

Offer not available in Canada
*New York and Iowa residents add appropriate sales tax.

BM-G

BIG BROTHERS/BIG SISTERS AND HARLEQUIN

Harlequin is proud to announce its official sponsorship of Big Brothers/Big Sisters of America. Look for this poster in your local Big Brothers/Big Sisters agency or call them to get one in your favorite bookstore. Love is all about sharing.

BB/BS 1A